UFOs AND *EXTRATERRESTRIALS*
ARE AS REAL AS THE **NOSE**

ON YOUR FACE!

UFOs and Extraterrestrials... Lou Baldin

UFOs AND *EXTRATERRESTRIALS*
ARE AS REAL AS THE NOSE
ON YOUR FACE!

Lou Baldin

UFOs And Extraterrestrials Are As Real As The Nose On Your Face

Copyright © 2011, by Lou Baldin

All rights reserved. No part of this book may be reproduced, stored, or transmitted by any means—whether auditory, graphic, mechanical, or electronic—without written permission of both the publisher and author, except in the case of brief excerpts used in critical articles and reviews. Unauthorized reproduction of any part of this work is illegal and is punishable by law.

ISBN: 978-1-105-27138-0

What follows are questions and answers concerning the reality of extraterrestrial beings on Earth, and their purpose. Numerous members at the Above Top Secret (ATS) internet site, asked questions anonymously, and were answered by the author. This segment began April 9, 2005 and ended April 3, 2006

Original content can be found at the Above Top Secret site: http://www.abovetopsecret.com/forum/thread133299/pg1

Questions and answers were edited for clarity. Some posts from the site were unsuitable and therefore not added to this book. Questions are in bold type.

We are not here to change the world, we are here so that the world can change us.

April 9, 2005

While enlisted in the United States Army, I was allowed access to extraterrestrial spaceships (UFOs). Inside the ships, I found real life "Alice in Wonderland" stuff. Distinguishing what was real or imaginary was a challenge. Inside the UFOs were other dimensions, a "Twilight Zone" of sorts. That is one reason governments around the world don't give credence to extraterrestrial beings and UFOs visiting Earth. Governments do not know what these beings are and have no ability to defend against such supernatural phenomena should it turn out to be of a hostile nature.

Governmental institutions are not inclined to admit inferiority to unknown space visitors. Those in the know, concerning Extraterrestrials, understand the superior nature of Extraterrestrials, and their highly advanced technology, and are terrified. What these beings are capable of doing with their superiority is horrific, therefore, sovereign nations intend to keep a lid on the phenomena by any means, including ridiculing those who talk openly about UFOs and extraterrestrial beings.

Can you go into more detail on what you personally have seen and know about ETs and their vehicles? How could anything be "imaginary" inside a UFO? Wouldn't everything inside be real? Why would ETs put fakery in their own vehicles?

Perhaps everything is real inside the ship, but while in the ship, the atmosphere is surreal and difficult to differentiate between reality and imaginary. The moment you step out of the ship the mind goes back to normal.

I do not believe it is about inferiority it is about suppression for government gain - not ours. They do not want us to know the truth - but it will prevail.

The governments are not in charge, concerning disclosure. If Extraterrestrials wanted to make official contact with the populations of the Earth there is nothing stopping them.

April 10, 2005

It's not that inside the ships is imaginary. It's simply that you are in two different realms simultaneously. What shape was the vessel? How big was it?

Being in two realms/realities simultaneously is confusing. The ship was about thirty feet wide, but once inside the ship it appeared much larger.

What type of propulsion system was used?

I was told, that the propulsion system was magnetic wave.

Did someone actually pilot the vessel or just turn it on?

The craft had no seats and no cockpit that I was aware of. It operated on its own, perhaps controlled by Extraterrestrial telepathy or some other unknown means.

In the practical art of war, the best thing is to take the enemy's country whole and intact; to shatter and destroy it is not so good. It is better to capture an army in its entirety than to destroy it.

The Extraterrestrials do not intend to conquer the human race, nor would they be concerned about preserving infrastructure if they did take over. In comparison to how the Extraterrestrials live, humans live in caves. Extraterrestrials are involved in world affairs, nothing happens without their knowledge or approval.

Explain what business you had entering the craft and if they are going to take 'action' in the future against humanity and make humanity privy to their existence.

The military never told me why they gave me access to the ship. My guess is that they did not know why and were following instructions from higher ups. I was in a ship; the ship flew away from this planet while I was in it. There was no sensation of movement, no G-force. I was standing up looking out one of the portholes and in a few seconds I was in space, the force did not knock me down, but the awesomeness nearly did. Extraterrestrials are not going to take over this planet they have always had control of Earth and the inhabitants of Earth.

So the "dreamland" is just that. A physical space on Earth mixed with a dimension shift. The source of the shift is a spacecraft?

I do not know if it is a dimensional shift or if it has something to do with the magnetic energy on the ship, which somehow alters or interferes with the electrical circuits in the human brain. The ship is definitely a dreamland, but it can be a chamber of horrors too. There were many unknowns inside the Extraterrestrial ship.

There were other people on the ship with me, perhaps four or five, but we did not speak. They were occupied with doing things and looking busy. I was in contact with an Extraterrestrial the size of a six-year-old child, but I do not recall what the being told me. It was not a question and answer session, the being spoke and I listened. I had many other previous encounters, but the details remain obscure. I was in army uniform yet those who gave me access to the ship acted as if they did not trust me, so there was suspicion and little conversation between us. They were not allowed access to the ship when it flew into space during some of my encounters, perhaps there was jealousy along with being suspicious.

Where exactly did the government get a 30-foot UFO?

Extraterrestrials are garrisoned on this planet and on the moon. They have bases in several countries in cooperation with certain governments. They let us play with some of their toys, take them for a spin, learn a few things on how to improve and upgrade our technology. Humans are on the verge of stepping into space, there is a lot of stuff to learn about that next big leap.

My military rank and clearance had nothing to do with my involvement with the Extraterrestrials. My involvement came about because of my ongoing contact with Extraterrestrials from childhood, much of that involvement remains hidden from me. My clearance to enter the ships was from the Extraterrestrials not the military. I was not a military experiment. The military was curious of my involvement with the Extraterrestrials, much like those posting questions on this thread, except that the military knows that Extraterrestrials are real and visiting Earth. The military is eager to know as much as possible about the Extraterrestrials, like everyone else, they can't quite get a handle on them and they are intimidated by that fact.

Humans are the inferior race in this equation, therefore, describing fantastical things when words fail to give a picture of extraterrestrial gadgetry I sometimes fill in the blanks with words such as pixy-dust. How would a nuclear physicist describe nuclear physics to a tribe of aborigines whose highest form of technology is throwing a spear? Or to the average person clueless in the understanding of physics? There is a huge gap between human technology and Extraterrestrial technology. Explaining things I saw and experienced in the ship is challenging.

April 11, 2005

You stated that you were in the Army. What year did you sign up? Where did you do your basic training? Did you go to college on the GI Bill and re-enter the service? What was your rank? Are you still in the Army? What bases were you stationed? What level of education do you possess? Have you done a foreign tour of duty or a tour that qualified you for hardship pay? If so, where were you stationed?

I enlisted in the army on January of 1970. My tour ended three years later, in 1973. My rank was specialist 4, my primary MOS (Military Occupational Specialty) was tank crewman, my secondary MOS was medical supply. My basic training took place at Fort Leonard Wood, Missouri. I was stationed at Fort Knox, Kentucky, Fort Ord California, Fort Hood, Texas, and did 16 months overseas on the island of Okinawa. I have some college.

I'm assuming that this encounter took place in Kentucky, between 1970 and 1973? Did the ship land on base?

I was stationed at several military installations. I received my "joyrides" more than once and at more than one base.

Was the interior all empty space? You mentioned no seats.

The ship was not a large open space it had rooms and compartments.

What did the windows look like? Could you see them from the outside? Were they tinted on the outside?

The act of entering the ship was strange. I found myself inside the ship, in other words, I did not walk into the ship, I was taken into the ship somehow. The ship had a main corridor that circled around the interior compartment like a hallway separating the portholes or viewing area from the interior of the ship. I was able to look out of the portholes. I did not notice if they were tinted, the view was clear.

Did you ever see any controls or readouts of any kind?

Controls and readouts appeared now and then in my mind and sometimes on floating round objects that followed me while in the ship.

What exactly did the "engine" look like? Was it in the center of the room you entered?

I do not recall seeing the engine or propulsion system, but in certain parts of the ship, I felt a strong energy force around my body, electrical or something like static electricity.

Do you know if there was a deck on the ship above, and/or below you?

Some ships had upper and lower areas some did not. The electrical force I felt had nothing to do with the movement of the ship; I felt it while the ship was parked in the VIP parking space on one of the military bases, and at other times too. The military brass never gave me permission to enter the ship even when it was on a military installation, it wasn't theirs' to give, they accepted it. The military does not own the ships, but they have "diplomatic" relations with the Extraterrestrials. Extraterrestrials have parking privileges on military bases. The military did not control who can enter the ships. The military never debriefed me because I never entered the ships on behalf of the military or the government. The military did not trust me to tell them what they wanted to know, they believed I was one of the Extraterrestrials, or perhaps one of their hybrids. (I later discovered that the military did debrief me. The military's black ops abduct those connected with extraterrestrials and attempt to extract information from them during abductions.)

Is there anything more you can tell us about the Extraterrestrials? What do you know about them beyond appearance?

I am not good about remembering faces of strangers let alone what the Extraterrestrials looked like during bizarre circumstances. I do not recall seeing any lizard types, or the big bug-eyed ones reported by abductees. Normal looking people have approached me on base and in civilian life that "stopped time" as we know it, and took me on board their ship. I may have been around those weird looking Extraterrestrials and they blocked the images from my mind.

What kind of material were the outside, inside floor, and inside walls made of, or what did they look like, what were they made from? Were you taken from the bases, or other locations?

Besides the bizarre circumstances inside the ship, the ship was a comfortable place. The materials were soft and had organic and synthetic qualities. If you can imagine standing inside a cloud, no pressure points on my body from the alien materials.

Did the military ever question you about what had happened while on board? How were you notified to come to the ship when it landed? What did you talk about with the Extraterrestrials while on the joyride? Upon this craft's return, superior officers asked not a single question?

Military people never "formally" questioned me, but I have observed certain "special" military people abducting other humans for specific programming. I knew those military people were humans because Extraterrestrials radiate energy that affects humans psychologically and physiologically, and these particular soldiers did not. I had infrequent conversation about human stuff with the officers, but they never talked shop with me. The army did not allow anything, or so it seemed. From what I could tell, the army officers went along with whatever the Extraterrestrials wanted. The Extraterrestrials were training them.

Have you ever reported your experience to anyone else? Or did you wait 35 years and finally decide to talk about it? Did you experience memory loss that is just now coming back to you?

My next question may seem strange, but I ask because of another case I read about. Were you ever a witness to something you weren't supposed to see while in the Army? Something other than Extraterrestrials, and not related to this story. Maybe you provided support for special ops or something?

I put off telling my story for a long time because of the stigma associated with people that communicate with paranormal beings. I have decided that what people think doesn't matter anymore, and I'm also becoming more aware as they allow me to remember more. I know what is out there and I am disclosing some of what I experienced. I was involved with some secret military stuff; many of us were during the Vietnam War.

I am fascinated. This gent has mentioned two things I was told years ago by a person deeply involved with craft (or alleged

craft), this guy was a military photographer and his story has never been told. I have not had contact with him in well over 12 years, but I recall his accounts of what he saw and experienced as if it was yesterday. Until this day, I haven't heard anyone ever mention some of the stuff he did, in any interview, net, magazine or any other place... except this fella here.

Can you elaborate on the secret military stuff? What purpose was the special programming? I'm sure your referring to hypnosis, right? And have you stayed in contact with anyone who might corroborate your story?

After the project was over we were split up and sent to new units, names were aliases, but it did not matter I had no desire to get back in touch with those people. I would be surprised if anyone came forward to collaborate, assuming they are still alive. They were a rough bunch that did not care about anything. Extraterrestrials can hypnotize anyone anytime. The soldiers on the ship were trained for things I was not privy to. Everything is on a need to know basis. When it didn't concern me I wasn't told. It is the best way to keep secrets. If the Extraterrestrials were concerned about this story, they would stop it.

April 12, 2005

Who else saw these crafts parked at Army bases? What was your assignment during the end of the Korean War?

I was born at the end of the Korean War, in 1952. Certain military people, civilian scientists and government officials saw these alien craft. When I entered the ship, there were a few people standing behind what was a protective glass partition. Guards posted outside the building did not appear to be aware of what was inside the building.

I'm not seeing why you were brought on board by the Extraterrestrials, nor allowed to be by the military (as you say, they agreed obviously to this). You've mentioned no specific training done by them, nor reported anything back to superiors.

There would be no US military superiority without Extraterrestrial technology. The military (US) receives large amounts of information from Extraterrestrials. Few understand how that knowledge is transferred from Extraterrestrials to the military. The Extraterrestrials do not hand the military or those working with the military, such as contractors, blueprints. Information is transferred partially through a form of telepathy, where information is uploaded into the minds of the scientists. I use the word telepathy because we don't have a word to describe higher forms of brain-to-brain transfers of knowledge, ideas, creativity, etc.

Why did the military 'select' you above others if as you say they allowed this exchange to happen? Did the Extraterrestrials convey to you what your mission was post contact? That is, did they say your role was to help create awareness about their existence?

My contact with Extraterrestrials began from the first day I was born and possibly before. I have vivid memories of my early contacts. The military did not select me. They knew about me before I joined the army.

April 13, 2005

Extraterrestrial contact is a big deal, and for those of us that claim to have it, it is a complex deal. We are not always fascinated by the prospect of our relationship with highly mysterious beings. Extraterrestrials are not like the neighbors next door, friendly or otherwise. Extraterrestrials can be your worst nightmare or they can be like angels. Most people that encounter Extraterrestrials are terrified for having done so, and have no desire to experience Extraterrestrial contact again. Extraterrestrial contact is not like a day at Disney Land; few people want to return after their first ride in an alien ship. Contact is not for the faint of heart. However, some abductees do experience enjoyable and fantastic experiences and look forward to more contact. Nevertheless, there are some hellish rides where abductees are taken "kicking and screaming" to horrible places.

Human brains cannot grasp and hold onto the overwhelming things seen and experienced when in the presence of Extraterrestrials unless the Extraterrestrials allow it. Those with contact live in two realities and information does not transfer from one of the realities to the other very well. Most abductees remember nothing of their experiences other than some horrifying situations. Those that have tried regression therapy to better understand their ordeals do not necessarily receive accurate information about their abductions during hypnosis. Extraterrestrials and sometimes the government can implant screen memories after abductions to hide what really happened. My experiences began before I was born on this planet. My mental awareness before birth was not that of a child when I first arrived, but that of an adult. The ship I traveled in took me to other places and I received a tour of the solar system prior to being dropped off on Earth.

One thing that I don't understand is, if you were the subject of abduction all of your life, why did these Extraterrestrials choose to invite you aboard their craft within the setting of the military base. Why bring you to the attention of the military? Also, sorry if I've missed this anywhere, but have you had any experiences since leaving the army and has the army monitored you because of this?

Extraterrestrials don't want to create panic in the military establishment and therefore are diplomatic about their doings by letting the military know who they have an interest in. Many have witnessed the level of nervousness between the US and the USSR during the cold war, sharing the same planet is not easy for humans. Extraterrestrials know about human paranoia and as far as I have been able to determine ETs don't want to rock the boat too much. I experienced Extraterrestrial encounters often after my military days. I am sure the military monitors me.

April 13, 2005

What I'm after is information about where ET's may have originated. Obviously if you can say "there's life within 50 light years of Sol," then you can start 'guesstimating' about how prevalent life is in this galaxy.

I wasn't told where they were from but they did tell me that planets like Earth and humans similar to us are the most common species in the galaxy. Planets with life on them number in the billions. In other words, we are not unique or alone in the universe.

Tell me more about these "fantastic experiences."

If someone handed you the keys to a Lamborghini and told you to enjoy the ride for a day or a week how would that make you feel? A Lamborghini is sweet; an Extraterrestrial spaceship is a far sweeter. Unfortunately, most people taken into a UFO are freaked out and they crap their pants. The anal probing mentioned my abductees are diaper changes.

Ever pick up a turtle and see the terror in its eyes? The turtle instinctively believes you are going to eat it and it will let loose. That is how most humans respond to Extraterrestrial contact. If you can get through the initial fear, the inside of the ship is a magical place.

Was anything else mentioned about the origins of life, man, or ETs? Since so many other planets with human-like beings are around, did they mention any having the same problems that we have here? Is Earth and its inhabitants unique in any way?

From what I learned, life as we know it has been around forever, trillions of years. Such information contradicts the age of the universe (according to our scientists) by a lot. I don't know if I misunderstood the ETs, but I figured they would know more than humans about the Universe and what is in it. Humans have yet to hatch from this planet called Earth, what could we possibly know about the age, or anything else, in the universe?

Visit any city on this planet and they have their own unique buildings and traditions, but they have one thing in common, crime, hate, rape, robbery, love, poverty, and abundance too. On this planet, we have the whole gamut of possibilities, from primitive villages to modern cities. I assume that type of gamut would be true throughout the galaxies.

Have you only experienced visualization of one particular extraterrestrial being?

I have experienced more than one extraterrestrial species, but don't know how many or what they look like.

Do you converse with them or do they merely communicate details to you?

They communicate with me I don't ask them questions they know what is on my mind and sometimes they give me answers.

Have you thought about taking a souvenir from your abduction?

There is no taking anything from the ship. Every object is a living thing, biological or machine, and the objects don't allow themselves to be taken lightly, or otherwise. Would you put something like that in your pocket?

How many do you believe are existent in the current human populous on Earth?

I have no idea how many are on this planet, but I know there are thousands.

Am I to believe that the fact that we are not unique as humans that they are unique in their own right?

They are not unique they come in many shapes and sizes, do the math, billions of star systems in our galaxy alone, there are many of what we call Extraterrestrials out there.

Next time they take you try to get information on some low-level simple free energy or anti-gravity or even how to get

"work" out of magnets as another form of battery. If you get a solid answer and relay it to me, I can build it.

April 14, 2005

Have you ever asked them what they are prepping you for? If you haven't told the army any of this, I bet they would want to hear the rest of it.

Once they fatten me up, I might make a good meal for them. The military knows more than I do, they also know how helpless they are in comparison to Extraterrestrials. The military only has contact with a few of the visitors to this planet and they know it, many Extraterrestrials remain incognito, hidden from the military.

You said that when an Extraterrestrial is close to you that you feel something, and you would not mistake that feeling again. Is that feeling something like déjà vu or maybe feeling strangely cold or a feeling as if you are being watched?

Extraterrestrials carry some kind of electrical charge and they radiate a powerful electrical field. There is a physiological effect on the human body when they are near as well.

If an Extraterrestrial was near to you would it be observing you? Can we acknowledge its presence in some way? Or even communicate with them?

We can't acknowledge them they have total control of the situation/encounter, that's why the governments of the world don't trust extraterrestrials. However, governments love ETs' technology exchange program.

April 15, 2005

Can you elaborate on this so-called technology exchange program?

I try to inject a little humor now and then, the exchange is one way, the extraterrestrials get nothing from us we get everything from them.

What are they really offering the government?

Like a child parent relationship the children receive, the parents give, and give, and give. ETs give humans receive.

Reverse engineering, and I have used the term myself, is misleading. There is no way we could reverse engineer ET stuff. ETs teach us and show us how to get to the next step of technological advancement the old fashion way, like teaching a child to ride a bike. The child falls off the bike until he or she fine-tune their equilibrium. That's why we end up testing things over and over again, before we get it right.

Test the reverse engineer concept yourself, try to reverse engineer your television from scratch, make the resistors, capacitors, transistors, integrated circuits, picture tube, etc. That should be simple for the average person (sarcasm). And the average person is what our best scientists are when confronted with Extraterrestrial technology; they understand nothing about it.

Televisions have been around for more than sixty years yet most people have no clue how they work. Make one from scratch? I don't think so. ETs gave us the means and know how to make everything we have.

Yeah I can see that... if science can back engineer an ET UFO it may just represent a good imitation or a decent model at best. Have you ever considered writing and having your story published?

April 15, 2005

Could you confirm that there was a slaughter of 66 human delta forces by the Greys in 1979 at Dulce base, is the government still doing Extraterrestrial exchange with the Greys, and do reptilians exist? Do you think after STAR WARS 3 and WAR OF THE WORLDS' showing would the government tell the shocking truth?

The government is concerned about protecting the people here on Earth, more or less. The military fires on Extraterrestrial ships all the time, after all, they don't know who the Extraterrestrials are and the Extraterrestrials routinely violate protected air space in every country. Extraterrestrials are intruders on Earth, or so, that is what the military thinks. The military has contact with a fraction of the Extraterrestrials that visit this planet, so there is a nervous trigger finger in the military establishment.

Friendly fire kills thousands of soldiers in wars, although we are not officially at war with Extraterrestrials some military people believe we should be. Those killed at Dulce may have been victims of friendly fire from other human combatants. Extraterrestrials are not allowed to kill humans due to protocol. However, in certain cases during wars, ETs have provided support for the killing of humans or aliens disguise as humans.

Governments can't tell the people about Extraterrestrials because they know next to nothing about Extraterrestrials.

You're sitting there typing to us that ETs are real, our governments aren't even doing that. Why can't they at least just tell us that much? Surely, they have at least some proof besides their own testimony that ETs are real. Why not show us the ET technology exchange program? They would receive flack, but it wouldn't be doubt casted upon their words. It would be because they've been lying for decades and most likely going to extreme criminal lengths to fund and commit this secrecy.

April 17, 2005

You didn't tell me about the Dulce base. Are the Dulce files true?

I have little information on what happened at Dulce. But I have been placed into an area that was underground like the Dulce caves, in a large cavern filled with strange machinery that was encased in huge metal containers. I was left there for a day alone, don't know why but it was not a fun time.

Could you explain the cavern part, you said it was not fun, were you punished?

Inside the cavern was a large metallic room. The room had machinery as that seen perhaps under a large city, like a power plant or water treatment plant, but it was completely silent. No city was on the surface only desert. The place was lit up but I don't recall the light source, whether it was florescent lighting (human stuff) or Extraterrestrial. There were no doors that I could see or find, I was in the cave and then I was in the metal building, compartment, cube, or whatever it was. Once I was in, I couldn't get out. I wasn't panicked but I had a bad feeling about it the whole time I was there. I explored the place for hours, there seemed to be no end to it. I wasn't punished it was like I was misplaced or left behind by accident. It felt like a void, I never felt so alone, like I was the only human alive. Everything has a life force, humans, animals, insects, and plants. Humans like to be around other humans and often gravitate to large cities to achieve that. There is energy around humans and their activities. The level of energy corresponds to the size of the crowd/city. Even in a desert, alone, you can feel and know that there are humans around, a few miles away perhaps, or in some small adjacent town. Inside that container or place, the energy humans give off could not penetrate the container. I did not feel alone I was alone; there is no worst feeling than that. It could be they were testing me to see how I handled total isolation from other humans. Perhaps the military or NASA, needed "volunteers" before they subject astronauts to long and lonely space voyages.

What in particular made the abductions so different from one to the next, I mean, there must have been a purpose to abduct you on each occasion and bearing in mind that these would not be simple creatures, it would need to be for a purpose that could not be simulated and different from the previous.

There are many entities in the abduction business, including covert government organizations. Reasons for abductions vary depending on who is doing the abducting. Certain experiments cannot be done openly in a free society. There is paper work, red tape, and bureaucracy that would stifle such activities if carried out overtly. Also, it would be very bad for public relations. Covert agents perform certain experiments using extraterrestrial equipment, and if they botch something, the Extraterrestrials fix it, sometimes. Abductees remember nothing of the experiments they are involved in, and in most cases are better off after the visit, for instance, no more cancer or other ailments that may have been bothering them.

Extraterrestrials care little about terrifying abductees because they know they will wipe the memory of the experience from the abductees' mind after the procedure. Abductions are negative experiences because the abductees have no control of the situation and panic sets in. A few abductees manage to put up a fight when their survival instinct kicks in, they scream, bite and swing at everything, but to no avail, the ETs simply carry them away. Sometimes extraterrestrials encase abductees in a rubbery substance (the movie "Fire in the Sky" is a good example). The substance immobilizes humans while keeping them conscious. Every experience and encounter is unique, some pleasant others not so pleasant. What separates the good from the bad encounters is the level of autonomy they allow abductees to have.

If you explored this for hours, and it had no end etc, I would like to learn some of the details of the machinery etc. I'm sure with your time spent you looked at them. During all that time did you ever eat?

The machinery had metallic looking skins or casings covering them. I didn't see gages, pulleys, wheels, levers, valves, only large odd shaped monolithic configurations. I call them machinery because that is what they reminded me of. I don't recall eating or drinking while I was a possession of the Extraterrestrials.

May 3, 2005

I am seeing a lot more use of Extraterrestrial pictures in raves, movies and subliminal art. Perhaps it is a conditioning phase to make us easier to accept what we knew all along. Question is: Will you forgive your government for saying it was a matter of National Security? Just watched The Forgotten. Good example as I thought the movie was about ghosts or the Devil.

Here is an experiment for those wishing to know a "tiny" bit of the feeling of an Extraterrestrial encounter. At night, no moon out, in the dark, in the woods, no lights around you, no flashlight and alone, anticipate an Extraterrestrial touching your hand. You can go into a dark basement (at night) alone and experience the same effect, if no one else is in the house with you. Stand in the quite darkness for fifteen minutes and you might force an encounter, you might also have a heart attack. Extraterrestrials are all around us, which is the creepy feeling we get when we are alone in the dark.

Extraterrestrials work at night and in the daylight too, but mostly late at night and early mornings, when people are in a deep sleep. The human mind can handle extraterrestrial contact better from a semi-sleep state, and that's where they keep you for the duration of time spent with them. It takes a large hair up your butt to meet an Extraterrestrial that is not in human costume and you fully awake and aware. It matters not how bad you may think you are (around other humans) when you are in the presence of Extraterrestrials, you become a helpless creature on the verge of going into shock from terror. I have been in attendance during abductions and I have witnessed muscular men cry like helpless babies even before anything was done to them.

I've had Extraterrestrial contact all of my life and I still never know what to expect. ETs have jobs to do here on this planet, giving us bits and pieces of information to improve out technology, medicine, education, war machines, and many other unknown things.

The wars we have and had, have been supervised by ETs, and made possible by them, perhaps formulated by them, for what ends only they know. Extraterrestrials are in control of everything, if they want this planet to be utopia it is in their power to make it happen, they can also make it into a hellhole worse than it already is.

From what I have learned, they are not here to make themselves known to the majority of the people of the world. ETs don't need to make contact with governments, they only do so because of some higher extraterrestrial protocol. They can do their work without humanity knowing about them, if they so choose. Since they have made contact with certain governments and individuals it seems probable that they have intensions of making themselves known at some point, to a larger portion of the planet. Perhaps humans need to make a psychological leap before we can handle them face to face. A leap that will not happen until we hatch from the egg we call Earth, and move out into the solar system.

What you describe isn't much different than the way human beings treat other species of life on the planet, in so far as the studying/controlling/research is concerned. Now we often respond this way towards certain species out of fear. Certainly, Extraterrestrials have something to fear from us as well?

Extraterrestrials are probably as fragile as tissue paper, but brawn and strength are nothing against a far superior race. We cage lions, tigers and bears (oh my) because they can easily tear us apart, however, these animals are at a disadvantage to our superior minds, and we can do as we please with them, with our technological advancement over animals.

Can the animal kingdom ever rise up against humans because of their claws, sharp teeth, and superior strength? Sure they can kill one or two people, those that are careless, otherwise never. Extraterrestrials are never careless around humans, but they have fallen victim to other Extraterrestrials (UFO crashes) ambushes, etc.

I was within 50 yards of an E.T.V. on private property. Are you saying this was an attempt on their part to reveal themselves to me, or just a mistake on their part for being so obvious? (Glowing brightly at night)

Compared to humans, Extraterrestrials are perfect, they don't make mistakes. Anyone who sees an Extraterrestrial ship (UFO) that close, more than likely has been inside the craft, and possibly taken on a leisurely cruse around the solar system. Abductees are taken for infinite reasons, programmed for something, repaired of something, illness, disease, etc. or even damaged for reasons only the Extraterrestrials know. They also take sperm, eggs and fetuses.

How would extraterrestrials take being chewed out by a human?

You take your children to the zoo and the best thing that can happen is hearing the roar of a lion, that is entertaining for us, as long as the lion is safely behind bars that is. The lion is not wishing us a nice day, it's also not chewing us out, its letting us know it would simply just like to chew on us. A human chewing out an Extraterrestrial might be equally entertaining for the Extraterrestrials. From what I have seen, humans are docile around Extraterrestrials, and totally under their control while in the ship, no chewing out happening.

Why don't the Extraterrestrials want to reveal themselves to us? Just curious if you know why.

ETs know how detrimental that would be to our development and wellbeing. If they came out, our lives would totally be disrupted, no one would go to work; everything in our daily rush for survival would come to a standstill. Who would operate the trains, plains, and deliver the food to the stores, gas pumps would go dry, and life as we know it would come to an abrupt stop. People would be so blown away that they couldn't function. Could you go about you daily routine if an armada of Extraterrestrial ships suddenly appeared in our skies? BTW they are here, but they remain incognito for our protection.

If ETs made themselves known there would be millions of people against what they would perceive as an invasion from space, and chaos would become a real problem. Formal contact with beings not of this world sounds nice for some, but is impossible at this stage of human development. Humans need to cut their teeth in space and become more in line with Extraterrestrials, before open communication is possible.

What about exploring inner space? Through a type of psychic-telepathic mission with ET? If that's how they communicate with each other, perhaps we should begin training ourselves in their methods.

ETs can get into your head and access everything inside your mind like a computer hacker. Plotting against ETs is impossible. Some ETs are essential to humans, and I believe that if they were not here shielding Earth, humanity might look much different, perhaps more chaos and more poverty, like in the Dark Ages.

When I was a child this "Hummingbird type thing" came up to me in the field by my house and it checked me out and scanned my mind or something! It wasn't a humming bird! I never have been able to explain it. Do the Extraterrestrials have anything like that? P.S. Everybody I'm not insane!

It's more like what don't the Extraterrestrials have? They have every gadget imaginable and mostly unimaginable by human concepts and standards. ET stuff is futuristic and magical compared to our stuff; much of it has life like qualities. Humans are slowly getting there, we have talking cars, coffee pots, microwaves, and robotics in their infancy. ET stuff can move about, make decisions, communicate, and take on many forms and shapes that often morph in front of your eyes. Some of the gadgets have more personality than the extraterrestrial beings. The buzzing gadget that came to you took you to the ship.

I don't like revealing such things because that's not my job and I don't know how it will affect the person receiving the information.

Therefore, I will rephrase. Such encounters can include a trip to the inside of an extraterrestrial ship. For the most part, abductions are harmless and can be extremely beneficial to the abductee.

May 4, 2005

Are you stating that ETs are omnipresent/omniscient? That they track all human movements at all times? ETs barging into your house uninvited would never be acceptable to humans either no matter what state of mind a human is in. Why do ETs not bother with treating humans with any dignity once they actually do show up for individual contact, but remain hidden to keep human civilization from freaking out? Why the seemingly arbitrary and highly selective help?

ETs have the technology to be omnipotent. Have you noticed that cameras are going up everywhere in your city? Have you ever driven in a neighborhood without seeing a single cop and the moment you go over the speed limit they are right there on you? ETs are infinitely more attuned to humanity than that, however, to what degree they get involved varies. ETs never barge into your home they permeate into your room. Apparently, their concepts of privacy and individual rights are vastly different from ours.

We hold a power over our children, we discipline them, go into their room without asking and treat them badly, as they often interpret our actions towards them, when in fact we are only looking out for their well-being. It's a matter of perspective. Why the selective help? Good question.

Why did they tell you to lay off the herb? From my understanding, it has been proven by the CIA that subjects who are stoned are very difficult to hypnotize.

They never said why on the herb. I think it has been proven that hypnosis requires a willing subject, in other words most people can be hypnotized if they want to be, as in quitting smoking, losing weight, and other desired human modifications. Extraterrestrials don't hypnotize, they program, like software in a computer hard drive. Nevertheless, we retain freewill rights. ETs' purpose is not to create robots out of humans; they will leave that to political and religious leaders to do that

Have you read Phillip Krapf's story? His books, "The Contact has Begun" and "The Challenge of Contact".

I haven't read Krapf's book, but "The Contact has begun" implies something new is about to happen. In the old days, the Extraterrestrials were the gods of mythology. Nevertheless, in this New Age environment many people need the affirmation of "Contact" because the gods (for many people) no longer apply. It has been unfolding for centuries. Now days, people have been somewhat primed by television, movies, crop circles, and abductions accounts.

When you said, "time stopped" you meant it only stopped on the ship, right?

That was a figure of speech because I don't know how to describe ETs taking me from point A to point B. I could have said they "beamed me up" but that's been over used.

So the military will fake abductions?

They don't fake them; humans have been trained to perform certain covert operations, which include abductions. I should have left this one out of my disclosure, so I won't elaborate much on it now.

You're saying you had the awareness of an adult while still a child? Is this something that faded over time or was you mentally advanced all through your childhood? I am curious.

It faded as I grew older, I was not a prodigy child.

How do you know about intergalactic protocol? What intergalactic protocol is there and how do you know of it? Is there a federation of Extraterrestrials?

I don't have details but when I have a question in my head they give me answers. The way they do certain things makes it obvious they follow rules. Those I have contact with are not a band of outlaws. However, there are extraterrestrial outlaws out there. Humans are not shooting down Extraterrestrial ships, other Extraterrestrials are.

You've said that Extraterrestrials can manipulate our emotions, so possibly this fear is being broadcast into these folks heads? Are you saying that a person couldn't condition themselves toward calmness in the presence of an Extraterrestrial? I mean, what can an Extraterrestrial do to me that a human cannot? Why would I be afraid of them?

Nothing works better than fear as an immobilizer. We would all like to think we could control our situations regardless of environment, but not true, an example would be a pride of lions, some meaner than others, however, their disposition makes no difference to us, we can cage them, sedate them, operate on them, kill them, do anything we wish to them, even eat them.

Humans have a mind and humans can outwit other humans, and other earthly creatures, unfortunately, and I know no one wants to hear it, or believe it, but ETs hold all the cards. There are humans able to condition themselves a little more than others can we are all unique. I see no reason to be afraid of ETs, but we humans are. Pick up a turtle off the road and move it to safety, the turtle knows not that you save its life, it pees out of fear because something strange picked it up.

Great analogy! I know that feeling!

May 5, 2005

The topics on this website really scare the shit out of me sometimes. How come so many people aren't granted the ability to really experience their time taken aboard a spaceship? Someone said they had a hummingbird experience and thought it was some Extraterrestrial spy object. You responded that they were on a spaceship and didn't know it. How come you get to semi understand what has happened to you and remember a lot of what has happened to you? What really boggled my mind is when you said that you remember being on spaceship before you were born on the planet Earth and when you saw Earth arriving in the distance you didn't know this would be your home...as in when you were in an embryonic state, or you were just a soul or something with no body. Wild stuff.

When we die we go somewhere or come from somewhere, relocated or stationed like some kind of covert military garrisoned on Earth. Oops, I let the cat out of the bag. My body is a mixture of whatever concoction the Extraterrestrials implanted in my mother's womb, and then taken on several test runs around the solar system before they let me loose on this planet. They then bring me in for the occasional tweak, checkup, or perhaps to have me clean the bathrooms on their ships.

Apparently, ETs have the ability, should they so desire, to convey some information to us, and understand us conversing back. I think that puts more burden on them to explain and justify themselves, and to make more respectful and formal diplomatic relations.

One would think, however, take a look at how well we humans communicate with each other, there are wars all over the place, always have been. We have problems communicating with our children (not bragging but I was lucky and had only a few problems with mine) but I was no angel as a teenager and certainly lack of communications with my parents was a problem.

Try changing someone's mine about anything, communication is not what its crack up to be. That may be why Extraterrestrials don't talk with their mouths, they use their minds instead. Extraterrestrials communicate with humans daily, on many levels, they can talk to us and do, and apparently they don't feel the need to talk with everyone.

How often have you talked to the president of the US, the pope, or other dignitaries? If the president or the pope had a one on one conversation with an Extraterrestrial yesterday do you think the world would know about it? Not likely.

Extraterrestrials can make communications easy, they can make themselves look like humans, and chat with you at your favorite drinking hole. How often do ETs do that and those they are taking to know? Many don't know they are taking to ETs, and ETs do it plenty. At this very moment and every minute of the day ETs are talking with humans, many simply don't know it.

Who says that advanced technology leads to more wisdom? Do we see much more political wisdom today than we did 2000 years ago in Rome? Not too much. There's a slightly greater degree of guilt over war crimes but that aint stopping Sudan.

Most people don't know what the Romans and other such civilizations had at their disposal, not much evidence remains. Once we get into space and set up colonies on the Moon and then Mars, China, US, UN, EU, Japan, India, and others all clamoring for a piece of the pie, do you think it's going to be smooth sailing? There will be disagreements, conflicts, and wars, over land and boarders on those planets too. Eventually Mars and the moon will unify under their own flags and separate from Earthlings as has been the case with civilizations here on Earth. That has been the pattern for thousands of years, who believes that will change? Extraterrestrials battle each other too.

If you do believe that Extraterrestrials are like benevolent parents whose job it is to guide us toward a higher state of understanding, then I am interested to know how you

personally feel this will happen. I mean, if you were taken on a star-journey while still an embryo and have had Extraterrestrial experiences all your life, you must have some kind of insight or opinion on how future events will unfold.

I think there is a misconception about what the ETs will do. What they will not do is transform our way of life into their way of life in a day, year, decade, or century, if ever. On Earth we have a large portion of the world living like they did four thousand years ago, simple huts, no sanitation, no clean and running water, mind-boggling poverty, why don't the advanced nations of the world cooperate and bring all these people into the twenty-first century? Because not everyone believes they should interfere with sovereign nations, regardless how bad off Third World Countries are. There is disagreement among the ET factions about the level of interference they partake in on this planet as well.

Personally I believe everyone should be brought up to a minimum of civilized standards. I would love to see this world transformed into a way of life similar to that of the ETs, they exist in what we call utopia.

Do you believe that these Extraterrestrials assisted the folks at Los Alamos to build the atomic bomb? Also, do you feel that Extraterrestrials will allow us to engage in nuclear war?

ETs assisted in the development of the atom bomb, without them, we wouldn't have nuclear physics. They also allowed the US to drop the bomb on Japan. In effect, they allowed a nuclear war to take place, whether they would allow it again is anyone's guess.

Bogalla living in a hut doesn't have to hit the alarm clock, worry about bill collectors calling him, car insurance, traffic, deadlines, etc. Which of us is really more advanced?

Yeah, fishing and hunting 24/7 sounds great, it's those added benefits that suck, flies and mosquitoes buzzing around them non-stop, human poop all over the place, the putrid smell might be good for clearing up the sinuses but that's probably not a good thing for delicate noses. They drink water that the EPA would classify as hazardous waste; they eat food that Fido would run from. They sweat and are sticky all the time during the day, and freeze their buns off at night. There are a few benefits to living in the rat race.

Advanced nations offer help to uncivilized nations all the time! The deal is the uncivilized nations (for example, those living in huts and who hunt food in the jungle) would be worse off if we brought them up to civilized standards that we know of. What are they going to do with a cell phone, a microwave, or a palm pilot? Civilizations like that are not searching for ways to

advance themselves. So, that's why super powers don't run in and set up an internet system in their village.

That sounds like a good excuse to let billions of people to continue to live in poverty, I'm sure many of them would disagree with your analyst.

There are obviously those of us whose lives are spent working towards the next big leap in tech and advancements in bettering our ways of life. These nations would greatly benefit from assistance from an outside influence.

Don't you believe that we are getting assistance from the ETs? It may be subtle but it's non-stop. The breakthroughs on the leading edge of science and technology are not by way of human ingenuity alone.

Truth or fiction, this thread is a great read, and I'm enjoying it (while eating dinner)

I recently listened to a gentleman on Coast to Coast AM that was talking about Astral Projection and other forms of out of body experiences. The host of the show asked him if he had ever used his ability to see the dark side of the moon, and if he had ever seen any "Extraterrestrial bases" or Extraterrestrials inhabiting the moon. The guest replied saying that he had in

fact seen Extraterrestrial bases and saw many different types of Extraterrestrials on the moon.

Now my question is, since you say that Extraterrestrials are always in control of human / Extraterrestrial encounters how does people like the guest on the radio show fit into that plan? Do the Extraterrestrials have any sort of control over people who can use their psychic abilities to initiate their own encounters?

Humans can't sneak up on ETs even in spiritual psychic form. The ETs allowed the encounter and provided the means of the out of body experience. Many if not all of those kinds of paranormal episodes are Extraterrestrial encounters; they are gifts where the Extraterrestrial presence is subtle and undetectable.

With ALL the technology and stuff that they have, what can they possibly get from us...what is it that we have, if anything, that they could use?

Humans have nothing that ETs need or could use, it's simply their job to do whatever they are doing here on Earth, so why don't they fix every little problem humans have? That's not their job.

When you said that you would 'know' when you have been close to one......Would this mean that you would also 'know'

when you are sitting at, say, a bar with one.....Would you get that same feeling?

Yes, I would get that feeling, but it's been a long time since I sat in a bar with anyone.

Am I to understand that you know for sure that these events are actually the work of Extraterrestrials? To say it another way, is it impossible for such a thing to happen without Extraterrestrial assistance? Humans can't astral project without Extraterrestrials?

There are plenty things humans can do on their own, astral projection is not one of them. Moving the soul out of the body is not like sacking groceries, or un-sacking them, it's not even in the abilities of "rocket scientists" this is the realm of the gods, ETs.

May 6, 2005

However, they are not ALL 'helping' us...and it is 'these non-helpers' that I am asking if you know? What they want from us?

The "non-helpers" are a mysterious bunch, what is their angle, what do they want from us? Surly they have ulterior motives, as you say. I can't answer for all of them, I don't know all of them. But, from the ones I do know about they too have jobs to perform on this planet.

An example would be basic training in the army, the worst time in my life, the drill sergeants were spawns of Satan straight out of hell. The drill sergeants hated us and on many occasions it seem they were trying to kill us rather than train us. It wasn't until I graduated basic training that I realized how valuable that hell-hole training was. They really didn't hate us or try to kill us, they actually liked us and were preparing us to survive a hellish war, should we end up in one.

Often what we perceive to be evil is in reality the exact opposite, it works the other way around too, good is not always good for us.

Technology from ET? Proof ? Cause that's a massive statement to say. Can you give examples?

I can't prove god, ETs, the tooth fairy or Santa Clause. However, there is a tooth fairy I have seen her on more than one occasion, she had a strange resemblance to my wife and put money under my daughters' pillows when they lost teeth. Santa Clause is more difficult but he exists too. I once had to fit myself into one of those red suits and bring gifts to put under the Christmas tree while the children peeked from the other room with my wife. Everything on this level of existence (Earth) is an allusion. Something or someone is behind the allusions. Children don't know who is behind those fairytales and they don't care, the end result is what matters most. The money from the tooth fairy was real, the gifts under the tree were real, and the technology that pops out of research laboratories is real. To whom we chose to give credit to is what is disputed.

The technology that seeps out of our laboratories, universities, corporations comes from where? Santa Clause? Scientists? Gods?

Can anyone know, can we point the finger at who is responsible? Hundreds of people, thousands of people, where do they/we get ideas? A whisper, a nudge, hard work, a breakthrough, a gift from Santa Clause. Ingenuity comes from hard work, desire, perseverance and luck. What is luck? Luck is a gift from higher beings, Extraterrestrials.

Extraterrestrials have jobs to do, they are not here to play footsies with us; they are here to impart information to humans. When they abduct people, it is strictly business, however, some of them have a sense of humor, and pranks are not out of the question.

Why are you on here? Has something happened to you that you can't explain? Most human specimens don't know they have ever had contact with ETs. Some people have bits and pieces of memories of Extraterrestrials, others only a strange feeling or deep curiosity about space and the stars above.

May 8, 2005

So I would think that if Extraterrestrials/ET really wanted to prevent humans from understanding them, they would better their amnesia inducing skills than anything currently in use.

Abductees remember what they are allowed to remember, nothing more, nothing less. The fact is there are numerous people that remember more than they are willing to talk about. They know about ETs very well and don't need additional information to validate their experiences. In other words, they are not going to be searching internet sites for UFO information, or reading UFO books. Many of these people are professionals in respectable leadership positions and will never divulge what they know, they don't need to. If they did, they would compromise their standing in the community. They are the same people that would call you crazy if you mentioned anything about ETs and UFOs around them. They shield themselves well.

People that are searching for the "truth" about Extraterrestrials are those with bits and pieces of memories of their encounters, and are trying to make sense of what happened to them, or is happening to them, some believe they are losing their minds, and need to know if ETs are real. ETs, in addition to whatever else they do with these people, intentionally leave broken memories in them as part of their (ETs) program to slowly condition mankind to extraterrestrial reality. Thousands of people with their cumulative UFO stories (not enough information to fill in the puzzle however) make up the catalyst that fuels the UFO phenomena.

Because of the accumulated accounts there are millions of people aware that something is going on, even though these millions of people have never seen or experienced UFOs and ETs themselves that they can remember.

May 9, 2005

I have read your posts on this topic and I'm simply fascinated on your story. Above all I'm a believer of your story and I am skeptic myself. I am only 15 years old. I got to high school and I do myself believe in Extraterrestrials and UFOs. But when I try and tell these type of things to my friends they simply dismiss it and ridicule me. It's sometimes nice to find a place where I can find others like me. I have only one question for now.

I'm sorry if you have already answered this question but how do the Extraterrestrials choose their abductees and are they chosen randomly? Or do the abductees have a specific mental advantage than another humans.

I don't know the particulars of how or why they choose who they do. My dad while he was still alive never believed in extraterrestrials, but told me that when he was a boy he saw three large flying disks a few years before the Second World War. He had no explanation for them but adamantly did not believe they were Extraterrestrials. Some people even when they see fantastic out of this world stuff can't make the mental leap that we are not alone in the universe. He didn't know it but he was being abducted on a regular basis. Many abductions run in the family. No one in my family believes in ETs.

If I were you, I wouldn't talk much about it at school, as you already know people will make fun of you. Even those that believe and have experienced ETs will seldom admit it. The subject remains taboo for the general population.

I'm one of those people who don't care about what others think of me most of the time. So I talk about UFOs and ETs at work, and around other people. Once I tell them all that I know they're like "Wow, that sounds possible and interesting" so don't be afraid!

Times are changing; more people believe or want to believe in extraterrestrials, so there is more acceptance. Still, if you are in certain jobs like airline pilot, teacher, clergy, CEO, scientist, politics, and the military, talking ET stuff is a sure bet to early retirement. It took me a long time to come out of the closet, my wife knew about my experiences, but I never told my children until they were older.

One day my daughter came home from school, she was in the fourth grade and rode the school bus. We lived in the typical neighborhood in one of the suburbs that were sprouting up all over the place. While on the bus ride to school a boy older than her came over to her seat and told her that he saw a UFO hovering over our house the night before. He lived three houses up on the other side of the street with a clear view of our house. She didn't know what a UFO was, but she was in shock that an older boy spoke to her on the bus, she didn't responded to him and he returned to his seat without saying anything else.

That evening after school she asked me what a UFO was, and why was such a thing over our house. I told her it was an unidentified flying object, I didn't elaborated and she shrugged it off and never brought it up again.

My children are much older now and I have mentioned a few things about ETs to them. However, they don't seem all that interested, if and when they become curious I will tell them whatever they wish to know.

May 10, 2005

Why do you think that all pictures of UFOs are blurred and fuzzy? Why do you think that all UFO sightings are summary described?

ETs are slowly making themselves known, eventually they will come out and everyone can take pictures of their neat flying machines and them, but I'm thinking it will not be for some time yet.

We have stealth aircraft designed to avoid radar and other forms of detection because we wish to remain incognito during reconnaissance/spying. The ETs have the ability to mask their ships in infinite ways, including making them very difficult to photograph. They are invisible most of the time and uncloak only when they want certain people to see them, however, they don't allow clear photos of their ships because they are not ready to make formal contact.

That is why most contactees can only give brief statements of their experiences. Ninety-five percent of what most abductees experience is blocked from memory. Regression only reveals what the Extraterrestrials allow, or want the person/s to know. Most of the time info from regression is material the ETs put there for the purpose of misleading. ETs will dictate information telepathically like questions asked of them. Seeing is believing, therefore, they don't want much of their stuff accurately described on the front pages of newspapers and other media.

Why are you still here, being able to speak rather than dead? Do you actually think that someone believes just because he wants to?

I'm still here because obviously I'm no threat, being slightly entertaining is not going to upset the apple cart of the military, the world, or the ETs. Obviously, the ETs want some of this out there, a little at a time; otherwise, no one would be able to tell their stories. The military can't "whack" people like me without permission from the ETs.

Proof is what makes belief a constant and not a variable.

I agree one hundred percent. Without proof, I wouldn't believe either and I believe one hundred percent.

Did you ever get straight answers from ETs on these obvious questions?

1) What precisely are they doing here, and why?

This planet is an incubator. There is more than one race of ETs here because there are many ongoing programs, like DNA manipulation, schooling, and incarceration programs. Humans originated from places throughout the galaxy and are being sorted out on this and other planets like this one.

2) What is the purpose of their limited, and apparently involuntary, interactions with certain humans?

They interact with those they use as vehicles to bring things into this planet, like technology, higher awareness and DNA material, to mention but a fraction.

3) Why certain humans, such, as, apparently, yourself?

I was willing to work cheap.

4) Why do they apparently allow marginal independent contact, but do not make full and open diplomatic relations with the population as a whole?

Earth populations would revolt against entities from other worlds. Not everyone wants ETs down here telling us what to do.

5) Do they believe this is ethical?

It is ethical to keep this planet from a mental meltdown, because that's what would happen if all of a sudden humanity became aware that there are thousands of ET ships on Earth, on the moon, in orbit around the planet, and throughout the solar system.

6) Why haven't they bothered to ask us about it?

We wouldn't understand the question.

If they had the ability to colonize the galaxy why is it not bursting with obvious EM signs that we would have seen with SETI. {Frankly I would have thought that if major ET civilizations with interstellar travel were possible, then SETI would have given a positive result the very first time it was turned on, as thousands of solar systems would be giving artificial emissions.

Humans have yet to hatch out of this planet (space exploration) and we believe that we can pick up advanced extraterrestrial communications? Humans are a few hundred years from that kind of ability if not a whole lot longer. SETI doesn't have any devices that can detect exotic ET stuff. There are thousands of Extraterrestrial ships buzzing all over the place right here on Earth and in Earth's orbit and our technology can't detect them, yet we point our equipment at places light years away and we expect to see what?

It wasn't that long ago that we communicated with smoke signals, and cuneiform tablets. The electromagnetic spectrum is a nice communications vehicle for us today, but it's not what the big boys and girls in galaxies faraway play with.

So ET/Extraterrestrial Beings are basically 'right under our noses'? They can cloak themselves and remain invisible, and I

have to admit that I always feel a presence here on Earth that I can't quite explain. Now, many people would say that what I feel is Universal Energy, or the collective thoughts of all organisms, or that I am overly suspicious in nature; but I KNOW that I am paranoid in thinking this way, and neither should anyone else. Perhaps the theory of thousands of ET vehicles/craft moving around and beyond this planet is valid.

Would you then agree, that there is an ET 'contain/hide our identity and technology trickle-down effect' being played upon human beings?

We are not contained on this planet by ETs (completely) we are contained on this planet more so by politicians that keep us grounded for personal agendas. They would rather spend tax money on other things. NASA is so fearful of losing funding that they ground their fleet for years every time a shuttle has a mishap.

The space program belongs to those who are not frightened so easily. The government has the money but they don't have the will to put people into space. The chains of containment will not be broken until private enterprise gets into the game. ETs have been infusing technological information into the hands and minds of people for a long time. They teach us how to build and ride a bicycle, but they will not ride it for us. The only thing that is keeping humanity from taking that next big step into the cosmos is the lack of backbone from the bureaucratic public sector.

ETs are not concerned about the speed of human development, nor are they fearful that we will bring our belligerence into the galaxy and contaminate the waters of blissful peace loving advanced cultures. Our nuclear technology, given to us by the ETs, is like a small firecracker in the realm of Extraterrestrial weapons. Our belligerence and war mongering is nothing but child's play, roughhousing on the playground. There are no ETs concerned about us causing mischief in the heavens, such a concept is absurd!

There's no evidence at all that any nuclear technology was "given" to us by Extraterrestrials. I'm a professional scientist and I've seen no development which shows anything but incremental human progress.

There is no evidence of ETs at all. We don't see the magic at work behind every day phenomenon like simple things as plants. Flowers sprouting from nowhere, leaves turning energy from the sun into apples, oranges and grapes popping them out from a branch of wood. The process is slow, nevertheless, it happens without our understanding it.

ETs deliver things incrementally, they don't drive up in a stealth bomber and hand us the keys, they put ideas in many peoples' heads and spread them out over many years, even centuries.

There is a very consistent chain of evidence from Otto Hahn and Lise Meitner observing spontaneous decay of Uranium to Fermi, to nuclear reactors created with Earth materials, and based on Earth physics known at that time.

Where do ideas come from? A perceived need, and a desire to meet that need, is the mother of invention, mother=ET. Many people ponder a problem until an answer comes to them. Some problems take longer than others to solve, observing spontaneous decay of Uranium, for instance. Had you the opportunity to talk to Hahn, Meitner, and Fermi, they may have told you they didn't quite understand how they came about with some of the stuff they are credited with discovering.

I'd sure like ET help on whatever they do to fly and communicate faster than light. But so far, there's no evidence they've helped us with squat.

ET showing us how to fly at the speed of light is putting the cart before the horse. Would you hand you five-year-old child the keys to the family car? What would humans do with the ability to fly at the speed of light at our present stage of underdevelopment?

If they want to help us, one month answering questions from the faculty at MIT would be amazing.

Are you sure that ET is not at MIT? ET is not going to accelerate dispensing information to bring about Utopia in a single swoop, there is a process, and they follow that process.

The world wouldn't freak out if:

1) ETs introduced themselves.

2) Didn't molest people against their will

3) ETs talked about themselves, and helped us, openly.

The world would freak out. Some people would see it as no different from a Hitler, Stalin, Churchill, or a Bush, claiming technological superiority and taking over.

1. ETs have introduced themselves to quite a few people.

2. I don't believe ETs are molesting anyone; however, they are quite intense super beings and exceedingly intimidating.

3. Humans would cease being productive in the presence of ETs. Expecting ETs to create the perfect world for them/us and why not, they have the capability to turn our whole way of life around, but that's not what they are here to do. How would they explain to

humanity that they can make Earth into a paradise, but they just don't feel like it?

Do you really think that 'the private sector' is going to be any more forthcoming about ET and help bring humans forward in life?

I'm not talking disclosure, which is not up to the government or the private sector. ETs are the only ones that can disclose their reality to the world.

There should be an age limit on here...I would not want my kids being exposed to half of this stuff.

Many people feel that censorship is the best way.

May 11, 2005

What we (as in say scientists from major universities) could use? Some ideas on an experiment which shows us a key physical principle that we aren't aware of now. We could then run with that. Right now, we appear to understand the basic physics of our everyday world, which is feasibly engineerable, extremely well. There doesn't seem to be any obvious major loophole. We can describe all physical objects we see on Earth damn well, at least w.r.t. basic science. There are anomalies still unexplained, but they are exotic things in observational cosmology towards the beginning of the universe, or at ultra high energies in particle accelerators.

You insist and believe profoundly that scientists in the past used lots of elbow grease to finagle their theories and inventions from the basic elements of this planet, and I agree it was their efforts and dedication that led them to the answers they so craved and eventually "received". But why are you and other scientists not following in their footsteps, doing all the work, pounding your heads against the wall when you inevitably run into that barrier, that fortress, that keeps secrets tightly and stingily from us. Why should ET give you info if they didn't give info to your predecessors, as you believe and stated in the quote below?

"Assuming that any moment of scientific creativity is attributable to ET Extraterrestrials is an insult. Where did Fermi and Hahn and Meitner get their ideas? By having lots of background knowledge and thinking about it."

Where did Fermi and Hahn get their mind, hands and ability to do research? From god? From Darwinian natural selection? Or perhaps from Extraterrestrials. Certainly, it depends on one's background on what they might be willing to believe. However, we humans had nothing to do with the creation of our own bodies and mind, some unknown supernatural force did. If that is an insult, then so be it.

Why is the interaction so one-sided? Why can't WE ask them about, oh, their music or literature, or anything about their culture?

How many of us are interested in our children's music, or in the latest fads, they are ensnared in? What if a bunch of MIT people went to one of those villages, where people still live as they did in the stone ages and told the natives about their taste in music, their literature or about the latest wonders, they have discovered in their labs. I bet the natives would really be excited. Same difference.

I have the feeling that either ETs don't' understand human society and feelings at all or they don't give a dam about us or any ethical reciprocity.

ETs know us inside and out, better than we know ourselves, that's why they have limited contact with us. ETs come in many different flavors, some care deeply. Most are indifferent and it's only a job for them. Then there are ETS that plain don't like us.

Did you mention earlier anything about your children being involved with ET? Do you have any idea as to whether they have been abducted or contacted by the ET/Extraterrestrials?

My children are part of the program, but they have no idea or any memories of their contact with ET.

Can you share some insights regarding consecutive generational abductions?

I have several brothers and sisters and none of them are involved, neither have any of them shown much interest in the ET phenomenon.

DNA is like a barcode, it identifies our basic equipment package, our location (Earth) our manufacturer (which ET species) and much more. That is why many people involved with ET go back several generations.

May 12, 2005

I don't think people would be upset if ETs said "it's your world and your future, you will have to make it yourself, but we'll be there to give you a hand, or at least think about it, if you ask nicely." I think that would be great.

People meditate in order to discover a higher awareness in themselves. Millions throughout the ages prayed to gods for guidance and favors. Meditation and prayer is simply telepathic communications with higher beings. People fixate on objects or ideas and focus energy on them, sometimes with supernatural results. Success usually comes to those most determined to get what they desire. The fact is there are higher beings among us; they have always been around us in various forms, spiritual, corporal, and something in-between. If you ask "nicely", they might give you what you want; after all, they have access to the secrets of the universe. They don't care what religion you are, or if you have no beliefs whatsoever.

May 13, 2005

I haven't sifted through all of the other posts in this thread yet, so correct me if I say something stupid. Didn't you say you were born and raised in Italy? If so, how were you in the U.S. Army?

I was born in Italy. My parents move to America a few years after WW2 and became American citizens. I was a US citizen through them and eligible for the draft, I enlisted.

In this world most have to get their own proof, no Earthling has the authority to hand out proof. I have proof but I can't share. Since I am able to remember many of my experiences I take that as a sign that I can speak about some of them. Many people know something paranormal is going on so I tell a few things that I have experienced to validate that there is something going on for those that are interested. What is proof for me? I have listed some in this tread, I have been inside ET ships. Most of the time I find myself inside the ships with no idea how I got there, I leave the same way. However, I have entered such ships through a vortex that has opened up in my bedroom, from where Extraterrestrials emerge. We talk and then I'm taken into the vortex and find myself inside an Alien ship. Once inside the ship I have patches of memory and no more. I talk about what I do remember, obviously the ETs don't want me or others to come back with more detailed accounts, just enough to know that there is something big going on in our solar system, and that the galaxy is swarming with civilizations millions of years ahead of us. ETs have given me proof and I have never asked for it. They give proof to thousands of people, but most will never admit to it, and many will take what they know to the grave with them. It took me fifty years to talk openly about my involvement. The proof is not "out there" it's right here on this planet for thousands, perhaps millions of people that have experienced it.

Well I for one am convinced of the existence of extraterrestrials. As a child I watched a UFO while sitting on the hood of a car with my football coach after a late night game. He was bringing me home after a game and we were driving on a small country road in Georgia when we both saw an object doing amazing maneuvers. After being completely stunned from what we were seeing my coach decided to stop the car in the middle of the road and sit on the hood and watch. I was only about 12 or 13 but remember it like it was yesterday. It moved in the sky like a firefly, back and forth side to side and up and down and stopping suddenly like it saw us. After about 15 minutes, my coach got scared and demanded we get back in the car and leave. I wanted him to flash the headlights at it but he was ready to just leave. The whole experience was hair raising to say the least. And the fact that

an adult was acting scared made it all that more real. The funny thing is the next day at school I was telling all my teammates and they were acting like it was a joke so I went and got the coach and told him to tell them what I was saying was true and to my surprise he acted like I was making it all up and he told the team that nothing of the sort ever happened. Imagine that! My point is even those people that experience these things sometimes they block them out or deny to themselves that they ever happened just to feel normal or to avoid embarrassment. Oh well, it is what it is. I am a 27-year-old computer tech now. And to this day I still think about that embarrassing situation as a child where I learned how people act about things they can't explain.

Understandably the coach wasn't willing to compromise his job and reputation, and did what most people that like their jobs do, keep quiet about the paranormal that they might encounter. Abductions are not always measured in hours or days some can be a few seconds or a few minutes in duration and therefore no lost time to speak of. Perhaps the coach remembered more than he wished to remember and was trying to deal with that new reality in private. You apparently don't remember much of it other than seeing the craft flying around and it is very possible that it was only the coach they came to visit since he was the only one with residual fear. Abductions can be positive experiences regardless of the fear and other bizarre things that may take place during an ET encounter. Some abductions are a one shot deal and never happen again.

Meditation and prayer are very different and you even contradict yourself in the first quote. Also, can you expand on the phrase "simply telepathic"?

I didn't contradict myself when I said "people meditate in order to discover a higher awareness in themselves." Meditation is mental communication with a higher power as is prayer. Unless you believe that the subconscious is just another part of the human brain and dies with the body at death, which it doesn't. The subconscious is a communications center with higher powers outside of the human body. That part of the mind is where we receive much of our "intuition" and other pertinent information that we call creativity. It's the place where we experience the thing known as "eureka", after pondering over a problem and receiving an answer. Prayer uses these same facilities. Telepathy is talking with other people or invisible entities in a non-verbal way. When people pray they usually do so in silent meditation. If they pray aloud, their thoughts are directed at certain deities, or objects. All verbal and non-verbal communications is monitored by ETs, or gods if that is your preference.

I applaud your courage to speak about your Extraterrestrial encounters! In my estimation, the dizziness and disorientation that people have when near Zetan-Extraterrestrial craft is due to a strong electromagnetic field, which is tied in with their antigravity wave propulsion system.

1. "Humans can't sneak up on ETs even in spiritual form. The ETs allowed the encounter and provided the means of the out of body experience."

2. "Many if not all of those kinds of paranormal episodes are Extraterrestrial encounters; they are gifts where the Extraterrestrial presence is benign."

I have to disagree with you on those above two points. The physical Extraterrestrials have more advanced technology and a greater industrial base than we have, to be sure. But they have nothing on us in the spiritual or psychic arena. In fact, my own experiences of investigation and research have shown me that they have no telepathic ability whatsoever. This is not to state that they cannot brainwash an abductee into believing that they have the ability to walk through walls, read minds, etc.

A prisoner who believes that his captors have godlike abilities is less likely to attempt escape and/or resist them. This is basic psychological manipulation and the Extraterrestrials

know full well how to do this with drugs and implanted screen memories.

I have found evidence that they are actually afraid of true telekinetic ability, simply because they cannot duplicate it with their machines. Yes, they have antigravity beams and paralysis rays, but they can't actually telekinetically move objects or create matter in any context. That is their weakness. They are intellectually and technologically gifted but spiritually primitive.

Compassion dictates evolution, not technology. They have the technology but they don't portray the spirituality. They are neither omnipotent nor omniscient.

Spirituality is a funny thing; no one knows exactly what it is. Although every living thing has a form of it including the ETs, except for those entities that are biological machines created as probes, or as a workforce around the galaxy as androids.

All living things exist at some level of awareness, presumably the higher the level of awareness the higher the spirituality. However, spirituality is use as a measure of higher virtue by those who claim to have lots of it. Here on Earth many competing rivals have claimed exclusivity to true "spirituality" or enlightenment, and all those others (those people or organizations with contrary beliefs) are imposters, heathens, and spawns of Satan.

Mormons, Catholics, all five thousand denominations of Protestants, Jews, Muslims, Buddhist, Anarchist, Communist, Socialist, Democrats, Republicans and the thousands of others that I haven't mentioned. These people and organizations claim to be more virtuous, more enlightened and therefore, more spiritual, than their competitors, therefore spiritually here on Earth has proven to be nothing more than a human ego trip.

We have a soul and so do higher levels of Extraterrestrials, but there are many machines out there involved in abductions as part of the ET workforce, perhaps that is whom you speak of.

May 14, 2005

The more accurate paradigm that I and other researchers espouse is the less popular perspective on the Extraterrestrial situation. It sells fewer books, not more. We further the idea that the Zetan-Extraterrestrials are in fact not benevolent, but self-serving and subtly imperialistic. Scores of abductee testimonial evidence corroborates and confirms this hypothesis.

I don't know much about the Zetans, there is a lot of stuff written and I have only scratched the surface of the UFO genre. I don't know which type of Extraterrestrials are dealing with me I do know that nice friendly ones have and some very ugly personality types too. The personality spectrum of ETs seems to be as varied as that of humans. As time goes by, I remember a bit more with each encounter, perhaps eventually I will have a better picture of what they are about. I have never been regressed and personally, I know it would be pointless since they can place whatever they wish in our minds. Nevertheless, I believe that I leave with a bit more knowledge of them after each encounter.

May 16, 2005

I am enjoying reading about your experiences. Don't worry about the people trying to ridicule you, they are not looking at the bigger picture. I for one am leaning toward believing at least some of what you are saying. You seem to talk very clinical about your experiences. Much of what you say makes sense and is quite logical, for example, why the various governments are very reluctant to disclose the truth to the general population. I would like to hear more. Do you believe/know if there has been contact between EBEs and ancient peoples? How long have they been "helping" humankind to progress? I also understand why you will/can not go into great detail about your experiences. Keep the information flowing though!

I'm sure you know that not everyone agrees that humankind has progressed, with or without the help of Extraterrestrials. Most people consider anything less than creating utopia on this planet unacceptable, especially if ETs are real and have the means to solve all our problems and do not. The Milky Way galaxy as well as most other galaxies are highly complex star systems, but not as chaotic as some cosmologist seem to believe. There is structure and accountability in the galaxies, but there are outlaws too.

Earth is an incubator and like any nursery there are many such incubators in each galaxy, millions of them just like this Earth. There are good caretakers, and bad caretakers. I'm inclined to believe that what we see as good and bad is not as simple as black and white when looking at the big picture. I believe this because I have learned more through adverse situations than desirable ones. Few of us will choose to go through hardship voluntarily, therefore all of us are thrown into such situations during or existence.

ETs have always been here and are everywhere. There are millions of planetary systems that are utopias whether Earth will ever be turned into a utopia I have no idea, but I doubt it. Everything already exists somewhere in the galaxy; there is no technology that we can imagine that doesn't exist now. Sickness, poverty, war, pestilence, hate, prejudice and a host of other calamities, are simply the apparatus of planets as Earth, and not a permanent condition of mankind.

May 17, 2005

I don't expect Extraterrestrials or ETs to solve all of our world problems. I do expect them to introduce themselves nicely, at a minimum. As a nice bonus, it would help if they could help us with some aspects of our life, which may include some of their advanced technology. With that, we could perhaps start solving our own problems a little bit better.

One hundred years ago, indoor plumbing didn't exist for the vast majority of people. There were no airplanes other than a few experimental ones. Electricity that would revolutionize everything and take mankind into the twenty-first century was slowly being introduced to mankind by (E)dison and (T)esla. As you can see ET has been helping us progress. Humans didn't get from horse-drawn wagons to space shuttles in less than sixty years alone.

So far, if they are flying around without our explicit knowledge and permission, they are causing us problems and doing nothing in return. Telling us it's for our own good, and then putting things into our mind is even worse.

They are not flying around without our knowledge many governments know about them. By placing things into our minds, we then turn around and put those things into blueprints, new inventions, new technology and an awareness that we can go into space, etc.

With reference to the military being behind abductions you said :

"They don't fake them; humans have been trained to perform certain covert operations, which include abductions. This is one item I should have left out of my disclosure, so I won't elaborate much on it now."

From this I get the feeling that there is something more that these EBEs are conditioning the human race for. Are we being conditioned for violence to be used in an intergalactic future war?

The only battles we are being conditioned to fight are the everyday battles of life. The ETs have millions of years of technological superiority on humans, they can fight their own battles.

Why would they orchestrate and allow the many conflicts around the world to continue? Why are they allowing our society to become more and more violent?

More violent than what period in history? WW2, WW1, Napoleonic wars, Dark ages, the Romans, the Crusaders, the Moslems, the Greeks, Vikings, etc. These are peaceful times compared to the insanity of the past. Why does ET allow belligerence? Several reasons:

1. Humans enjoy violence, hence the movies that are most popular coming out of Hollywood.

2. It is easier to plunder than doing the work to create things.

3. Successions of peoples and societies have created a sense of history, legitimizing the human illusion that we originated from this planet, savages evolving through the ages.

4. More than one ET group is involved on this planet and they introduced competition between the races for those reasons.

5. Everyone on this planet more or less, chose to be here, to be challenged by a void, a yearning in their soul for greed, hate, envy and the need to quench the thirst for blood thirst, are a few of the reasons.

6. We use fertilizer in order to produce healthy and beautiful flowers, the best fertilizer is manure.

7. To appreciate love, peace and tranquility some need/wish to experience hell first.

8. ETs accommodate those needs and requirements in each of us.

Your posts are fascinating...keep them coming!

    Will do.

Are you saying that these EBEs only started helping us around 100 years ago?

This world didn't require a giant leap forward until it reached a critical mass of population, where it could not feed and house the numbers of people coming in without a major shift in technology. That point in time was the turn of the century. Mankind is precisely where it should be, technologically speaking. That was true one hundred years ago, one thousand years ago, etc. We receive the appropriate technology for the times we live in.

This is a long process, so this tells me that time means nothing to them? Is time perceived differently by the ETs? Do you know whether they are capable of inter-dimensional travel?

Time is an illusion. Go into space away from planet Earth and what do you use to measure time with? Our twenty-four hour system is based on the rotation of this planet, and its movement around the sun. I point this out to demonstrate how fickle the whole idea of time is. ETs are not constrained by the illusion of time. They don't have time clocks, they don't need to be anywhere at certain times. Higher life forms in this galaxy are not constrained to time and schedules. It's a fairly new phenomenon on this planet too; it became increasingly more important with the industrial revolution at the turn of the nineteenth century. Eventually it will not be as important a few centuries into the future here on Earth.

Extraterrestrials are capable of inter-dimensional travel, humans are too, our souls can travel on that super highway with the guidance of ETs.

Why aid us in creating weapons of destruction like the A-bomb when it would be more beneficial to aid us in creating for example food that grows in any climate, or a way to prevent global warming, a way to stabilize the climates throughout the world? And what about revolutionary cures for the most common diseases? If the Earth population didn't have to worry about cures, wars, etc, we would focus our energies into advancing the human race and we could already have been populating the stars by now!

ETs are not here to turn this planet into utopia, what you see is what we get. The illusion of what many perceive as life as you quote above is only that an illusion. We all see the world from unique perspectives; those you believe are suffering may in fact be experiencing something necessary for their particular plight in life.

To what end are there millions of "incubators"? Why nurse us through life?

There are millions of planets in this galaxy that are exactly like Earth, same type of people same kind of problems. They nurse us through life because there is no other way to get us from point A to point B.

Great posts! I like that they are longer and you have a more personal tone with your answers. It's like you're lecturing us from the Extraterrestrial perspective without you really knowing if you're part Extraterrestrial or what. You seem sincere and I like reading this thread. Anyone who shares personal info has a bit more credibility. I suppose you could even make the personal details up, but there are details to your answers that ring true.

Would you agree then that the Extraterrestrials are like "God" in that they sort of sit back and allow good and evil (free will) to do their thing but they are "minding the crib" so that we don't wreck ourselves?

ETs are technical advisers, teachers, slave drivers, your best friend and your worst nightmare. They don't sit back and watch they are neck deep in mankind's affairs. We have free will, although it doesn't always feel like it.

They mind the crib, and are now preparing the house (Solar system) so that we can crawl around some of the rooms (planets and moons). It is obvious to some of us that in the next few decades, humans will be stepping out of the crib and venturing into space. ETs are preparing the way but will remain behind the stage scenery so that we don't become distracted.

We are entering a phase of phenomenal change and the problems on this planet are only a diversion, not a deterrent to what is ahead. While many fear the future and believe that life on this world is going down the toilet fantastic changes will happen right under their noses. Many will participate; many will remain asleep.

I guess that's a nice thought, but who is the governing body? Who controls Extraterrestrials and tells them what they can and cannot do to us?

There is a hierarchy and the upper echelons of ETs remain shrouded in mystery, much like the worker ETs remain shrouded here on Earth.

May 18, 2005

Unless I am way off the mark and the EBEs are planning on helping/aiding humankind to a more meaningful existence before we are 'allowed' to venture into space.

The world will never be a perfect place in the minds of everyone. Your idea of utopia, right and wrong, true happiness or whatever is not necessarily shared by the six and a half billion and growing other Earthlings, with their own unique perspective of what makes a utopia.

I live in a prosperous country amongst people who have good and great living conditions, yet if you talk to them some are not happy, they are concerned about the future, the economy, their children, gridlock in the large cities, the politicians, sickness, death, getting old, etc. In general humans tend to be pessimistic about life regardless of their economic condition, there are plenty of optimists, but they are the exception. There never will be a Promised Land that will suit everyone here on Earth, that's one reason we have so many wars, few agree on how to make Earth a better place.

ET took mankind kicking and screaming through the Industrial Revolution, they will take mankind into space regardless of the unfinished problems many perceive we still have on Earth. Not to say that we as individuals, communities and nations shouldn't do everything we possibly can to help each other, after all, that is the fine line that separates man from beast. Many of the answers to the problems on Earth will only be found in space in zero gravity, and super clean labs, from which will emerge new advances in medicine, electronics, and agriculture.

ETs are not cuddly they lean toward tough-love.

I am interested to know your views on the theory that an advanced people once inhabited the Earth many thousands of years ago, before "official" civilization began. Yes, I am talking about an "Atlantis" of sorts. This was a civilization with a vast knowledge of the stars, precession, the constellations, building, and understanding of the world around us. They allegedly flourished around 15,000BC - 7,000BC, and probably earlier, are thought to have built the Sphinx, and after a disaster of sorts, the few survivors spread throughout the world. They taught their knowledge to the early Egyptians, the peoples of S. America, and the Far East, amongst others.

ETs were here way before those dates you mention. They worked openly among the native-experiments and had colonies, and cities with all the magical apparatus of their home planet. More than one race of ETs resided on Earth and some people believe that perhaps some battles took place between those races. There were battles, but once the time for humans came those ETs in charge simply destroyed much of the evidence of their existence and the existence of other ET encampments, or infestations.

ETs never left Earth. As humans became aware of their surroundings the opulent and sophisticated life style of the ETs clashed with the primitive lives of humans. ETs covertly blended into the societies they set up and became leaders, priest, senators, teachers, and nobility. Smaller colonies of ETs continued to squat in areas devoid of human population. ETs live amongst us to this day, in primitive cities, but some chose to commute. It's only a short ride to any of the planetary suburbs located on neighboring planets, moons, and mother ships, cruising the solar system.

I was thinking about this last night, and I was wondering if you could tell us the sequence of events from you being "told" that there is a space ship waiting, to you actually stepping on board. Did the military come and tell you that it was time to go on a trip? Were you on base when you were told? Or did you have to travel some distance to arrive at the ship? Did you just drop what you were doing and go, or did you have a specific time that you had to embark, like "at 1800hrs you are to report to Hangar 15 for a trip on Spaceship 1"?

The military is a well-oiled machine but highly bureaucratic. Every second of every member's life is accounted for. Nevertheless, of my three years of active duty several months of it remains unaccounted, completely blanked out of my mind. Much of that blank space was while I served overseas.

Prior to entering a ship I was fetched by an NCO and dropped off at a hanger and told to go inside, an ET telepathically briefed me beforehand. Most of the time I never saw the exterior of the ship, I walked through plywood corridors that led into the ship. Sometimes there was no one around not even guards that I could see.

Much of what goes on inside the ship remains in the ship. At times, I have a clear understanding of everything I did while in the ship, but when I try to put down on paper my detailed experiences or verbalized them I am hampered. ETs enjoy making us look foolish and they give us (contactees) just enough information to achieve that.

When you came back from your trip and disembarked from the ship did you just go about your business? Did you go home to rest, and were you given any leave time by the military after such trips? Or did the military let you come and go as you pleased? Were you debriefed when you got back from these trips?

Afterwards I had a few beers. The military never "officially" gave me more time off than the thirty days per year. Since I experienced missing time, at least in my mind, perhaps they allowed extra leave. I could not come and go as I pleased during "normal" duty. I don't recall being debriefed it may have happened and then blocked by the military or the ETs.

When I was younger (17), I was diagnosed with Circaidian Discronism. Dr.Bartell in Wichita Falls Texas made the diagnosis. He told me at that time not to worry. It was very rare, and the number of potential patients worldwide would never justify the development of any drugs to specifically treat my disorder. He said, but hey you know the guy that wrote Lonesome Dove lives 45 miles from here, and he has the same thing you have! And I'm like O.k., but, so what does that mean? He tells me if a sleep disorder could make you Famous this is the one to have!

I'm not famous, but I totally understand what you were saying about time! I know, because I'm always on a different schedule than the average person. We Humans are not tied to the 24 hour rotation of the Earth, I'm living proof of that!

As you know our biological clocks are triggered by daylight and nighttime based on the Earth's rotation. People like you have problems conforming to that cycle perhaps you spend more time out there in space than most people. Extraterrestrials' biological clocks run on different frequencies, assuming they have one, while on their ships their bodies are not weighed down by gravity so they need less energy than if they existed only on Earth as humans do. While in space the human brain detects the loss of gravity and the absence of darkness and we can literally go without sleeping for longer periods. As far as I know, ETs don't sleep at all.

Due to the lack of gravity and the brightness inside the ships, the human mind and body are not taxed much, no jetlag, little or no fatigue and no mental exhaustion, which may only be a feature of extraterrestrial technology built into their ships. That translates to less food and drink requirement. I don't recall eating or drinking while on the ships. Obviously to keep the kidneys from failing there must be some system that compensates for liquid intake. The flipside of traveling inside ET ships for extended time makes returning to Earth a mental and physical drag.

May 20, 2005

Is our government in a stalemate right now with these advanced souls? Are they still showing us technology advancement? By the year 2012, will they start to make themselves more known to the general population?

There is no stalemate that would require equivalence between humans and ETs. ETs infuse people on Earth with new knowledge at appropriate stages, and it will go on for a long time as long as humans exist. We humans are still playing in the sandbox with little shovels and buckets, but bigger stuff is coming off the assembly line. Some stuff takes years before the public becomes aware of it. New ideas and technologies continue unabated to be introduced across the board, not only to the military, but to individuals, entrepreneurs, industry, and universities. The "exotic" stuff falls to the military and their contractors first, because the average Joe shouldn't be running around with dangerous materials that only select ET approved scientists and physicists know how to play with.

Will they show themselves openly around 2012? I would be surprised, however more people will be working with them and some will know.

What kind of feeling did you get when you interacted with these beings? Did they show any emotion of any kind? Or was it more like the worker drone kind of syndrome?

My early encounters were casual almost friendship like. As I got older they became distant, they were around me but not face-to-face while on the ship. ETs in human costume off the ship could fool anyone, they are eccentric, but for the most part, they communicate like humans. I have had some horrific encounters but it may have been my misinterpretation, they may have been showing me some horrific disaster or something in the future, an Earthquake or battle scene. I'm not psychic, and can't predict things but I have felt the pain and fear and seen some strange happenings projected in my mind or in front of me like a movie while on the ship. Perhaps it was movie night with ET and the feature film was some horror show, otherwise why expose me to situations I can't do anything about?

Worker drones are part of the ET program. The drones do the manual, tedious and dirty work. They are highly advance machines that are difficult for the human mind to comprehend. It's as if your dishwashing machine can move about the house collecting dirty dishes, your car running errands for you and changing its own oil and doing its own maintenance, etc. Drones process abducted humans same as nurses taking your temperature and blood pressure before the doctor (ET) sees you. And like some nurses they are impersonal—it's a job and they scare the crap out of those they handle.

Did you feel anytime that you were being manipulated? Or does it feel as if more like you are the pupil?

ETs manipulate the same way a boss, a teacher, or parents do, to get you to do something you might not want to do. Are they manipulating me? Possibly, I don't like writing all that much or making public appearances. Am I a pupil? More like cheap labor.

Also can you describe your altered state? What were your emotions like in this state? Did it feel like you were in a dream state of reality, yet you were in the physical?

For abductees, the altered state is possibly brought on by confusion, extreme fear and disorientation. Something like giving a speech at the Academy awards and fumbling all your words. Some of my encounters were anxiety free and my state of mind was normal. They can make things comfortable for us. Much of the fear that abductees remember and report is due to the drones that process them. Fear is also used to block out many of the things that go on in the ship.

The state of mind is not dream like, it is somewhat normal, with blank spaces, however, some instances have no Earthly description.

There are regions of the mind most people know nothing about until ET takes you there—then try and hang on to your sanity!

May 22, 2005

Thank you for answering my questions. I think what they were showing you was a possible future on Earth. Maybe to enlighten you so others will also get the hint on why it is so important on why we must change the way we think, the way we eat, and the way we live.

So have you ever been to area 51? If you are not allowed to talk on this, could you say yes or no to the question, and I will leave it at that.

Area 51 is famous because many people believe that's where, if Extraterrestrials are really visiting Earth, they are hiding out at. I have been to several places where ETs are "hiding out". Most of these places I only see from the inside so I really don't know where they are located. I'm never aware of everything in such places. They don't have signs telling you where you are once inside these building. ETs don't consider that information pertinent, especially since what they are doing is covert.

How fast did that ship get into space?

There is no sensation of movement and the ship is in space in seconds, if not quicker.

When you talk to your wife about these Extraterrestrial encounters what's her response? And yet you would think women would be more open to this.

She believes, there's been a few things she was able to see to convince her.

All and all you would think the Extraterrestrials would get tired of saving us humans from our own demise over and over. I wonder how many times they went to our ancient civilizations and tried to balance us out.

It's their job, plus they don't get tired and bored like humans do while doing their jobs. I believe they enjoy their work immensely. They have excellent working conditions, fantastic equipment to work with, travel benefits, and a great retirement plan!

The ETs don't need to get comfortable with us, we have to get comfortable with them and that's a pretty big leap for us. It will happen over time. I don't know where they are, concerning their level of spirituality, I believe it to be quite high, much of our contact is with their machines, which are intelligent but lacking in the area of spirituality.

I have never had an encounter with an Extraterrestrial or anything Extraterrestrial related, but my mother did see UFO's

over a nuclear power plant close to where I live in 1974 or 1975. They were described as balls of light. There were several of them, they moved across the sky at great speeds and would stop on a dime hover and shoot off on different angles. My mother is not one to fabricate anything. In fact, it was a friend of hers (an ambulance driver) who came and got her late at night to come and see this. He had seen it before. The night he came and got my mother there were reporters there and I think it was captured on film. So not having ever seen anything myself, my mother is the next best thing.

Anyway, In reading your posts you seem very sincere. I have read that we have at least a few different races of Extraterrestrials here on Earth. The Sirian race is on a technology exchange program with a group of people that are a secret government agency on the surface but are a group within a group which is not known by the government. They give us technology because on their planet their ozone layer has been depleted and they have been forced to live underground. Their skin is very sensitive to the radiation from the sun due to the evolution that has taken place from living underground. They need to genetically modify their DNA. That's where we come in. It's a matter of survival. They are not here to hurt us. We are helping them survive. The Greys are also here to perpetuate their species. They have an exchange system set up as well. We have a very rich genetic pool here on Earth. From what I have read, some of these Extraterrestrial civilizations do not any more. The Extraterrestrials need to perpetuate their species by experimenting with our genetic pool. The government is the organization keeping this under a vale of secrecy. I don't think the Extraterrestrials would mind everyone knowing they were here. But our brilliant Gov. thinks it would create a mass hysteria if all this were made public all at once. They are conditioning us. Piece by piece they feed us. We as a collective whole will be able to accept it soon enough.

We also must remember that these Extraterrestrials are just another form of humanity. We all come from one GOD. They have DNA just as we do. Theirs is just in another state of evolution. Ours is in it's infancy. But as you can tell, by the fact that they are here, they did not integrate so well on their planet either. They screwed up their planet just as we are. If we had access to all of their technology at once, we would probably not need oil or any other type of energy that we pay for. The Extraterrestrials (or brothers from distant planets) could give this planet technologies that would certainly put us on the right track to stop killing our planet, but then who would be most affected. That's right, the top money manipulating families in the world. The one's that control many aspects of our lives behind the scenes. They have 99 percent of the world's wealth, and let us play with 1 percent. Do you think they want to give up their biggest revenue generators? It's an exchange set up between the Extraterrestrials and the government and the guys behind the cloak (who really run the government and the stock market). I am sure we will be conditioned soon enough, and the Ultra wealthy realize something needs to be done about our approaching energy crisis anyway. They just need to find a way to make as much money off of the new technologies as they did off of the old. The Extraterrestrials that are here are not to fear. Their ways are much different than ours, but if you think about it your neighbor's habits are much different than yours. We as humans have come to evolve into something where we think that in order to survive we must fight for everything as an individual. We have put up a wall around our soul. We all stem from one place, let us function as a collective whole. Free your heart and your soul. We are one.

I don't know about those Extraterrestrials or their motives that you mention in your post, perhaps they are renegades. The ones I am aware of are not in need of anything we have, instead they provide incremental information that we need to advance to the next stage. These ETs are not from a dying planet, they are from highly advance systems in this galaxy in need of nothing. In our galaxy, there are no shortages of any materials and those with the technology can harvest whatever they need indefinitely. If they have the abilities to travel to this plant then they have the technology to solve such petty problems as those that you mentioned.

There is a higher power that rules over our solar system and this planet and it's not a bunch of greedy people hording resources unless they are renegade ETs or put in place by ET. There are no humans calling the shots here on Earth, that's only a smoke screen. Technology is not kept from people by CEOs that have yet to figure out a way to make money on it. The technology that we receive and end up using is often dictated by ETs, not CEOs.

I have never myself seen one (UFO)...that I can recall, but my father has seen them a number of times while living in Upstate New York. And it goes further back than just him. His Mother and Father have also seen them a number of times living in the same area. If it is true that it happens within generations...than could it be possible that I have witnessed them also, but do not recall it?

From what I have seen it tends to run in families, my two children have no clue, yet I know they are involved. In my humble opinion, it sounds like you are too, perhaps on limited bases. Most people have no idea they have been abducted, some remember a little, others more, but never by accident.

I have always looked up to the skies in complete wonder, and pondered how small we really are, before I should have been wondering the meaning of life (around 5 or 6 years of age). Then recently I woke up from sleeping with a start in the middle of the night, and the last thing I remember seeing before I awoke, was this face about a foot from my face and I knew as soon as I awoke that it was some type of Extraterrestrial, but that's it. I need to learn as much about this subject as possible. I don't know why I am so passionate about it, but it drives me day after day.

From your statement in that paragraph you have visited with ETs, and to confirm it they let you remember the little that you do. Another clue is your deep need to know or remember what you have experienced while in space. Most people enjoy looking at the stars, which has nothing to do with ET visitation, but those that have seen the stars from other perspectives during abductions are left with a strong desire to do so again.

The Extraterrestrials I am talking about are far from renegades. Technology exchange programs do not get set up by renegades. I am not suggesting the Extraterrestrials you are talking about are from a dying planet. You say there is no

shortage of material, how about DNA. Our planet is a genetic pot at the end of the rainbow. You said you have blank spots in your memory. You were led to Extraterrestrial ships by your government. Do you think they were taking people for joy rides for fun? There is a reason you have blank spots in your memory, and the Extraterrestrials you have been in contact with didn't take you for a ride without a purpose. I realize here on Earth we don't really call the shots, the Extraterrestrials could do whatever they wanted with us with their technology. They are obviously friendly, but they aren't here just to help us, our DNA is very important. I didn't say that CEO's keep technology from people. The people that I am talking about eat CEO's for breakfast. We have R & D think tanks on this planet that are even shielded from the NSA. That is whom the Extraterrestrials work with. Even the Extraterrestrials don't work with the Gov. The IQ of the people in Gov. is pathetic therefore the Extraterrestrials have no use for them. There are also technologies that can increase your IQ by 500%, letting you have access to your super-conscious. These technologies have been given to the group of people I am talking about. They dilute them and they are passed to the NSA and the NSA dilutes them again and works with private sector companies (bell labs) to get them out. So yes, the Extraterrestrials are helping us, but we are helping them in return. You were on that ship for a reason. You have had memory replacement

technology used on you. That's where the blank spots are from.

ETs that are visiting Earth have thousands if not millions of years on humans, don't you think that such advanced beings could simply create or make any DNA they required? DNA is complex for humans no doubt, but not for highly advanced super beings. However, they do manipulate our DNA and use it on intermediate species, human/alien hybrids, but I don't presently know much about such programs.

What was it your wife saw that made her a believer?

My wife was curious like most people about ETs, I told her they will scare the hell out of her but she didn't believe me, and was certain she could handle it. Besides, she said, "how bad can they be, Will Smith kicked their butt in the movie Independence Day, and Sigourney Weaver handled that freaky Extraterrestrial in three episodes of Extraterrestrial, very well." When people think about ETs they use the only references they have, which is mostly from television, movies, and fiction novels.

Anyway, she got her wish and caught a glimpse of one in our living room one night. They were there for me and they decided to let her see one of them, knowing about her desire, they granted it. She's been a firm believer since and does not want to meet any of them again. I never seen the women so frightened in my life, I thought she was going to have a heart attack.

There are some Extraterrestrial races I believe to be very spiritual and some that seem to have their own agenda. Have you ever been in contact with the praying mantis Extraterrestrials? Also you have said you went to other locations, did they have different Extraterrestrials there then the previous ones?

Not aware of praying mantis Extraterrestrials, I have little recollection of the facial features of any of the ETs I have encountered.

I find your posts very interesting and sincere! As a matter of interest, what does it mean when you get an inkling that they are coming?

They come mostly in the early morning hours. Having insomnia most of my life I'm usually awake in bed. When they enter the room, my whole brain becomes electrically aware similar to a florescent bulb when placed near a high-energy field, and a loud sound fills my ears. No one hears the sound but the intended, my wife sleeps right through it, they keep her sleeping.

I have met them during daytime, they were garbed as humans, and their energy field affects me, sometimes causing stomach cramps.

They affected certain electrical things including my car when I took them places in it.

How does one prepare themselves for that? How does one overcome that fear?

There is no preparing that I am aware of. I have known them my whole life and they still scare the heck out of me, although, I also have comfortable encounters with them.

Do they come anyway and just erase the bad bits afterwards?

Yes, they can throw you off a sky skyscraper just for the experience (yours), and then make it all better, figuratively speaking.

Scientists are only paying attention to 10 percent of our DNA, the part that creates our proteins. Mystics and scientists alike do not understand the other 90 percent of the human DNA template. Everything, whether it's a biological environment or a state of mind, requires adaptation on the part of the person undergoing an experience. Adaptation is the primary intelligence designed within our genetic code, and it is this intelligence that is awakened, or triggered, with certain stimuli.

There are higher vibratory frequencies within our DNA that can be triggered through catalytic images, words, or sounds.

Our DNA is designed to respond to natural imagery, words, tones, music, and other external forces. Yes, they can manipulate DNA, and they do, but our DNA is a 3D map of proportions unknown. It is far more sophisticated than anyone realizes. We here on Earth have DNA that is relatively unspoiled, or not tampered with. We have something close to what the first source gave us. Many Extraterrestrials need our DNA map. It let's them solve their Rubik's cube, so to speak. We are soul carriers, and the soul is also part of the other 90 percent that our current scientists think is junk. It is only because they cannot even come close to understanding it. Do a little bit of research, you will see what they know.

So to answer one of your questions, yes, of course they can create their own DNA, but will it be able to carry a soul? Modifications push them further from the originator, GOD. We all come from one. Our soul lets us communicate with our origin, right now on a super-conscious level, but soon we will be given tools to access our super-conscious, and know that we are all connected through our souls to GOD. I am speaking scientifically and I say this because many people believe the soul is a myth or something inanimate, but it is not. It is as scientific as anything has ever been. If you created something and gave something life, would you not want to be connected to it? Would you nurture it and hope it would love you? We

here on Earth (original to Earth I mean) have put up walls as individuals and have practically disconnected ourselves from society. We have gotten further and further away from what we are supposed to be. It is ok though, because we all make choices good or bad. We are what we are and we will be shown the door and it will be a choice to walk through it or not. I am personally very optimistic about the future of humanity. I think this age of individualism and thirst for power will end.

You bring up fascinating stuff about DNA. Perhaps instead of only 90% of it being in the spiritual realm why not one hundred percent? All matter is made of atoms, atoms are further broken down into quarks, quarks into strings and strings are nothing but exotic vibrations. In other words, matter is only an illusion, a byproduct of spiritual reality. ETs have a handle on this phenomenon, they can materialize and spiritualize at will.

May 23, 2005

By early morning hours, do you mean 1, 2 a.m.? As you are drifting-off?

> Usually between 2-6 AM.

When you describe the brain lighting up, is it a similar experience to say, thinking the light has come on in the room while your eyes are closed with a whooshing noise? Followed by opening your eyes to find it is still actually dark in the room?

> Sounds like you've been there.

Is your family ready to be beamed up yet? I know mine isn't not yet anyways. There's truth to this post, that's why I found it ironic. This happened when I was going through I 93 towards Flagstaff and we were on a lonely road that had the feeling of something eerie. The guy in front of us kept swerving and falling asleep at the wheel. Well let's just say that this cloud on the horizon kept following our car. Then I see red, blue green, magenta color. The hue around our car was purple. I rolled my windows down viewing this .And it was about five to ten minutes it followed us. Next I send out a telepathic message so to speak to them that my families not ready yet. And then its like it just moved forward like it was doing a routine check of its stomping grounds. My wife recounted the same thing. I don't remember hearing any noise from it. But then again who knows I was driving fast when I rolled down my windows. My wife and I had that weird silence and feeling like we were being observed.

My family likes terra firma; they don't like it when I occasionally bring up the subject around them so I try not to. It appears you remember the chase in detail, but not the visit, which is common and possibly a good thing that you don't. Visiting with ETs is not a preferred family adventure.

What you have said in this post really peaks my interest. Thank you so much for sharing everything that you can with us. That noise that you describe that you hear when they come visit. That noise was also there when I awoke with that Extraterrestrial being in front of me. Everything you say seems very truthful to me, almost as if I already knew these things. I will continue to read this thread and hopefully, we will hear much more from you. Thanks again.

I would also like to share a dream I had about 2 or 3 years ago…A bunch of different people (I do not know in my waking hours) and I were all scrambling to get out of this one hanger type building with all these different hallways. There was a large countdown clock on every wall that I saw, a digital clock, and it was counting backwards very fast. We were all running and people were screaming, and we were trying to run to safety, but from what I don't know. Then at the very end of the dream, the clock runs down to zero and we all just holding our breath and close our eyes...then I woke up.

The dream was one of those that felt as if it was no dream at all but really happening. I will never forget that dream for as long as I live because the feeling I got from it was of sheer panic and impending death if we did not get out of there before that clock went to zero. I would love to hear your thoughts on this dream

I'm no dream interpreter but perhaps it's a personal message to you that after death, we wake up to a new reality. Death is the number one concern that most people share. When we wake from a dream we cease to exist in that dream world, in essence we die from that world and wake up in this one. That's the same with this life, at death we wake up to another existence. There is no true death only a continuous stream of life with many branches and realities.

After your last comment to me it all became a little more clear. Thank you so much for being so helpful. I will continue to read this thread and learn from it more and more...thanks again!

May 24, 2005

I wonder if those effects are the same for the Extraterrestrials. Do their minds feel as though they have been drugged as well? I wonder if they have just become accustomed to it, or if they are affected at all. Perhaps they are not affected at all, but when they spend too much time in our atmosphere, they become disoriented? Just theorizing.

Planet Earth is ET's playground; humans are more "alien" to Earth than ETs are. They are not affected by placing cups of water around the house, they cannot be locked into a room, nor can earthly germs harm them, they have been involved with the creation of this planet and everything in it for eons. Their minds are not affected by the Earth's environment at all. However, many humans are; allergies, flu and a host of other earthly diseases plaguing humans. ETs have been in this type of atmosphere before humans and are well adapted to it. ETs don't get sick, or disoriented.

What do you know about ET technology? Like their electromagnetic pulsed crafts.

That it is a lot more exotic than we can ever imagine, it can easily cloak and move through solid objects.

What about hand held weapons do they possess them? They are scouts so maybe they possess hand held weapons. I mean they must encounter hostile territory somewhere in our universe. Geez, imagine if you were to actually view an intergalactic war, this probably makes our nukes look like grenades. They probably have anti matter weapons that would do massive destruction if need be.

Extraterrestrial ships have been shot down on this planet, since human technology can't do it that leaves other ETs. I haven't seen any of their weapons systems, they don't need such things against humans, and I don't think they (those other ETs) can use them on us either. No doubt there are battles taking place, there are billions of solar systems in this galaxy, which equate to hundreds of millions of highly advanced races, chances are disputes happen.

I guess it would be safe to assume that all Extraterrestrials who visit are more advanced than us, but not all Extraterrestrials are equal to each other in terms of technological development. Therefore, would it be safe to assume that the Roswell Greys were shot down by a more advanced race, so that we could recover the craft?

A better assumption is that they purposely crashed a few dumbed-down ET ships with lifelike androids, we wouldn't know the difference.

They all probably saw us split the atom, and said hey, look what they can do. Then the Greys might have come in for a closer look and fell victim to a sneaky idea from someone higher up on the food chain.

Oppenheimer, Fermi and others had ET playmates when they came up with their atom bomb building equations. Geniuses are not so stupid that they would tell anyone where they get their best ideas; otherwise, they wouldn't be viewed as geniuses would they?

As for the notion of continued life after death, I buy it. My mother is a very religious person and she's very much into the idea of halos and the Pearly Gates. The standard idea for most people I guess. But a month after my grandfather died of emphysema, he came back for a short visit to her bedroom one night to say goodbye I guess, according to her. He said don't worry about me, I'm fine...but the message for her before he was gone was "It's not what you think." Which I think means forget the halos and Pearly Gates because it's not anything like what most church people would like to believe or imagine. I told her he's just further down the road and we'll catch up with him later. Now, what he's doing, I have no idea, he didn't tell her. I guess he's not allowed or it's too complicated.

Religion is the great pacifier for many while they are on Earth, that is religion's purpose. The other side is not that much different from Earth for most. For those expecting to sit around playing the harp it's going to be a big shocker, people have jobs over there too, oh horror of horrors! Those that enjoy staying busy, productive, and creative, they will have their heaven.

(Response to belligerent question, not added to this book) Sorry that you had to stoop this low, perhaps you'll get lucky and your friends won't see your post on this thread. However, the least I can do is give you an answer. I know you'll love it.

Drake is wrong, wrong, and wrong, he was and is way off the mark of reality, and he is proof that a higher education may provide a better income, but certainly not wisdom, intelligence, or knowledge. According to his equations, we humans are very special and unique in this vast universe of endless billions of stars and planetary systems. That's not scientific its plane ignorant. Granted he is coming from the belief that all life simply happened by chance, which is certainly the current worldwide psychosis.

We can't use that logic alone to prove that there are all these Extraterrestrial races either, as that logic can explain giant invisible onions as well. We won't know until we find it and get proof. Making up your own reality isn't healthy, let's stay with ours.

Which reality, the one that kept people believing for thousands of years that the Earth was the center of the universe? As many people continue to believe today. The one where for thousands of years everyone believed Earth was flat? I know those analogies have been over-used and apply to everything including grandma's secret cookie recipe, but they are hard to beat. You live in the world that makes sense to you, what else do you have to go on. Some people have more to go on, different experiences than yours and others, and therefore their realities are different, unique. You can't project your reality onto anyone else. Some people live sterile existences and wear the blinders prescribed by the particular society they happen to live in. There are over six billion people on this planet, ETs have removed the blinders from a few million of those people. You may say that I am brainwashed or delusional; however, I'm not the one who believes trillions of solar systems are devoid of life, that is plain ignorant.

People found that out by actually exploring, learning and thinking. They didn't just say, my life has no wonder in it, I KNOW! I'll suddenly think there are all these extraterrestrial races everywhere. Listen, I believe anything is possible, the universe is only what is known. Unknown is infinite, that's where wonder comes from. I don't take that unknown and suddenly transform it into the known from my own ideas. That

would not only take out the wonder in life, it would close my mind and make absolutely no sense.

When an Extraterrestrial race comes over here, explains where they are from, etc. or we get proof of them coming here or being out there, I won't assume they are here or even out there. I can understand the possibility, but as far as we can go on, I can only say there is a BIG chance of Extraterrestrial races out there. I stay mentally healthy, understand the possibility of anything, but do not go on something from my own ideas as our combined reality and tell people things I have no idea about.

I didn't make all this up because my mom neglected me while I was growing up and I compensated by creating these imaginary friends. My life was not worse than others that lived in my community and my mother didn't neglect me.

I saw Earth from space more than once, not a dream, not an illusion. When I was very young some fifty years ago before the USSR and the US put people into orbit, before any television shows like Star Track, and many Extraterrestrial movies, and books I was running around inside a space ship with other children and I often looked out the ship's portholes and saw huge globes (planets and moons) hanging in the darkness of space.

126

I lived in a small village with no modern conveniences, televisions, radios and books of fiction didn't exist for us. There is no way my mind could have created what I experience without having some reference such as television, books and stories. My parents don't believe in ET, so they didn't tell me stories about such beings. Too bad you can't push the envelope a bit and stretch your mind around stuff like this. I guess you'll have to wait until it happens to you before you can believe, nothing wrong with that.

The ET's job is not to make everyone believe in them? I mean free will is taught in almost all religions and ways of thinking in general, so free will lets one determine if you will believe this or not. I don't think they need all of us on this planet to believe in them...the message is out there for us to come to our own conclusions. They know that, and I think that is just fine with them. Just like not everyone believes in the same God or that there even is a God, the same is true with ETs. Just my humble opinion though.

Should ETs want full disclosure to happen it would be easy for them to do it, they obviously don't want that. However, they let it permeate out slowly through crop circles, abductions, movies, books, and people like me who seek lots of attention. Most will simply not believe period. Look how long it took to figure out that the Earth moves around the sun and this planet is not flat, even though simple instruments and common sense could have disclosed such facts. Some people will believe, not because they are easily fooled but because they know instinctively. Most will continue to graze on the same old sod (beliefs) because that's what everyone else is doing. And that's fine, like you stated, they will come around when they are ready, or not, that too is fine.

Howdy! Question, to see the Extraterrestrials one must go to a dark place or out in the country, be alone in the early AM? Did I get that right? Why will this event scare me? Are they hideous?

What I was getting at was that if you want something bad enough you can make it happen, including an Extraterrestrial visit or abduction. ETs can pick you up and even visit with you in Time Square in broad daylight if they wish without anyone seeing them except you. You don't need an ET to feel fear late at night in a dark forest alone by yourself with no weapons or flashlights. But if you can handle that for about a half hour or more you will have a tiny bit of an idea of what abductees feel when ETs pick them up. I don't know if they are hideous I don't recall exactly what they look like, but there is something about them that brings the fear of god to the surface. Perhaps ETs control the situation by projecting things into the mind because they can make it an encounter with them a pleasant experience as well.

I wish they'd get a move on. I haven't had a decent night's sleep in ages. At least then they could email me and make an appointment.

I hope you are not losing sleep because you are waiting on ET to visit. Our lives do not revolved around ETs. They do their jobs and we have to do our jobs on terra firma. It's ok to believe in something but don't become obsessed with it. Believe it or not I'm not obsessed with ETs. I simply put a little information about my experiences out there for people to contemplate.

I have a simple question for you. If Extraterrestrials are superior to us, and there are numerous races of Extraterrestrials, then somewhere down the line there are Extraterrestrial races superior to other Extraterrestrial races. So my question to you is, who do you think is at the top? Something has to create an Extraterrestrial.

We have six billion plus people on Earth. By some estimates, about two billion are Muslim, one billion Christians, and maybe another billion Buddhist that leaves two billion for everything else. More than three billion humans believe one god created everything. What came first the chicken or the egg? Darwinists believe the egg came first, Creationist believe it was the chicken. Scientists believe the universe is about fourteen billion years old and came into existence in a split second, the Big Bang theory, not much different from what the creationist believe. But the universe could easily be ten times older than that and much more, who's counting? If it is then it throws the big bang theory out the door. It's possible that the universe is not only infinite, but that it has always existed, constantly remaking itself at the centers of galaxies and exploding stars. So in essence, intelligent life could have existed for trillions upon trillions of Earth years and perhaps it has always existed and nothing was "created", certainly a paradox for the human mind to chew on.

I've been reading this thread and am absolutely fascinated with what you have to say. I believe every word of it, and I think it's incredible. I want to thank you for sharing your story with us. I have a question for you. Throughout the last few pages there has been talk as to how Extraterrestrials are trying to help us and stuff of the sort, would you say that the Extraterrestrials are only trying to help us, or could they possibly have created us? I know that's a bit, out there, but I was just curious.

What we see as brilliant technology and scientific breakthroughs is child's play compared to what exist in the real big galaxy we live in. Humans were planted here many eons ago and nurtured by certain ETs. However, the body is only one element in the equation, there is an everlasting soul plugged into each body.

There are many levels of ETs involved in the process we call mankind.

May 25, 2005

That's really interesting. Are you saying that the universe could have just simply existed? I have been thinking that lately. But there could be a top dog as well, but it's all so hard to understand. The idea that the universe simply existed, which is what I feel you are hinting at, is very interesting. If this is so, do we really have a purpose after "hatching from this nursery"?

The idea that the universe has always been is harder to swallow than the existence of one all-powerful god or that ETs are real, or that we are intelligent apes. We humans get comfortable with something and would rather die than give it up. The idea of a perpetual universe would throw monkey wrenches into many beliefs (religious and secular), overturning the whole concept of what matter is. What I mean by hatching is spreading out into the solar system, building cities on other planets, moons and in space and eventually creating a mega complex of cities containing billions of people.

The purpose of humanity is to design and build the extraterrestrial structures and in so doing add exponentially to our collective knowledge as we discover and work with new and exotic materials found on the other planets. Humans are individual cells creating a bigger self, like cells that multiply and fill-in the cranium of a human brain. Thousands of years from now the solar system will be glowing with human activity with a greater range of knowledge at our fingertips. Humans will be closer to understanding our origins and whom it is that pulls the strings.

There is no death and some people come back to this place after they expire. Others will remain in the spiritual sector and continue their work from there. Some humans will become other types of beings working in this solar system or one of the trillions of other star systems in the galaxy.

First off thanks for sharing your experience. Stepping back to your time(s) that you have left Earth and on the ship. I am curious to know the impact on your body. We are all aware of the chemical reactions that occur in our bodies that are constantly changing so how did your metabolism feel after the voyage? How did your body feel? How did ET compensate for your cellular activity? Did your stool look any different when you got home? (Not trying to be funny) I am just trying to figure out how things impacted you anatomically and physiologically. I think the mental, emotional etc etc has been covered nicely with the prior posts.

As you know here on Earth metabolism is nonstop to meet the demands of mind and body 24/7. But in space, inside ET's ships things are different. The body and the mind require a fraction of the energy we use while on Earth and that fraction seems to be met from the glow of energy radiated by the ship. Entering the ship is physiologically easier on the system than leaving the ship. There is a difference adjusting to the gravity and the metabolism going from near hibernation back up to full speed, creates a drain on energy, but it's usually of short duration. However, there were times I felt like I worked in the coalmines for a couple of shifts. There is a noticeable difference in the bodily functions and byproducts on return. But that's also true when I go on vacations her on Earth, jetlag, time zones, change in diet, lost baggage, etc.

May 26, 2005

I'd just like to say this whole thing has been very interesting to read. I've been lurking here for a little bit and this is my first post, very interesting stuff!

May 27, 2005

Do the Extraterrestrial crafts have a gravity device in them? Did you float around while up there in space? Did the speed move so fast like you weren't moving at all? Did your body age or become ageless? Well buddy that's it for questions for now, but there is always another day.

I didn't floated, nor was I aware of a gravitational pull on my body. There is no up, down or sideways in space but there is a sense of equilibrium, standing up and walking is the same as if you are on Earth less any fatigue, so the gravity or whatever force that keeps you from bouncing around the ship hardly tax the muscles. There was no sensation of moving when the ship beamed around at neck-break speeds, there were no harnesses that I was aware of, I wasn't strapped into a seat. I don't recall seeing a seat; perhaps they only put them out for VIPs. I'm thinking that since there is little if any wear-and-tear on the body while in the ship that the ageing process is suspended during those periods spent with ETs.

I believe your story, but you seem like you think these Extraterrestrials are God. Sorry to bring religion up on here but I've been Christian for a long time but then I always had that feeling that there are things (infinitely) more than what we see I think I have had contact because whenever I see a

picture of one I remember strange experiences I've never had and I get stomach cramps.

I don't believe that Extraterrestrials are gods, they never claimed to be gods, to me anyway.

I feel as if I'm being watched while I'm alone sometimes it gets unbearable and when I see pictures of Greys I get stomach cramps and other feelings , how can we tell them not to send the programmers(androids) and ask them to come instead?

ETs and their machines will not hurt you, that's not their purpose. If you are evil or have done something bad then you will have to make amends, if not don't worry about them, in fact they may be there to protect you. If you have done something wrong, and you wish to change, they can help you without face-to-face contact. They hear every thought you have and you can communicate your wishes to them that way. Bottom-line, go about you daily business and don't worry about them. They will do whatever job it is they need to do and you don't need to be aware of it. Because of the nature of what they are humans have a natural fear of them, "fear not" because there is nothing to fear if there is no willful evil in you.

Is there anything I can do to make them make themselves noticed by me, not at night though. I have enough trouble getting to sleep as it is. Just so they can acknowledge me?

ETs are not here to entertain us that's why most abductees don't remember much, there is nothing good to remember in many encounters. You don't have to do anything for them to notice you they know who you are and deal with you according to whatever reason they are in contact with you for. They make the call on how much you will remember, if you remember little or nothing, then that's for your own good. Any concerns or requests you have they know about. Forcing an encounter can be a double-edge-sword because you will then know without a doubt that they are real, but the encounter may not be a positive one and you might even beg them to erase it. Why are some encounters so bad? Because they might show you something about yourself you would rather not know.

Since I started reading your thread I have found myself less and less scared. Also, the night visits have been gaining in intensity. Just three days ago, after we had talked about the lights and the sounds you had mentioned I had the most intense experience yet. It is hard to put into words. I asked you about the anxiety felt before a visit is due. Since last week, a new factor has been added. I keep getting the thought of "Is it okay to come?" "Are you okay?" running repeatedly through my head. Don't know if you could shed some light on that. I am feeling less and less like lashing out as I used to, but it isn't helping me get any sleep!

They have an interest in you that only they know what that is, however, it may not be necessary for you to remember what and why they have this connection with you. They always work behind the scenes. In certain cases, they will gradually let you remember things, but it can be a slow and long process. ETs are extremely different from us, their appearance, the energy they emit, and the fact that they speak into your mind and know all your thoughts puts us at a disadvantage. There is little or no casual conversation with them, a stark difference between them and humans. They may sense that you want to remember more and are conditioning you for that eventuality, assuming, it is ETs placing such ideas in your head and not you. Nevertheless, no need to lose sleep, there is nothing you can do about them, they can't and will not harm you.

I am at heart quite skeptical so I am open to the possibility that it is all wishful thinking on my part. Whatever it is, it has taken a long term problem of mine and made a turn for the better with me and for whatever little part your posts had in doing that, I thank you. I have no intention of pushing it and just intend to let things unfold at their own pace.

July 26, 2005

After reading this entire thread, I got to hand it to you. You somehow managed to get through this thread and maintain. Some fascinating answers you give to some of the questions asked of you. I believe many of your answers to be in all probability, likely correct. Either that or you have read one too many science fiction books and assembled your own perspective from the cumulative imaginations of those book's authors. But your descriptions of the "somewhat blurry" experiences and ships are nearly identical to other information I have from someone who has "been there and done that." Like many here, I can't be 100% sold until they land and make it known in the open. But I have really enjoyed reading this thread, and I hear ya!

I do not read science fiction books. My experiences are real and I relate them the best I can. I understand that it is difficult if not impossible to believe that Extraterrestrials are here without being able to see them, but the real mystery is not why many people don't know about them, it is why so many do. Most that know about ETs will never admit to it because it would jeopardize their careers.

Considering after 9\11, Iraq war, and tsunami don't you think that ET's should show themselves?

ETs show themselves every single day, they are in contact with certain people on this planet as advisors. However, most don't know they are dealing with ETs, those that do don't tell.

You worked for the military so what did the military think about the bible revelations?

The military is a big community of people with the same mixture of religious beliefs as the civilian world. That's true with the top brass too. Some believe as you do that Armageddon is just around the corner, others don't know what to believe. Those that know and deal with ETs are the most confused of all. It's like being in a lion's den with no weapons for defense. These lions (ETs) can consume us in seconds should they wish to, but that is not why they are here, well most of them anyway.

There is no end time, no Armageddon as talked about in the bible and other ancient literature with worldwide destruction. However, there will be a major shift in technology and standard of living as we gear up to meet the challenges of the space age.

Most people will not even notice the changes, so for those waiting for the big change or revelation to be taken into the sky by a savior will be disappointed, not going to happen. However, people have been taken into the sky in ships, it's been going on for thousands of years. The trip usually doesn't last long and they bring them back.

Wow. I've read all this thread and it's very interesting. I noticed it rather died out at the end of May, and you seem to have bumped it yourself yesterday. I have a notion that there's still something you're trying to get out that you're holding back. It would be great if you'd just come out with it. Does it have anything to do with the first four words you used to start this thread?

What you've written to this point is fascinating, although I remain skeptical. There's obviously something going on, I'll agree that's as real as the nose on your face. I'm just not at all convinced it's what you report it to be. Best of luck to you, though.

Once upon a time there was a blue planet "third rock from the sun" and all of its people believed they were at the center of the universe, and why not, the sun (star) circled their fair planet once every day, surely that meant that the gods favored them out of all the other star systems. One is apt to believe that is a fairytale yet it was what the average person believed for eons. Now days most know that the sun is stationary yet we still believe we are at the center of the universe. Millions perhaps billions of people still believe that the gods have favored Earthlings above the rest of the billion of endless star systems out there. Certainly, there are people that are willing to believe the possibility that some of those other planets have microbes and other inferior life forms that are eager to evolve and perhaps become intelligent as did humans on this planet.

This thread is about Extraterrestrials from space that have traveled billions of miles in fantastic machines and they have been doing it for thousands of years and will be doing it for thousands of years to come.

They do this without human approval because they were here first and they are infinitely more complex than humans are. An adult does not need to ask his five-year-old child permission to do anything; can such a child give any usable advice to the adult? The child depends completely on the adult, without ever understanding anything about that adult.

July 29, 2005

It sounds like you are speaking about your experiences with one type of Extraterrestrial on behalf of all the different Extraterrestrials. Maybe you are programmed or led to believe that they don't make mistakes and that they are god-like. Maybe Clifford Stone was programmed by the Extraterrestrials to believe in 57 different manifestations and was made to believe that they do make mistakes. Which is how Extraterrestrials were captured and ships recovered and studied. Maybe he is right in his testimony, maybe you are right in your testimony. Who can know!?

Let me put it this way, I know there are thousands of Extraterrestrials coming and going, and living on this planet many people know. What are the odds that nothing is ever found by the civilian population, ET litter, UFO parts and Extraterrestrial bodies? Nothing is found because they make no mistakes. Ships and Extraterrestrials, or most likely androids from crashed ET vehicles that are in the possession of various governments and their militaries, were planted for the purpose of the awaking process mankind is undergoing.

I don't know how many Extraterrestrial species there are visiting this planet and I doubt anyone knows. Four to five hundred billion star systems in this galaxy alone equates to countless possibilities.

Nevertheless, it's a big puzzle and the pieces are highly dispersed among the population. The awaking process is slow and drawn out perhaps to avoid a kink in the program that would throw everything off kilter.

July 30, 2005

I had an encounter with an Extraterrestrial once, granted it was through the TV. I felt an emotion connection with the Extraterrestrial, I forgot the movie, but yeah, I had dreams for days after seeing the movie.

Perhaps you should turn off the television and go outside every now and then. People that believe we are alone in the universe need to see a psychiatrist. Then again, most psychiatrists believe we are alone in the universe. That fact alone should tell you something.

You say that they can't and will not harm people, yet there are numerous reports of people saying that experiments were performed on them that caused them pain. Not to mention that these people are taken against their own free will. So what is that supposed to mean?

Much of the pain comes from the horrendous fear triggered by the very strange Extraterrestrial encounter. That fear intensifies the whole experience, the slightest touch or movement around the person is cause for alarm and panic. In the midst of the terror, one can create all kinds of horrific scenarios in the mind.

It also depends on who is doing the abducting and for what purpose, but the vast majority of those taken are retuned in the same physical condition as they were before the encounter. Some will be better off, perhaps leave with a slight improvement to their DNA or with a physical ailment repaired. Other than a slight skin blemish on a few abductees little evidence of abuse is present.

Since they know everything about us, then why are there so many people out there that WANT to meet and be taken by ET's , yet it almost always seems that the ET's take people who do not want to be taken or know nothing about ET's? Again, against free will.

Those that want to meet ETs have the glamorized version in their minds like "Star Trek" and space travel in fantastic ships by entities that have figured it all out and live in utopia civilizations somewhere over the rainbow. Which is all true, fantastic trips for some and the ETs do live in utopia compared to humans.

Regretfully ETs are not here to provide joy rides to the inhabitants of Earth, although for some that is one of the benefits of the encounters. ETs have jobs to do, complex jobs, which include taking people against their will. Only in a few democratic societies do humans have the illusion of "rights", in the rest of the world no such fantasy exists, apparently ETs don't follow that line of thinking either.

I'm still a big-time skeptic but you have me convinced you believe. Not sure what value there is in that for you, but there you go. Hang in there.

It's understandable that some people need proof of things unseen. But much of what billions of people accept with little hesitation, like natural selection (Darwinism) and one powerful and often angry god, comes with no proof either.

Darwin had many good ideas about the origins of life yet he never came up with proof. To this day none of what he espoused, theorized and believed strongly in is provable, although much of it makes sense to those that have nothing else to hold on to. His lack of proof doesn't receive the same criticism from the scientific community that other disciplines and philosophies seem to garner.

Nevertheless, unlike religion and its secular counterpart (Darwinism) both pretty much based on conjecture, thousands of people have experienced extraterrestrial contact, real physical contact, yet those who haven't experience this physical contact refuse to believe them.

How can one prove they hugged their child last week, the hugging can be recreated, but that does not prove you hugged your child last week. Can we take the child's word for it? How do we know that the child wasn't having the same delusion? Perhaps the child's deep need for a hug is behind this delusion?

Not believing in something because one lacks personal experience is not rational, applying that concept across the board would leave few things anyone could believe in.

July 31, 2005

Ok, then what is this "job" they have to do?

Since they are illegal aliens without work visas they could get into big trouble if I tell.

Either that or you just don't have an answer which is more what I think. If you know so much , why are you on this site talking about it? Why not go get yourself proven sane and then tell your story to people that can actually make your story known to the masses?

The level of skepticism on this UFO board tells me that the general public is not ready or interested in knowing what is going on. People live in a cozy bubble and have no real need to leave that make-believe world. Can anyone really be proven sane? Or for that matter, insane?

I have attempted to get my story out but few are interested, so I post bits and pieces on this thread.

The nearer the truth I get the more preposterous it sounds so I keep it toned down and somewhat believable and still few believe.

This is not a UFO board, it's a conspiracy board. And did you know, there are possible explanations for UFOs that do not include the existence of Extraterrestrials with physical bodies,

AKA the precious Grey hoax. Try thinking in terms of non-human intelligence and non-physical entities that should get you back to waking up there. It's not unfounded skepticism.

I don't speculate or conjecture about extraterrestrials, I know they are real, and are here. Because you don't know does not negate the fact that they are real. You can go ahead and believe we are the center of the universe if you wish you have plenty of company.

August 1, 2005

Just so we're clear, we are in about 90% agreement. And I'll submit I could be wrong about the other 10%. Is it possible that you experienced everything you experienced and there was no extraterrestrial involvement? That a government with fantastic secret technologies and virtually unlimited resources could have pulled this off and "allowed" you to come forward to share what you believe to be Extraterrestrial interaction? I'm not being accusatory, I'm just asking. And I'm still interested in whatever you have to relate. And to further clarify, I'm not suggesting it must be either "A" or "B". I'm open to the possibility that there may be extraterrestrial activity AND governmental/powers-that-be efforts to fake same.

Not a chance. While in Italy during my early years of life, post WW2, I was in ships that flew into space in a blink of an eye and I saw Earth and the other planets from these ships looking through the portholes. Those were my first experiences. Italy was like a Third World country at the time, devastated by WW2. The village I lived in had no radios, televisions, or any concepts of space travel, bicycles and horses were the main form of transportation.

Years later in America, I was in the military, during the early seventies. I was privy to much of the leading edge technology

America had. The SR-71 spy-plane used for reconnaissance over Vietnam, Laos, Cambodia, China, and the USSR was secret and leading edge technology at the time and the general public wouldn't know of it for many years after the war was over. The SR-71 was a toy in comparison to what I was flying in, back in the early nineteen fifties, many years before the SR-71 was even on the drawing board. I was able to compare our American technology with Extraterrestrial technology while in the service. How can I put it, ours tinker toys, theirs pure magic, no comparison whatsoever, not even close, not in the ballpark, we are infants they are Einstein's times a thousand. Even our Sci-Fi stuff like Star Trek is embarrassingly insignificant in comparison. ETs have thousands if not millions of years advantage over humans. The us military and the secret governments are afraid of these ETs and their magic machinery.

Like I said in my earlier post the nearer I get to telling the truth the more bizarre it sounds and the more people that will think me nuts. So how the heck do I tell my story and make it believable short of dragging an extraterrestrial out into public? I tell my story for those who are interested in knowing the fantastic possibilities that are out there, no one need believe it, but it's true all the same.

1) I won't call you 'nuts'.

2) I'm interested.

I appreciate your willingness to be forthcoming. Nobody knows who you are anyway, so I'd advise you to not take anything personally. Obviously, I have my own theories. I'm trying to be open-minded enough to not discount out of hand those things that don't support my theory. The big problem is that virtually all the available evidence supporting a definite EBE presence is anecdotal, so we're left with attempting to somehow make a judgment call about the person relating the story. Is it a fifteen-year-old kid with a vivid imagination, or a lonely middle-aged guy with an attention Jones, or someone with a serious mental issue, or The Real Deal? You've got my attention.

What if I were to ask the ETs for the cure of major illnesses, and they gave it to me and I posted it on this thread, once verified I would be considered a genius, a god, or possibly that I was telling the truth about Extraterrestrials.

ETs know the cure for everything that ails humans, they could make everything right on this planet with little effort why don't they?

However, what would a sudden cure for cancer and other diseases do to the economy? Countless billions of dollars are spent researching these plagues in the US alone, trillions more throughout the world. Thousands of scientists, lab assistants, nurses, doctors, janitors, would be out of work. Hospitals, pharmaceuticals, supporting industries would go bankrupt. The domino effect would take down homebuilders, bankers and the slew of industry that supports them. Any major and abrupt change on our planet would be devastating. If one Extraterrestrial ship showed itself and made it known that extraterrestrials are real Earth would be doomed. It would be as if God showed up. Everyone would expect Got to take care of their every need and God better get to it or the whole shebang will go down the tubes very quickly. Millions of people need to show up for work so that six and a half billion people don't starve to death. That is why proof is not forthcoming.

My account (all true) and those of others are harmless because the vast majority will remain unconvinced and sedated to reality, as it should be. However, these stories serve a purpose as do movies and books of extraterrestrials regardless of how far off the mark they might seem or be. Only a few people at a time need to become aware of what is really going on in this big fat universe, that way there won't be any major disruptions.

From the stories my parents told me about Italy around the time you mentioned - I think 3rd world was a compliment. Their town was obliterated because they had an ammunition factory there and "zee Germans" liked to play the game of "Level that Town". I have my own reason to believe you.

January 5, 2006

Has our government asked any ET's to deliver us a cure for aids?

The governments of the world are like children at the candy store asking ETs for anything they can get.

Why would the most powerful men in the world want to lose their superiority over society?

The most powerful men and women are not that powerful, they die, get sick, have heart attacks and strokes, power is fleeting and non-existent.

Our government is controlled secretly by negative Extraterrestrials.

ETs in charge of this planet have a mandate, and they are carrying it out.

People have no faith or trust in mankind so they pin all their hopes on altruistic creatures or beings to fix all that ails us. It doesn't matter that there is not one shred of evidence beyond anecdotal stories to support an almost zealous beliefs. By pegging the hopes on Extraterrestrials for righting wrongs and fixing problems this looks more like an excused resignation to

accept that nothing really can be done. So it will be their (Extraterrestrials) fault for allowing it to happen.

Without extraterrestrials, humans would be up a bigger creek. The difference between humans and ETs is that ETs don't require recognition, they do things and keep their deeds hidden.

Why then don't they fix all the problems? They have fixed many problems millions of problems. Look at human history through the Dark Ages; look at today, some improvement took place.

How long does it take to fix humanities' problems? The world is a big and complex place and problems are taken care of at the appropriate rate for this type of planet.

It might be a good idea to start again from the very beginning and tell us exactly what you experienced start to finish.

I'm sure you would agree that this is not a run of the mill tale; to say the least this account is a very complex phenomena. There is a reason people like me don't tell their stories, much cannot be told, and what is told has to be done delicately.

He is telling the truth I can tell. Don't ask me how, I just know. Thanks for coming forward and sharing your experience.

Do you believe that when capitalism finally collapses, and a peoples socialist society begins to rise from the chaos, when

resources are finally shared, when class structures and poverty are understood as VIOLENCE. Then will the Extraterrestrials show?

Capitalism is not going to collapse; resources are created as they are needed by industrialized and free societies. ETs don't need to show themselves openly, they haven't for thousands of years and they aren't' going to start now. However, they have contact with thousands of people every day, most will not talk about it due to the hostility towards those like me that do come forward.

Perhaps the surreal effect is caused by the massive emfs produced by these crafts.

Electro magnetic force (Emf) is very strong but there are other factors, the human senses are much more keen when inside the ship and we humans are not use to keen senses, which creates confusion as the brain is bombarded with new and awkward information.

What mandate do ETs have? By all means, spill your guts. Tell us on this board every fact and detail you know, no matter how miniscule. Just like the Ghostbusters, We're ready to believe you!

The mandate involves each sovereign country and each country has their own unique challenges and requirements, the mandate can also involved individuals and their problems or inner needs, but ETs only facilitate people that know what they need to make the next step in their lives, there are over six billion people on this planet, ETs have their hands full.

Makes sense. We are use to operating only at certain limited levels and anything like that introduced I'm sure sets off all kinds of visual and auditory experiences. Perhaps the pharmaceutical companies are trying to rewire the human to where they can operate more on their (Extraterrestrials) level. More so than not rewiring the chemistry. As far as them taking over who's to say they haven't been in control all along.

The pharmaceuticals are like every other industry, they make good stuff and bad stuff but in the long run humans move forward ever so slowly, except for the last 100 years where we had a major spurt. Few want to admit that ETs are in control, not even those that know ETs are real and been around for some time.

January 6, 2006

Life elsewhere is probable - I say this purely on the math, so many galaxies, so many suns, some must have the right chemistry. But that's not to say it's anything like people expect Extraterrestrial life to resemble. Can you support your claims with some evidence? A photo, a video?

I do have a rock; a meteorite that was given to me many years ago. I even tried to break it open to see what was inside it when I had one too many drinks, again, many years ago. Obviously the stone is not proof of anything, meteorites are everywhere, but they never told me if it's from this planet or some other planet or moon or even from other star system. I'm sure I will receive some flak for posting that I have a meteorite from an extraterrestrial but ET would not let me video tape or take pictures of their ship.

Indeed your thread really answers many of my questions, But I would really like to know the answer to the ultimate question. What are we and why are we here, what purpose does it serves for the Extraterrestrials to aid us during our changes?

It's best that most don't remember who they are and why they are here, for one that information would detract and add nothing to their present experience on Earth. Without the aid of ETs there would be no escape from this planet, no moving forward, no advancement in technology and no hope for mankind, Earth would be a dead zone. Humans helping humans is like the blind leading the blind, yet few people understand that, or are aware of that reality. The vast majority need not know any different, which is how ETs want it.

January 7, 2006

I am curious if the plant, Salvia Divinorum, helps the human mind connect with Extraterrestrials and allows contact on many levels? From my research, the herb, Salvia Divinorum, seems to bring the human soul or spirit or mind to a level that allows them to travel throughout the multidimensional realities of the universe instantly to experience many things. One of the many things that people state during Salvia Divinorum "trips" is the essence of visiting Extraterrestrial worlds and meeting Extraterrestrial beings. I'm curious what your thoughts on this are.

This is the first time I have heard of Salvia Divinorum it sounds like LSD, I never tried that either. If you are asking if I take drugs, I do, an aspirin once in a while, and I have a glass of wine with my meals.

If you're for real, please give us something tangible to go on. Even if 10% of this is true, you're talking about changing people's entire world.

100% of what I said is true, but there is little chance that the apple cart is going to be overturned any time soon. Most people are locked into their illusions, however, ever so slowly, ET unlocks the minds of thousands of people, and these people suddenly notice that there are billions of stars in the night sky, and their curiosity begins to unfold. How many people do you know that need or want their view of the world to come to an end? No one is going to be dragged "kicking and screaming" into another reality, into the truth of what life really is about.

Proof would shatter the illusions of this world for all, but all are not ready for the next big step.

Having had smoked the SD, I would say no. It is just mildly hallucinogen and lasts only a short period of time. I felt that the only things that were affected by it were colors and physical sensation was a little "trippy" (was stood up but felt like I was lying on my back if that makes any sense) and I felt very hot on the inside of my body and cold on the outside of my skin. I was able to still talk to my buddies and had no sensation of heightened spiritual sensation and definitely no multi-dimensional travel. Salvia may make the person believe this if they were so inclined in the same way any other hallucinogen may do. If you really believe that taking an hallucinogen will give you the ability to think you can see/do/experience things, then your mind will be tricked into experiencing things that have not actually happened. That's why people may use hallucinogens.

He is telling the exact "current situation" of mankind. We are just on the same "understanding frequency". All the Best.

Very exciting read! I was curious about the et's reproduction. Since they are much more advanced than us, do they reproduce as we do or do they conceive by scientific methods?

The ETs that are here, the ones that make contact with humans are strictly business and show no signs of gender. There are Extraterrestrial tourists but they don't have contact with humans that I know of. The Extraterrestrials that are in human "uniforms" (skin), have bodies that are anatomically correct, but whether they function or are sterile I don't know, my feeling is they are sterile. How they procreated on their planets is a blank. However, they do have facilities in our solar system that house hybrids, many of them, but these hybrids are not for this planet or for this solar system that I'm aware of at this time.

Seeing as how this thread was revived with questions of your credibility, maybe you could take a picture of this meteorite and post it. Surely, that is not too difficult.

I will have to go dig that rock out of the basement; it's buried under some of my other space junk paraphernalia stuff, ha, ha. I will post it tonight or tomorrow

UFOs and Extraterrestrials... Lou Baldin

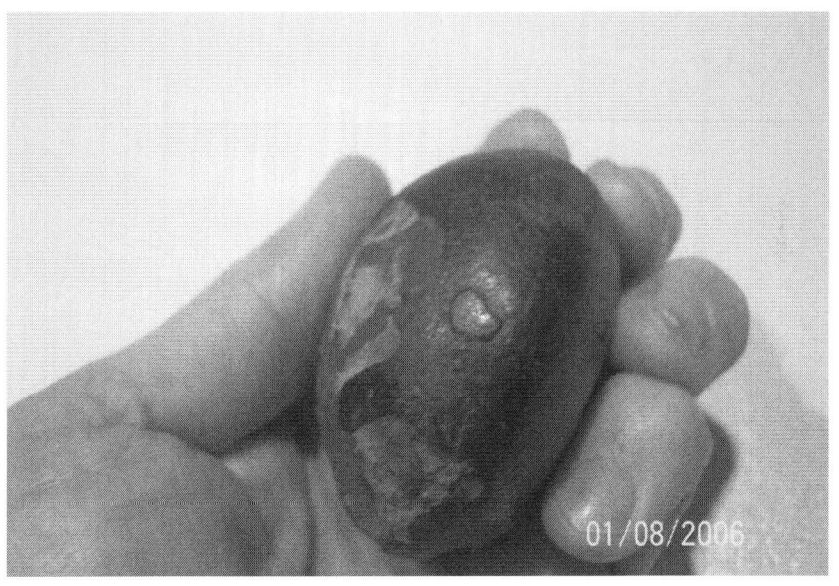

UFOs and Extraterrestrials... Lou Baldin

01/08/2006

01/08/2006

January 8, 2006

How many times have I read this stuff before, those rocks look like garden stones.

Most people wouldn't know a diamond if it were not polished and in a display case at a jewelry store. What is your expertise in rocks? Are you a gardener? Or is your BS degree in "true skepticism". It doesn't take much education to be a skeptic; even a child can be one. If you are an archeologist, then say so and tell us what kind of "garden rock" that is.

Q1. Is it cold to the touch and does it absorb heat from your hand thus warming the 'rock'?

The rock is cold and hard, it is 2 ½ inches by 2 inches. Weighs about a pound

Q2. Did you ask for this rock or not? If not, then why give you it if you aren't to have any proof to show the masses?

I don't remember if I asked for it. If they wanted me to present proof, they would have given me something more believable, a rock is a rock even if it is from another planet or solar system. I have said that this rock is not proof of anything; it's only part of my story. ETs are not interested in proving themselves to the masses; if they were, they surely wouldn't need humans like me to do it for them.

January 8, 2006

It certainly looks like a meteorite, having the burnt outer layer, and looks very similar to others in the Stony Meteorite class posted at this website. *http://www.meteorite.fr/en/news/*. And it looks very similar to the ones on this page from that website. *http://www.meteorite.fr/en/oriented/default.htm*. That yellow colored mineral looks strange though, and I don't see any other meteorites with the same color. It could be due to some oxidation from a mineral. If I were you I would have it checked out, it may be unique and valuable.

I didn't post it as evidence or proof. I don't have a picture of ET handing it to me, and even if I did who would believe it?

I'm not saying it is, but it shows that you actually have a meteorite, and at the least you were able to back up that part of your story. Nice pics!

You say the Extraterrestrials follow 'rules' of some sort (Except for the Outlaws I guess), with these rules, are there any 'rights' that we as humans have? Or are we just considered 'animals' to them in a sense?

Humans have a soul, the animal part, which is the body is only a vehicle, nevertheless because of the soul every human has immeasurable value. People in prison have immeasurable value also, yet they are not treated well, so they believe they have no value, and in many cases, it's true. Our situations whether bad or good in this life are not a statement by ETs that we are nothing but animals or commodities. However, our lives are not accidents, or coincidences, everything we go through or experience on this planet has a purpose a reason.

Also, how does one attract the attention of the ET's in regards to one being exceptionally spiritual or intelligent? I mean what causes an ET to decide who to 'abduct' and reveal things unto, and those to avoid?

ETs are not attracted to personal spirituality, intelligence or good looks. ETs work with everyone on some level. Most people don't need to understand what makes the engine in a car operate, to operate a car. ETs work in similar ways. ETs are the engine that makes thing go, hidden underneath the hood.

I know I have many health problems myself, wish they could fix me up since I have no real healthcare/insurance.

Doctors have a purpose, but they are only one small part of the equation to good health. America with its state of the art health care industry has more sick people than do Third World countries. Therefore, the best health care is not the total solution. Extraterrestrials don't have doctors and hospitals as we do on

Earth. They don't get sick or ill, their bodies and minds fix things before they break. Accidents are practically nonexistent for ETs.

Human minds are equipped to fix many things that ail us. The human mind is designed to fix anything and some day when people realize the power that resides in their head health care may become obsolete.

You never know, perhaps ETs will sneak in when you are not looking and fix you up. It happens all the time.

So, the ETs basically are so advanced in technologies that they have conquered the spiritual realms? It sounds like they are guiding the evolution and growth of our spirits/souls through reincarnation, from what you have stated earlier.

The physical realm is an illusion and is only an extension of the spiritual realm. Everything is spiritual energy of one form or other. Considering that the universe is without beginning, and will never end, and that souls have the same inextinguishable qualities, reincarnation is a vehicle for many kinds of adventures, such as learning, vacation, growth, punishment, reward and a gamut of other objectives.

Do you have any idea what type of religion the ETs ascribe to? Or what their philosophy of life and the universe is?

Religion has its purposes on Earth, community, extended family, and many other things but not for war as many speculate considering the history of religious wars. Religion, as humans understand it, doesn't exist at higher levels, the level where ETs resides. Philosophy is for those who can only guess about life and the universe, humans. ETs are not philosophical creatures.

Do ETs believe in a Multi-dimensional reality, in regards to copies of us in parallel universes/etc living out other probable lives?

Multi-dimensional reality is a reality, but we only exist in one reality at a time.

I know you have stated that it is like 'pixy dust' in a sense due to just how advanced their technology is. Therefore, understanding it/them at our level is nearly impossible.

We don't understand their technology because when we are placed into this planet those memories are erased for the duration of life while here.

In regards to our minds healing ourselves, is this done on a physical chemical level? Or is it done on a spiritual/reality altering level? I am guessing when you say there are some that have the ability you are talking about the faith/psychic

healers? Also, what is stopping most of us from utilizing this? Is it evolutionary or is it more or less a state of mind?

Since there really isn't any physical anything, everything we accomplish is through our spiritual energy. The soul can tap into a vast energy source; some people like to call it god. Everyone has the ability to tap into that energy, most deny it for a multitude of reasons. Some faith/psychic healers have discovered it, most have not. I think we can all agree that the state of mind is more than half the battle to any achievement.

So are you saying that the Physical World is a form of Technology? Almost "Matrix" like that was created/manifested from the spiritual realms to create a type of 'university' in the physical where we can live, learn, experience, and 'play' the game of life and then return? If that is true, then the ETs and UFOs we see in the physical are nothing more than 'vehicles' for them to interact with the physical world. With that said does that mean that we are equal with the ETs on a spiritual level or are in fact ETs ourselves, one consciousness, one energy? And that we take turns "playing" and learning in the game of life and when we die we take a different 'role' in the game either in the spiritual or physical realm somewhere in the 'game universe' of sorts?

I thank you for taking the time out to answer all my questions. I hope you aren't developing carpal tunnel from all the typing. If so, hopefully the ETs can fix that for you.

You put it very nicely into a nutshell. I think you know more than you are letting on. However, most people will not buy it; it's far too simple a concept.

For as long as I can remember, I have had vivid dreams that have slowly shown me reality, my world, the universe, and a multidimensional existence. Many times in my dreams I 'awake' in my dream into another vivid, life like reality, I am someone very different, and it's confusing at times. This happens on several other levels at times making it extremely hard to wake up.

There are physical abductions and there are spiritual abductions where your body remains in bed and they take your soul for a joy ride. Both types of abductions can be difficult to wake from if you panic, many people panic. Abductions are opportunities to visit with people on the other side, they are sessions to help you get through a hardship or a difficult problem in this life, and a gamut of other reasons.

I don't know if I have ever been abducted, if so, I don't know why they haven't fixed my health problems. I do know that reality exists on so many other levels, that outside of the very

universe is another and another and in a way that is hard to comprehend. There are an infinity of infinities of realities and creation and spirituality where the soul exists on an infinite level and I honestly feel that beyond all that there is another reality being the soul that the very souls that are connected in the essence of the group mind, "GOD" are attempting to discover and evolve.

ETs can make things easier for many people, but everything we go through is by design. Sometimes you can renegotiate a life change during abduction, most of the time you can't.

I wonder at times who I am? Where I am from? Who was I? And even if I am a God of sorts? I wonder if the people around me are real, and are there 'fake humans' without souls mixed with others like me, who indeed are 'real', and what not? How did I, who I am, to be picked to live this life in this body at this time?

God implies perfection so if you were a god you would know without a doubt. We run into fake humans every day, figuratively and literally. Unless you are here for some kind of punishment you chose to be here, you just don't remember signing that contract.

Honestly, I feel like my body is nothing more than a 'controller' that allows me to participate in this reality. Very hard to explain, maybe you can understand where I'm coming from? I do have a question, has this 'revelation' of the true nature of reality affected your life? Your beliefs, philosophy/religion?

I was raised as a Christian, and I understand the purpose of religion, but like I said earlier religion is a thing of Earth and other planets that are similar to Earth. Same with philosophy it's nice to have if you have nothing else. Problems we encounter in life are illusions and finite ones, philosophy for some, reality for me.

January 9, 2006

What are your thoughts on the connections of the "fall" of the human race/mind caused by Satan and ETs? Is there any link between the bible, spirituality, and the physical realm whatsoever, and where is it leading to?

Religions and other belief systems are fables created by ETs as a component of life on Earth and millions of other planets like Earth. In the book of JOB Satan is one of god's servants, he works for the big guy. Good and evil are illusions, programs running on this computer we call Earth. However, there are rewards and consequences for our actions based on that program, murder, rape and a host of other criminal activity will not get you brownie points on the other side but more hard time on planets like this one. Your next tour of duty is determined by your actions on Earth, more and better opportunities or fewer and crappier ones.

I'm sorry but I can't accept the simple concept of us in heaven saying "I'm bored, I think I'll erase my knowledge and experience cancer on Earth!"

Some people believe that if they are good and believe in certain things that they will be rewarded for all eternity with playing the harp on a soft cloud forever and ever. Others' believe that they will be given a bunch of virgins to play with, their own personal harem. Some are relying on not coming back as insects.

Then there are those that believe this life is all there is, you die and become worm food. None of that stuff is true but most will not be allowed to know it until they die and get their personal evaluation.

Cancer, like everything on Earth, is by design. I don't think anyone signs up for cancer, but you never know.

Do the Extraterrestrials ever allow individuals to 'move' to other planets within current lifetimes? Or is that something that waits until the next lifetime?

They do, but some of these people are dragged kicking and screaming to their new location, for reasons I'm not aware of. There is no eternal hell like in the bible, but there are some places and conditions even on Earth, that feel like hell is forever.

Yes, I am a gardener by trade at present - but I'll probably get piss bored with that too. I quite fancy a job in the stock market or a jeweler perhaps. Sorry - but until I see something that hits me on the nose, that kind of evidence, then the grey areas will stay in the skeptical box.

Since everything on Earth is an illusion, it's unlikely that your nose is going to take a hit from something real. If you wish to get a small peek at reality, you will have to step out of the box that the vast majority remains trapped inside of. Stepping out of the box is not easy and very few people do it. Those in the box call us crazy for leaving the box. Imagine that.

I have read the first couple of pages of this thread and the last five or so. A few questions if you don't mind:

1. So you are saying the bible is a fable. Are you saying Jesus was an ET? Also, who will 'evaluate' us on the other side?

Jesus was and is an concept, a well-crafted concept. You will be one of the judges on the panel, the harshest judge on the panel, and you will throw the book at yourself. Once we cross over our flaws will glow like hot coals and it will be our responsibility to correct those flaws in order for us to move up. No one else can do it for us.

2. Are you implying that there is no god, Heaven or Hell?

No old white bearded man running the whole show, or a mother Earth type either. No eternal hell for the masses of non-believers, but some of us will need to place ourselves into hellish predicaments to remove certain flaws. If we don't do it voluntarily it will be forced up on us.

3. You also say that we don't end up here by accident, we in a way signed a "contract". When you sign this contract, do you know where you will be born? For instance, do you go into it

knowing if you will be born into a family in a third world country? Or a rich family? Or is it all random?

You will know exactly what you are signing up for, most of the time it is 100% your call. Random can be found on a slot machine and is an illusion, if you win, it was given to you, if you lose, it was taken from you. How many people walk away with money in their pockets playing random machines?

4. Do you astral project? Visit the astral plane?

I don't astral project.

5. What are your feelings on the NWO, is it real or paranoia?

Concerning New World Order (NWO), humans have never run anything, never will, Earth is a place of learning, a playpen, can be a wondrous place to explore and enjoy or a hellhole to try to survive. Earth has something for everyone both good and bad.

As Real as the Nose on my Face? I can touch my Nose. I can let others see and touch my nose. I can prove my nose exists. I can go to any doctor and/or specialist and have them prove beyond any doubt that my nose is in fact real and therefore exists. I can submit samples for study in the effort to prove that my nose does indeed inhabit this world. Extraterrestrials on the other hand. Well.....debate. None of the above can be done and there simply aren't any Extraterrestrials aside from

a few questionable photographs, stories, and accounts. When will we get an Extraterrestrial that we can examine like the noses on our faces?

This world is a hall of mirrors, to see your nose you have to look in the mirror, if you are happy with what you see your search is over. If life as you know it suits you, you need not search any longer or at all. The illusions of life were created for a purpose and it serves that purpose very well. However, there are those who are allowed to know a few other realities and those people know who they are. The rest only see nonsense and there is nothing wrong with that.

First off thanks for the interesting reading, I've been following the entire thread with great interest. Dang, the upper post just gives me the creeps, really, I get shudders from pictures of Greys, they just freak me out, and I feel bad when I see a picture of them.

Maybe you know the reason for that? Seems like something subliminal to me. As for abductions, well, I really can't distinguish a dream and an abduction, I have had a huge fear of ET since I was a little boy, maybe 5 or so years old. Most nights I look into the sky with fear, and at many nights I wake up in the middle of the night not remembering anything, sweating like hell and the first thing I do is I look at the sky, thinking... Extraterrestrial... am I nuts?

You may have had contact with drones they are unpleasant they do a job and kick you out the door when they are through with you. But usually they only treat adults that way. I haven't had any bad experiences while I was young, I played with others my age inside the ship, sometimes it was parked above Earth other times it flew around the solar system and we got to look out thought the portholes. I hear many stories where people like you describe abductions at an early age and being afraid. Many visits are for medical procedures and ETs don't use anesthesia so that may explain the fear/pain.

We humans are afraid of many things including life itself, one can only imagine when faced with something extraterrestrial and incredibly strange, our brains are not wired for that kind of experience. No point fearing ETs they have our best interest in mind, even the drones can't hurt humans, humiliate and put fear in us, yes they can and do.

Have you yourself seen an Extraterrestrial? If so how do they appear? Are any of the photos floating around on the internet of Extraterrestrials real? Or at least come close to what they look like, for instance this one?

The one in the picture looks familiar, but many creatures we call Extraterrestrials or ET are machines, drones and have the personality of a wet rag, they don't communicate at all they only process humans or their souls with little regard for our delicate feelings. Those ETs that have communicated with me telepathically have an appearance that is impossible for me to describe. Of all the pictures and drawings that I have seen on the internet none ring a bell for me. For some reason ETs rarely let me remember their faces.

Where did the ETs get the idea for these religious beliefs and fables? Did ETs just conjure them out of thin air or do they have some connection with the past events of our world?

ETs have been around for billions of years they haven't just fallen off the turnip truck, they probably know a few more things then we humans do.

You sound as if you're saying we pretty much have no free will and have already signed up for exactly what we're getting on this plane of existence. Why then should we be punished or rewarded for anything we do here? Are the rewards and consequences a part of what we signed up for as well?

Not all of us are here by choice, as I stated in my post that you conveniently ignored. When you sign up to improve yourself for whatever reason you sign up for the whole ball of wax, otherwise where is the challenge? If you come down here and become a bum, a criminal, or what have you, then there are consequences for those "decisions".

"None of that stuff is true but most will not be allowed to know it until they die and get their evaluation."

Again, evaluated by whom? Evaluated by people who "signed up" to be evaluators for things we have no control over?

When you are in school, don't you do self-evaluations along with teacher evaluations, and parent evaluations? Between lives, there are evaluations by a number of entities that know you, and help you with your problems.

"Cancer like everything on Earth is by design, I don't think anyone signs up for it, but you never know."

You go on later to say:

"You know exactly what you are signing up for, most of the time it is 100% your call.

So then, we do sign up for terminal illnesses? I hate to nit pick your posts like this, but what else can you expect when you put so much stuff out there.

Why do we sky dive, drive racecars, swim near sharks and do many other stupid things that can and do get us killed or injured? For the challenge perhaps. Terminal illnesses is a huge challenge, assuming someone picked that from the bag of tricks they were offered, it could also be punishment for a past life infraction, that we didn't choose, but was thrown into the mix of things we would have to pick from.

"Jesus was not an ET, nor a man; he is a fable, a well crafted fable by ET."

So Jesus wasn't even a man who ascended the physical realm and reconnected with pure spirit through compassion (as did many others such as Buddha, Krishna, Mohammed), he was just another fable huh?

All religions and beliefs are fables and so were some of the players. As far as ascending through acts of compassion, even harden criminals have compassion, but compassion alone will not clear anyone of infractions with the law, we still must pay the speeding ticket when issued.

"You will be one of the judges on the panel, the harshest judge on the panel and a throw-the-book-at-you kind of judge. Once you cross over your flaws will glow like hot coals."

How can we be judged for predetermined illusions? At what point did we go from pure beings to having flaws to correct? Was that at the signing of the contract to be thrown into this world? Maybe that's where the idea of Satan comes from.

Most souls while on Earth don't know they are illusions. We humans put up with speed traps and sobriety check points because even good people will break the law if they get the chance to do so. We have leeway within predetermined issues, enough for the occasional shenanigans. You can often get away with things on Earth, but nothing slips by ETs and they will point out your shenanigans, everyone of them.

"It is your responsibility to correct those flaws; no one else can do it for you."

You say it's our responsibility to correct these flaw, no one else can do it for us, then you say:

"There is no old bearded man running the whole show, or a mother Earth type. There is no hell, but some of us will have to put ourselves into hellish predicaments to remove our flaws. If we don't do it voluntarily it will be forced up on us."

So now, it will be forced up on us? HUGE contradiction.

It will be forced on us by ETs, not a bearded old man with an attitude and a smote inclination. As a comparison to what you label a contradiction, take the military, most people would never complete military basic training if it were up to them, most are forced through it kicking and screaming, yet now days everyone in the American military volunteered to go through basic training. Most are glad that they weren't easily let off the hook and are proud of their accomplishment. The fact that they needed persuasive encouragement to get through it was for their benefit.

I'm not sure whether I believe everything in your story, but I just have to say that most of what you say I agree with 100%. If this is a hoax, you've done a hell of a great job! I've had a few encounters with UFO's, one of which was olive drab with USAF painted with white on the side (happened in northern Michigan). I don't have any questions, just wanted to give you a pat on the back.

January 10, 2006

Do the ETs constantly 'browse' or 'download' our Internet for study? Or do they already know everything on Earth in an instant through some sort of 'consciousness/spiritual download' in a sense? Do the ETs ever get online and chat?

The idea of prayer came from ETs. Essentially, prayer is a form of communication with them. Our thoughts have frequencies like radio transmissions, but the frequencies are too high to be picked up by human equipment, ETs pick them up instantly. Six billion plus brains on Earth and all of them have their own unique frequency, like finger prints.

ETs do get on line and chat. Most humans don't know about ETs and that they can communicate directly with ETs so ET uses the conventional means of communication incognito. No matter which god people believe they are talking to during prayer, the messages are picked up by entities such as ETs. Sometimes ETs respond to requests.

Earlier you stated that SETI was in essence a waste of time since it can't pick up the 'high tech' signals the ETs use, due to our primitive state of technology. But what about picking up signals from other primitives/like technology civilizations? Since you stated there were millions upon millions in our galaxy alone.

There is no need for the primitives to communicate with each other. The distances will never be traversed and physical contact completely out of the question. Eventually people on Earth will build cities on many of the moons and planets in this solar system, but the human race will never leave this solar system in the flesh. Countless people alive today will move on to other more advanced planets and solar systems and enjoy contact with a multitude of other life forms, things that will boggle the mind even once the human blinders are removed. Others will return to this planet or other cities in space that will be built in the next thousand years, so either way it will be a fun time for most, but not everyone.

I brought up Salvia Divinorum before as from what I have heard, the origins of the plant are really unknown, the species was *never* before discovered except for a very small pocket of growth. Many who have partaken of the Herb state they experience inter-dimensional travel and travel throughout the universe at overwhelming speeds. Experiencing Extraterrestrials worlds, walking amongst Extraterrestrial beings, etc. Many times, they are 'regarded' but most of the Extraterrestrials seem indifferent or not concerned with their presence and folks are usually 'noticed' but ignored when visiting these other realms/planets. That's why I asked your take on it. Perhaps you can ask the ETs about Salvia Divinorum? It has been theorized that the plants were

genetically created by ETs and placed here as a communication tool. There is no Lethal Dose possibility, and it has so many safe guards in place it almost seems like it is an advanced software program in many respects. Like the holowdeck with all safeties enabled.

ETs can take anyone to any place in the galaxy and the universe if they want to and they do. However, the human body never leaves the solar system, when ETs take people out of this solar system the body remains in bed or in a container inside a ship. There are synthetic and organic drugs that will do many things to the mind, but taking the soul out of the solar system is not one of them. Being under the influence of drugs does make it easier to be in the presence of ETs and ETs can take you and show you many things without you leaving your bedroom. I'm not allowed to take drugs and I have access to ETs.

In your last post you wrote a heck of allot of Fiction. If it's not fiction, where are you getting this information?

I don't write fiction, I get my information from the horse's mouth, ETs.

Those are pretty grand claims and I imagine you'll want to share this proof or evidence to support everything you write is true. Can you post the comprehensive evidence here in this forum so we can review this proof/evidence for ourselves? If

you can't supply this, then I will presume it is fiction and based on unfounded speculation borne of wishful thinking.

I don't speculate or do wishful thinking, I write what I have experienced and seen with my own eyes. If I had proof and was willing to share it I would be on my way to my next life.

There's nothing wrong with Fiction or curious imagination, but writing Fiction as Factual information seriously damages the already battered core of UFO/Extraterrestrial foundation. Please post some facts and or proof to support your statements.

There certainly is something wrong about writing fiction and claiming it to be the truth. I wish people would stop doing that. However, if they did stop, much of what's on the internet and written in books concerning UFOs, religion, Darwinism, cosmology and much of physics would have to be discarded as fiction.

No one has extraterrestrial proof because ETs haven't put it out there for people to have. ETs don't want the proof out there, until they do there will be no proof. Only factual stories like mine.

Good to see you back again. You were quiet for a while there. Anyhow, just wanted to get your opinion on recent developments since last we chatted. What is your take on the

move by numerous governments jockeying to be ambassadors to ET, i.e. Canada and the UN.

Since ETs have always been here on Earth they have no need of ambassadors. People are frustrated because many suspect that something is going on and their governments are not addressing the ET issue. Obviously, the UN, which sees itself as the world representative would throw their hat in the ring, and Canada needing to show the world that it is a progressive country would do so too. But the leaders are only placating, sucking up to, certain citizens and doing some grandstanding in the process. I doubt that the UN or Canada are serious in wanting to alert the world about Extraterrestrials. Nor are they so naïve to believe that ETs are not here. Any country with an air force knows ETs are here and not the least bit interested in "take me to your leader" diplomacy.

How about this recent jump in space travel technology? Mars in 3 hours and all that? Sort of, oh look! We had this idea since the 50's; maybe it would be a good design for space travel. Like, they have been probably using it for years and just want to make it public.

There is no such thing as new technology, everything already exist somewhere. There are people and places on Earth that don't have cellular phones and computers, fewer and fewer places. ET ships exist and some day that magic technology will be just another part of everyday things like former magic stuff as electricity, phones, radio, airplanes, the horseless buggy, and sliced bread.

The military is playing with some flying machines now that would boggle the minds of everyone on this planet if people knew about them. ETs are releasing fantastic toys at a rapid rate into the hands of certain governments, only slowing down to give us time to incorporate such magic into our everyday reality. Everything we have today is magic, the airplane, computer, electricity life itself, yet because people are accustomed to those things they don't see them for what they really are, stuff of the supernatural.

Sometimes bits and pieces of truth are found in fiction, objects like the "water container" that is used for "space travel". It might not be a water container and it might not be space travel.

Fiction holds more truth than what people call reality. Fiction talks about space travel, other inhabited worlds, magical star ships, all true stuff. Reality talks about what we can observe, taste of touch. For thousands of years humans observed the sun going around the planet, therefore, that was reality. Today those with both feet firmly planted on the "reality bandwagon", believe that billions and billions of star systems are void of intelligent life simply because ET hasn't picked up the phone and called us back.

Between you and me, we know my Extraterrestrials are the superior Extraterrestrials. And they have ok'd you to disclose all your proof to this board by tomorrow. Now you believe me right? Cool. Can't wait!

Since your higher-ranking ETs gave me the clearance to release the proof to you then so be it. I can only show you the proof everyone else must ignore this post. Go look in the mirror, what you see was created by ET. Not buying it?

Is there any human technology that could create your eyes? Your hearing, your taste buds, your heart, lungs, billions of cells that replaced themselves every few days without you being aware that the body you resided in today is not the same body you were in last week, and the week before, all the way back to when you were born. By the way, before you were born, at the very beginning of you, two strands of microscopic DNA joined together and began creating your body, they built the most complex machine known to man and did it in less than nine months.

What have you done in the last nine months?

January 11, 2006

If ETs 'listen' to and comprehend each and every mind and all of our thoughts at every moment of every day and they do this to all life in the universe, then what do they do with this 'data' that they collect? I mean, is reality itself, a large distributed computational computer that is churning out probabilities, possibilities, within multiple dimensions of reality?

You know that all radio and television signals are perpetually drifting out in space. Vibrations live on forever. Every thought, every action, and though we can hide behind, names and monikers, everything that is yours can be traced back to you or whoever it originated from for eternity. Data is not collected as it is in a computer, classified and stored away. Whatever we generate follows us wherever we go like military records. Probabilities and possibilities are human level concepts and are not part of what we are.

Do ETs relay this data to God? And that's another question, have the ETs met God? Or is God still a mystery for them? I'm guessing the true reality is still a small part of the whole picture of the super reality.

I hate to ruffle feathers, but there isn't one point where all power emanates from. The universe is billions of times larger than what is perceive by mortals or seen by satellites. The universe is really a big place and is occupied my countless billions of distinct energy forces like a school of jellyfish/ galaxies. Human reality is a pinprick on a strand of vibrations that make up the smallest part of an atom. Super reality is the outward universe that we humans will never know anything about.

What is the best way to get in touch with the 'good' ETs? You said to sit alone in the dark and concentrate on thinking of communicating with them. Are there specific thought patterns that they look for? Specific incantations or rituals that can call them?

ETs hear your thoughts. When I said to sit alone in the dark, I was referring to a tiny bit of the fear factor that a person would encounter when they are face to face with ETs. People believe that being inside a church, synagogue, mosque, or spinning a prayer wheel, will enhance communication with their deities, not true.

Incantations, rituals and chanting not only annoy humans it annoys ETs too. Strait talk is good enough. ETs hear your thoughts while you drive to work, go shopping, taking a bath, while you are having dinner, talking behind your boss's back. In other words, humans have zero privacy.

Are 'angels' and 'demons' other forms of ETs?

Angels and demons are often the same coin. They are also separate beings with specific duties.

You said that a majority of the Extraterrestrials are the 'drones' and the guys who run the drones are rarely seen or remembered, correct?

Drones are soulless machines that operate autonomously but also at the discretion of ETs.

If our bodies are the creation of the ETs, then why do they fail and have so many problems?

Humans do have freewill and they can abuse or misuse their bodies. Look at how some of us treat our cars, houses and other things entrusted to us. Nevertheless, many flaws are programmed into the body, like a car assembly line, different products go into certain cars by directive.

How do you know that Jesus was 'made up' and if so, why would they make up Jesus and create an institution of religion as oppressive as Christianity?

I was told. It's not the institution of Christianity or the other religions and beliefs that are good or bad, it's the people. Everyone is tested on this planet for the reasons of proving to themselves what they are truly made of.

What is your take on 2012? Sorry if this has been discussed.

2012 will be one more year that we have to pay taxes, get up and go to work, take vacations, be happy about the good things that are happening and sad about the bad things. There will always be wars, rumors of wars, famines, and natural disasters, and signs and omens that the world is coming to an end. The world is not coming to an end, but all that other stuff happens otherwise we will never get off this planet. Life and death is one and the same, we die here on Earth and wake up and live in another place. It's been that way forever. Unlike here on Earth most of existence is fantastic.

Thanks for all the quick replies! Hope all the questions aren't getting annoying. If they are just ignore me. What about the Prophet Yahweh guy? Was he a load of bull or did he really have the power to summon UFOs.

He had the power that all of us have, to make fools of ourselves.

I have been reading and seen many things. There is no one place or sitting that cannot be discredited or made to look the way it did. Before I get the label as just a nonbeliever of UFOs, I am a believer in God! I would love to find out some real info on UFOs or something.

I do not think that we are the only ones out here! I know that 50% of the sightings of UFOs are just Experimental Aircraft. The one thing I do know and I would say most of you guys would say I am right on this is. If We were out in space looking at some planet that had a race of beings that acted like us on it, would you make contact?

If you could help the people of Earth would you?

Do you know anything about "Project Serpo Project Exchange Program" that has been discussed in another thread on this site?

I have read some of it, there was no exchange of humans for aliens as mention in that tread. Humans are taken to other planets every day and returned the same day, some remember their experiences, most don't. The government has sent certain scientists on learning expeditions with ETs, however most trips off planet are by ordinary people picked by ETs without the governments knowledge, and some are returned a bit less ordinary.

Are there any cultures that had some sort of resemblance to that of our own, you know, same technology, cultural and political issues of similar nature to ours? If so, out of curiosity, what were they like?

There are numerous planets exactly like Earth, so much so that if ETs plucked you from this one and placed you into one of the others you wouldn't' know until you tried to find your house and make contact with your family and friends, they wouldn't be there.

Whether or not any of this is true (if there is such a thing), your outlook (insight?) on religion is one of the most rational and sensible I've read. I must admit, I've spent the past couple of hours trawling through your history of posts as far as it would let me and one thing that struck me dumb, is that your entire posting style and opinions are consistent - Even on the old board, even in subjects totally unrelated to UFO's. Sure, it could be the consistent ramblings of a madman, but I think we both know that's not true. Curiouser and curiourser cried Alice.

"There are many planets exactly like Earth, so much so that if ET plucked you from this one and placed you into one of the others you wouldn't' know until you tried to find your house and make contact with your family and friends, they wouldn't be there."

Do go into depth on this.

How is it possible for there to be other planets just like Earth? Well if Darwin is correct then it's impossible. Darwin did his job very well, so well that millions will go to the grave believing in Darwinism, and they will get the shock of their lives when they see him on the other side, perhaps playing Darwin on some other planet. The great thing about dying is that it only last a few seconds and then you are alive again somewhere else. The place you wake up in will be a temporary place, a fantastic city that you will never want to leave. You will be in spirit form and in complete ecstasy. You may be there for a short time or hundreds of Earth years (time as we know it is non-existent there). From there you will be sent to any number of planets, or back to this one. New planets and stars are created every second in every galaxy. There is no tossing the dice as Einstein once said of god. ET doesn't toss the dice either. Planets are created for human habitation.

There are planets at every stage of so called evolution. Many people will remain with a planet from beginning to end. Start out as a member of a primitive tribe and end up cruising around the solar system many lifetimes later.

For those thinking about suicide in order to go to a better places, forget it. Unless one has a very good reason to suicide, those who do it will be returned and presented with additional challenges, more difficult than what they ran away from.

January 12, 2006

Thank you again for all your hard work in responding to every question we ask. It means a lot to me that you don't 'overlook' questions. I am curious, are there such things as GHOSTS? IF so, what are they and what do ETs think of them? Have you ever seen one?

When we die we can revisit places on Earth before being reassigned to another situation. If we die and were involved in something sinister we may remain here searching for some kind of resolution. Some people are attuned to other souls more than what is normal and sometimes they pick up the vibrations of these poltergeists that have lost their way and are haunting places.

Are there humans who 'work' with the ETs and remember 100% of everything they do with the ETs? If so, how does one 'get a job' with the ETs?

There are many such people and they are cognizant of their duties with ETs. Also thousands carry out ET orders without a clue that they are working for a higher cause. Their paycheck may come from an IBM or government agency or some fast food restaurant, but they work for ET. You may have a job with ET. It's their call on how much you will know about them.

I know time is an illusion, but is "Time travel" possible and has it been utilized by ETs to try out various items, see the end result and for them to return and correct it/etc for a more favorable end result?

Trial and error is a human level activity so ET is not out there experimenting with getting things right. One might think that it could be extremely boring living an existence where everything has been figured out and they might be right. Time travel is a complex phenomenon; I have been shown a few things before they happened so it must work on some level.

You stated earlier that the human body is the work of ET engineering. So does that mean that everything we classify as 'organic' is in fact a type of 'synthetic' that we currently have no knowledge of?

Everything is a machine, plants, animals and matter itself. Souls are the only exception to that rule.

You also stated that this reality is a complete illusion. If that is the case then are we really here in this physical reality interfacing through this body interacting with real physical objects? Or is it more of a matrix type situation where we 'jack into' the matrix through an interface? Or is it more of a 'holodeck' type situation?

Our souls are attached to the bodies we reside in, we are here inside a machine we call a human body, the pain is real, the joy is real, hate and love are real. They say you can't take it with you when you die, not quite true, everyone leaves Earth with plenty of baggage. All the pain you caused to others and yourself, and all the joy you created for you and others, that all goes with you when you die.

I was thinking the other day about what you said, and it made me think of Star Trek and "Q" and how the ETs were basically "Q" in a sense. So if what you said was true earlier, then Star Trek is probably more accurate than most of the other TV shows out there eh? Or maybe Firefly?

Everything the human mind can imagine and that is not much, is being played out in millions of star systems throughout the galaxies. Galaxies are never ending wonderlands created specifically for us.

I'm so glad that this thread is doing the rounds again, with a new audience this time! I was there the first time round and was bitterly disappointed when the thread died. This is one of my favorite posters here on ATS and I am more than happy that he is willing to share his experiences with us! Keep up the good work and long live this thread!

I hadn't been following this thread and posted here by accident (it was really weird, because I was sure I was replying to a PY thread). However, "serendipitously" if you will, I must agree with you that this thread is fascinating. While I am skeptical of many things that he may post, I must also concur with those who point out that his descriptions of "what comes next" are intriguing. In my case, what intrigues me is how closely many of the details match what I discern in my meditations, including memories of possible past lives -- and deaths -- and what happens after that. I may end up reading the thread backwards, but now that I'm subscribed to it, I think I will as my time and interest permit. There are no coincidences.

"Suicide for no good reason is unacceptable and those who do it will be returned and presented with additional challenges often more difficult than what they ran away from."

Hi, I have been reading this thread for just a couple of days and have found it extremely interesting. If you are making all of this up off the top of your head, then you have got some really incredible persistence! (Not that I do think that). Anyway, what you said above is very strange because I had a really weird dream the other day, and just before I woke up a voice (I say *voice but it was inside my head)* explained to me this exact concept. That if you commit suicide simply because you are depressed, or for no good reason, you will not have solved anything and will be in the next life just as depressed as or worse than before. I just thought it was odd that you posted that around the same time of my dream.

I also wanted to ask you, are you getting all the information that you are relaying here from the Extraterrestrials, or is some of it from your own mediation or whatever?

I don't meditate, everything that I write that inspires readers is from ETs, they refuse to claim the rest.

What about dreams, what are they?

That's your brain shuffling through the work load it receives every day. ETs can talk to you without freaking you out while visiting you in your dreams. People in your life that have passed can also visit you in your dreams.

What is déjà vu?

Have you seen the movie "Ground hog day"? Think that's not possible, think again and again and again.

Any famous presidents that you know of that had contact with ETs?

Every president beginning with George Washington knew and met with ETs, so have certain other world leaders.

The Dulce base, is it real?

Dulce may be the least of places ET activity is going on, too much publicity.

The sherman ranch in Utah, know anything about it?

http://www.rense.com/general32/strange.htm (its a long but very quick read)

There are thousands of ETs on this planet every second of the day coming, going and permanently garrisoned here. Strange things happen for many reasons but mostly to keep people away or to deflect attention from other places.

You say dreams are just thoughts from real life, but people who OBEE say it's actually your soul on the astral plane. Do you even believe Astral Projection is real?

Astral Projection can't happen without ET, it's an abduction of sorts, where the soul is siphoned from the body and taken places mostly via a ship or capsule, OBEE is a real deal.

January 13, 2006

As to whether this person is speaking the truth or not, it doesn't really matter either way, for in the absence of evidence or antecedents, everything else is pure speculation, but personally, being an open minded person (not that open till all the brains fall out), I do find some of his statements thought provoking.

Amongst some of them, like the current dispute about everything is a machine, he may be ahead of his time, for already we are in the process of understanding more of nanotechnology and creating it for everyday appliances, e.g. biological computers, particle machines, etc. Will a tree be discovered one day to be nothing more than a programmed instructed object made up of biological particles? The line between living and non-living things is getting closer as we rush headlong into this century.

I have a million questions to ask you, but I'll start with just a couple to keep things simple. You say that everything here is a machine; plants, animals even our bodies. The only thing that is real is our soul. If this is the case, at what age do our children have their soul inserted into their bodies? Is it when they are still in the womb or is it earlier or later maybe? What

about stillborn babies? Did they die or just have no soul in them?

Souls are inserted after birth, but sometimes just before the baby enters the world. Stillborns and babies that are aborted receive no souls.

You say that our "real" selves chose to put us on this planet and they would be the harshest judges when we leave (die). Does this "real self" live on another planet somewhere? If I had a spaceship and it could be possible to visit this planet, could I then go and shake the hand of my "real self"?

No, you are here in your body and when you die there is a period that you go through before you regain complete awareness of who you are. Some souls reach this awareness immediately upon death others spend time trying to grasp what they are, having entered a kind of limbo zone.

Is this a REAL extraterrestrial or not? If not please enlighten those that think otherwise.

http://www.abovetopsecret.com/forum/thread190504/pg1

Not real. ETs control the situation they don't make mistakes and get caught on camera. However, poltergeist can be mischievous and so can humans.

Is there a question that you "don't" know the answer to?

Everyone has the capacity to know. The human soul can tap into the vast library of knowledge that exists in the universe. Seek and you will find. Blame others for your predicament in this life and you will remain buried in ignorance, denied access to such libraries.

Why are these ET's focusing in on our planet is it because their population is so large they could almost have a few focusing in on every planet or are we just next in line?

A city large or small is like a galaxy and there are many galaxy some large some small. Each city has enough daycare centers to service the needs of the cities; each galaxy has more than enough ETs to service all the needs of each solar system. ETs have jobs like us, but not the eight to five kind. ETs love their jobs. Once you leave Earth, depending on who you are and what you have accomplished during your existence here, and other places, you may have the pick of great jobs or return here or some other planet and be a rock star or president or a coal miner, dishwasher, etc.

What is your opinion what will be accomplished in the next 50 years? Will the ET's begin giving us even more at a time or will they stay with the same pace?

They have opened the flood gates of technology coming into this planet because Earth is on the brink of hatching out into the solar system. Perhaps not as fast as many people would like, but maintaining the illusion that humans are doing it on their own is important.

What do you think about these ET's appearance? Do you think it is customizable like ours? Or do you think maybe they are all relatively the same?

ETs are unique as are all souls. What is reported by abductees is window dressing, they can take on any appearance and so can their drones and machines.

Maybe the universe is like our "playing field" for our souls. However the reason why our Earth fights is because we have been a planet that holds all the newcomers. Like Earth is basically square one. You live your life here then when you "die" if you did good you will maybe be sent to another planet but if you are bad you will be kept on Earth or a planet similar or worse.

There are new souls, but billions of souls on Earth today have been around for some time.

This is why the Extraterrestrials are trying to help us. They have been here a while and know how the game is

played....maybe some of them started out on Earth as cavemen. So the reason why they have high-tech gear is because they earned it. kind of like a role-playing video game.

ETs aren't trying to help they have been helping throughout the history of man. Without adult supervision, ETs in this case, Earth would be like a schoolyard without supervision, total chaos. A hell no human would be able to escape from.

You make some interesting points, and I appreciate you trying to answers as many questions as you can.

Belief is personal in my opinion, so people should take from you what they need, and never force their opinion of you onto others. I guess reading through this thread, something jumps out at me - and please correct me if I am wrong.

Coexistence with Extraterrestrials will never happen in our lifetimes - or what we perceive as lifetimes – period? In the sense that - I will never be able to walk down the street holding hands with my ET friend talking about music of another planet and seeing other humans doing similar. In essence that would be life (me or you, now) and afterlife ('Extraterrestrials') coexisting on the same reality(here on Earth)? Which by definition, and partly due to our limited understanding, cannot happen - or can it?

ETs have always coexisted with humans. In the in-between zone depending on your level you will interact with many entities, family and friends from past lives and future ones on this Earth or one of the many other planets. BTW, this planet is fine but it is very low on the intergalactic scale concerning things to do, like comparing a small town of 200 people with a city like New York City. Holding hands and walking down the street with ETs, not happening.

All that jazz about sharing tech with ET - the human race "BOLDLY GOING" etc etc etc - is rubbish. Current space travel and exploration is token, hope is given & taken to pass the time - so basically folks - live life, do good, help others etc, and wait for death, as then you will truly be free to experience the wonders that await us all.

Even after humans build cities throughout the solar system, "Boldly" traveling in a starship out of this solar system is extremely unlikely. However, there are solar systems that have multiple suns, and there are star clusters where "Boldly" Going to other stars in fantastic Star Trek kind of ship is a reality.

People living in the Western World are clueless to how bad many people on this planet have it, more than four billion people live way below poverty. The rest might count their blessing if they live above the poverty line. Strangely, more people in the west and well-off communities commit suicide or sit around waiting for death than those that live on the edge of hell, in Third World countries. I paint a nice picture of what's to come after life on Earth, to encourage those who believe that life as we know it has nothing to offer. This life is very important and what we do with it will determine where we end up next, use this life wisely

Who gauges "GOOD & BAD"? - I have always had a problem with that one.

Your flaws, if any, will be as plain to you as a swollen thumb having been hit by a hammer, after death.

Just to add, I firmly believe there is Life out there - possibly even some visiting us - however I make that assumption purely based on what has been presented to me - via books / print media / schools, etc. In saying that, I've been told that space is infinite - so I must assume there are infinite possibilities of existence, thus my personal belief in ET. For all I know, and because I assume I am sentient, all that material could be falsified (for whatever reason - which would be irrelevant anyway) and we are nothing be a 1 or 0 or a automated Lego set or whatever.

Your soul is priceless and there is a huge amount of energy expanded on your behalf, as is true for all of us.

January 14, 2006

Hi, I'm interested to know what you think of the Starship Capricorn correspondence:

http://www.starshipcapricorn.org

The website is updated daily, posting the telepathic communications between starship personnel, mostly Helena, and a human here on Earth named Lavar. Recent posts indicate that First Contact is happening right now! My thoughts are that this is a genuine correspondence and an accurate one.

There is no "Starship Capricorn", sorry

January 15, 2006

What makes you so important that the army would have you inside a ship that they want to keep a secret on? Why would the army have it when the Air force would be the people to get it? I totally believe in UFO's but not your story.

I never said that the army owns the UFOs, not the real ones anyway. The US builds fighter jets and sells a few to our allies, but what they sell them are inferior copies to what the US has. Likewise, the air force and the army both have ET ships that they recovered from crash sites. But what they have are junk that the ETs let them acquire through supposed crashes. ETs land their ships on many military installations, army, navy, air force, and marines; ETs have VIP parking privileges at "all" military bases in the world. No military or government owns any real ET ships, however, the military is allowed certain and restricted access to such ships.

The military and world government have no say on who can enter real ET ships, ETs make all those calls. I know my story is unbelievable if you want the real truth tune into one of the major news stations.

Great story, very logical and most of it is well thought out. Great to see a story that doesn't drone on and on about self-pity over humanity. Normally people are devoid of logic or so

desperate to find greater meaning in their lives that they are completely delusional when it comes to 'conspiracies.' Your story isn't perfect; if it were there wouldn't be 30 pages in this thread.

Ever since I got suckered into buying that Above Black book in high school I've been coming back to these types of websites every few months to see what's going on. I never post or contribute, but this was the first time I saw someone posting something sensible. It's finally brought me some closure over the $15 I wasted on that book!

You really think that 'the private sector' is going to be any more forthcoming about ET and help bring humans forward in life?

I'm not talking about disclosure, which is not up to the government (public sector) or the private sector. ETs are the only ones that can disclose their reality to the world.

Not going to embark on private verses public, that's a discussion for other threads."

He means that private enterprise is full of risk takers that can and probably will invest lots of money into sectors monopolized by the government; such as space travel. If one

company makes a mistake, it will not cripple others attempting the same hurdle, such as the government entity. Private corporations and free enterprise are definite keys to advancement in any type of technology race. Competition breeds ingenuity.

Exactly, NASA is a huge government agency in fear of losing its prestige, power, and taxpayer funding. If the private sector had been allowed in the game twenty years ago, there would be hotels on the moon and in orbit around the Earth by now. Governments serve the status quo and are slow to change and adapt. America is the leader in the world only because of private and free enterprise, but those freedoms are being curtailed by the day. Free enterprise is under attack by those who believe that government is the great equalizer concerning quality of living and resources. Unfortunately, that is not true, every industry where government rules has lagged far behind free enterprise. NASA is one of these stagnant government industries. Private industry with a fraction of the trillions of dollars that NASA has received from the taxpayer would have given America a real and viable space program.

January 16, 2006

You continue to fascinate me with your comments. But please tell me, how do you come by such information? Is it given to you by ET? I guess it is! Does ET know that you communicate with us on ATS? If so, why do you think they let you talk to us?

ETs know, it's their way of communicating information to those able or willing to hear it.

If military bases give ETs VIP access. Can you tell me is there any bases in the UK that allow this? There is a fairly large US military base near where I live, would this be a good place to go UFO spotting?

Not a good place, a UFO can appear anywhere; there are no accidental sightings.

What about Darwin's evolution theory?

Much of Darwinism is a matter of opinion and little else. A lot has been invested in the belief of Darwinism and therefore it must be upheld and protected by those whose livelihood depends on the status quo. All countries have come to depend on that false religion. Life as we know it from the day we are born depends on the belief in Darwinism. Darwinism is ingrained in our learning and scientific institutions and without it the house of cards will fall. That's why it is forbidden to teach anything else in the American public schools and universities. A lot is riding on Darwinism, but like all false doctrines, Darwinism's time is about up and it will eventually come crashing down by the weight of its own absurdity.

Can you tell ET to get in touch with me or anyone else on this forum? Why doesn't ETs want everyone to know about them? If they did, presumably they have the ability to communicate with everyone and chose not to? Are they waiting for something before they give full disclosure?

ETs are aware of those that wish contact with them, when and if that ever takes place with any certain individual is known only by them. At this stage of the game, and for the foreseeable future, contact with humans is mostly business and not pleasure. They have the ability to communicate with everyone, but they know the big picture and they operate within those parameters concerning those they make contact with. Full disclosure is not on the table, when and if it will happen they are not saying.

I'm still reading this discussion carefully since I discovered it weeks ago. If sometimes somewhat dubiously. Still, this is one of the most convincing things I've ever read (For that, I gave "way above"). Just a few questions (no need to answer all):

1) If you're saying that Darwin's theory of evolution is incorrect then what is? How did everything evolve, if it did at all?

One can say that the model T Ford has evolved and split into many lines of Ford cars over the decades. Humans were behind that evolution not luck or chance. Humans haven't evolved over the centuries, there were different species of humans throughout the centuries and there still are. Homo sapiens of today are the homo sapiens of yesterday. Humans haven't changed only their surroundings, cultures and technology have.

2) When was the last time you were in contact with these beings?

Have you ever been out of contact with people you know? Family, friends, work associates. If not face-to-face, we managed to keep in touch with them by cell phones and or other means. ETs stay in touch with slightly more advanced technology than we humans do.

3) Surely not all ET races never make mistakes ?(Referring to EBEs capable of traveling to Earth) As you said there are millions/billions of different races all at different stages of evolution and technological progress and by what you've told us the US is already in possession or close to being in possession of vehicles capable of space travel. Of course, it's

220

common knowledge that the human race is eons from reaching a utopian, errorless state of existence. So perhaps, could there be EBEs who make mistakes?

None will admit to it.

5) If one finds the concept of being abducted, no matter how harmless or good natured it is, would ET, out of empathy, not abduct or erase memory of the event completely without the abductee having an inkling of what had happened? (Btw, I'm paranoid) I ask this as an old friend of mine always tried to tell me stories of being abducted with perhaps the same strange qualities you describe (obviously, he wasn't as knowledgeable as you are of the whole situation you claim is real). So say these beings are real, no thanks, no matter what, my mind wouldn't be able to comprehend something of this magnitude. Thus I approach this topic of ETs by telling myself I believe it's true but in the back of my mind there's always something saying it's not.

ETs knows the breaking point of those they come in contact with, they seldom push pass that point.

I sometimes appreciate the concept of only revealing ETs when mankind is ready as I have often thought about the negative and devastating impact it would have on the world and it would probably ruin a lot of lives if you think about it.

That's why full disclosure hasn't happened.

January 17, 2006

What is your opinion of Ouija boards? What do we really communicate with when we use them? Can I use one to communicate with ET?

Ouija boards are toys/gadgets for both humans and poltergeist, can you trust either? Ouija boards are nothing but wood and plastic. In the few cases where poltergeist answer questions the answers are playful but can be devious. I wouldn't recommend using such a device to make serious decisions in your life. Poltergeist can hear your thoughts when you seek them out, a door often best left closed. ETs are aware of our thoughts regardless of whether you seek them out or not. ETs can communicate in many ways including directly to your mind, in dreams, and nightmares, again not information you want to take to the bank. Chances are you have had physical ET contact, but they can't leave you with those memories because they might encumber your daily life. Knowledge from ETs bestows an unfair advantage to those receiving it, therefore ETs limit total recall and in most cases, any recall about the encounter with them.

You mentioned that my ET encounter hasn't dramatically impacted my life, true, but I have known them before I was born, and they maintain regular contact with me. I'm sort of acclimated to them, nevertheless, their presence can be extremely intimidating at times, especially when they are not in human costume or in the dark of night. In comparison humans, intimidating other humans is child's play. I'm sure you haven't read many abduction accounts where the abductee was delighted about the contact. Intellectual contrast between ET and the human level mind makes casual conversation with the higher beings nearly impossible and most of the time unpleasant.

If ET gives people this information, only to blank it out of their memory afterwards, then why bother? What is the point of letting people in a fugue with unanswered emotions and feelings in their heads? Surely, that is as encumbering to their daily life, as knowledge of their visits, or fear of the unknown factor should they visit again?

The Wright brothers remembered how to build and tweak their flying machine, but they didn't remember their visit with ET, the source of the information for the flying machine that they built. There are abductees that have problems integrating what they have received during abduction, perhaps they were told to change certain destructive behaviors and they refuse to do so; and then they are unsure of what is causing their inner conflict. Under those conditions ETs may let them remember parts of their abduction to let them know, and let others know, those that eventually will hear about their story, that humans are not alone in the universe, it's like hitting two birds with one stone. Most of the abductions stories that people hear about are from such people, the ones that remember the nightmares, the probes, the scary Extraterrestrials and their ships. The abductions no one hears about are those from people that are pillars of the community, scientists with breakthroughs in their fields of research, etc.

ET abductions serve primarily to inject new ideas and technology into the world and to help individuals who are seeking assistance with certain personal problems. To answer your last question, helping people doesn't always mean treating them with kid gloves, sometimes the best medicine leaves a bad taste.

So human ingenuity amounts to nothing? Everything we are and everything we have accomplished is thanks to ET? If that were true, I would be seriously depressed. I can understand that singularly we can be stupid animals at times, but as a part of a larger group collective I thought we added up to something more than ET's version of a Sim-Game.

You can always go on the assumption that it's only my opinion and nothing more. ETs don't do everything for us we are here for a purpose, but that purpose is not necessarily the occupation we find ourselves in, but it could be. The big stuff like flight and splitting the atom were big steps for planet Earth and were inspired by larger than human intellects.

That we have no power over our future and need to be constantly shunted into the right groove for them. I think the concept of Extraterrestrial Abduction is firmly rooted in the collective consciousness right now, and not exactly as a very positive thing. Does ET understand the concept of beating a dead horse? How could they possibly come back from such bad PR?

As a human being, you have all the power you can handle. Some people can handle more power, others need assistance at every turn, welfare for instance. Everything ETs do is for us not for them. America dropped two atom bombs on Japan, Japan is now America's closes ally and not because they fear America.

Not only can't we advance by ourselves technologically we also need them to act as Agony Aunts? Yikes. If ET is so Extraterrestrial in the first place, how could they possibly comprehend the personal problems of an entity (us) which is as Extraterrestrial to them?

ETs are Extraterrestrial to humans, humans are not Extraterrestrial to ETs.

A bit of "tough-love" then? ET obviously doesn't like Gene Roddenberry or the Prime Directive. Or are they just trying to clean up the neighborhood?

Have you seen the neighborhood?

January 18, 2006

Please tell me why this is the case. What is your definition of a poltergeist anyway?

If you could put on magic glasses, you would see a soup of entities everywhere you looked, like a crowded dial on your radio, each entity representing a unique frequency. Such beings know the rules of the game and can observe, but not interfere with humans unless the contact is initiated by a human, in which case, the human may become an object for fun or danger. We can communicate with loved ones that have passed on simply by thinking about them. What humans see and understand as difficult situation needing resolution carries little weight on the other side and is viewed as a child's complaints or simple naive curiosities. Poltergeist can be what we call ghosts and even ETs. The dead as we call them are more alive and aware than any human on Earth.

I can understand that ET would not like to be engaged in idle chitchat, but in all fairness, if I was to speak to ET the last thing on my mind would be to talk to him about the weather! But why do you say unpleasant? What could possibly be unpleasant about talking to a greater mind?

When talking about ETs the intellect differential is vast, like talking to a pet that doesn't know you, the animal is spooked easily by the human. There are ETs that take human form and make conversation with them possible, many people have had contact with them they just don't know it.

Ok, so here's the real deal: I am aware of ET's existence, and I am not going to go loopy if they talk to me, and I want to talk to them, or rather I want them to talk to me. So how do I initiate this? Is there anything that I can do that says to ET that I am 'ready'?

Only ET knows when you are ready, but being ready is not a prerequisite for an encounter. Can you imagine the line that would form if ET had an open door policy?

Do you know what your purpose is here? Is it possible for us to know what our purpose is?

Our purpose is anything that helps us move forward in this life. If you can get through the illusion of difficulties we all are presented with and remain happy and content you have achieved your purpose, everything else is only filler.

Another thing that occurs to me is if ET is so intelligent and so busy going about their business, do they appreciate the brilliant things that humans do like a beautiful artwork or our music. Do they have a sense of humor? Do they think we are funny? What about a sense of adventure? What do they think

of our movies? The ETs that you portray seem so scientific, does ET have time to play games?

They tape some of our stuff to their refrigerator door. They never get my jokes so I would say they have no humor. If you could see from where they are coming from, their cities, cultural centers, entertainment districts, etc, we come up a bit short. Remember how fascinating the playground at the park was when you were young? How about today? Some ETs were once or twice in our shoes.

What you've stated over the last few post seems to imply that it's not humans who figure things out its the Extraterrestrials who implant the thoughts in our brains so we think we figured it out. Why would they do that? I mean surely it would be much more healthy for a civilization to evolve on its own and if they kill each other or don't advance that surely means that they aren't beings that are fit to handle the powers that the more advanced beings have (who acquire their technology through natural intelligence).

I'm going to post a disclaimer: Things on my thread can be hazardous to the beliefs which are standard issue from our learning institutions. Unfortunately we can't have it both ways, you either believe in one or the other, its oil and water and they don't mix well.

We are not a civilization we are individuals living in a civilization here on Earth. We are not a colony of ants or a herd of cattle, or robots, nor are we zombies. We are each unique individuals with souls forged in celestial furnaces by the gods. We enter this planet alone and we leave it alone. We don't come and go as a society, herd, colony, or zombies.

No civilization acquire anything on their own, intelligence or technology. Just as we have children, and our children have children, each generation of parents takes care of their children otherwise there would be no children.

Surely, a civilization that got itself to where ever it gets is far better than one that's almost "cheating"? You could look at it like this: Why, if Bob wants to get big and strong, would he take steroids instead of doing it himself? Why doesn't he get there himself doing the more healthy alternative: lifting weights?

Individuals are free to get from point A to point B however they choose. How they do it will determine their next test and eventually their next hunting ground somewhere in the galaxy.

What about the first civilization that ever was, how did they get by? (What was first the chicken or the egg?) Is ET just going to keep leading mankind, blindfolded, forever? What's the point of having a civilization that has no independence? A

civilization that couldn't survive on its own? (Even if you say they won't ever be left on their own I think it's still an important principal).

There is no beginning and there is no end we exist in a loop, both the chicken and the egg are one.

Thanks, great answers! Completely answered my questions. However, (I know I'm delving into the realms of philosophy here but...) there's just one thing. I just can't grasp the concept of existence almost playing over and over again in a loop. If I were to take this literally that would be saying that I have been at my computer typing this post an infinite number of times in the past and will do so again an infinite number of times in the future. This brings me to the question: If the physical realm is just like a music track on a CD player playing on loop setting (same track repeatedly) surely, this track has an amount of time. How long is the loop? If I were some ultra superior celestial being watching over me right now how long would I have to wait until I can observe the same moment again? It's been proven that the human brain cannot comprehend the concept of infinity (I wonder if anything can) so it's understandable that I would question your statement.

The loop is infinite and if you live forever, and you will, you will never experience the same thing twice unless you want to, or are forced to.

And finally when I read what you said about looping existence the biggest question that has ever existed popped into my head (If you can't answer this and, understandably, I doubt you can, please take it as a rhetorical question:).Why does everything exist? Why isn't there just nothing? Surely there must have been a start somewhere or at least a reason for everything to exist in this exact way.

For there to be nothing something has to be, there is no light if there is no darkness.

Result of ADD I think too much about things.

You are asking stuff that many adults don't want to know the answers to. Nor could they handle the answers. Some of this stuff can be a burden if you choose to believe it because you still have to live in a world that is fast asleep and being one of the few that is awake is a challenge not suited for everyone. For some, keeping this stuff in the realm of philosophy might help.

Is there a possibility of an infinite world where there is always a greater being? For example: Let's say somebody owns a cat (indoor cat) in this world. The cat is almost like us and we are

the ET's. The cat lives in the house and has no thoughts about the Earth because it is too big to comprehend. It can look out the window and see the Earth but unless we, the Extraterrestrials, can bring the cat outside, it will never find out about a greater world. So there's the cat with us being the Extraterrestrials. Then there's us with the ET's being the Extraterrestrials. Therefore, if this is true then the ET's must have another life form, which is greater than they are. That would mean they live in the universe and the greater life form can take them out of the universe just as we can do with the cat. If this is true, there should be a never-ending cycle.

You might be on to something there!

I would stake big money on fear being the major cause of Japan being friends with us after we nuked them. Remember Kobe? If not fear, then what exactly would endear them to the US? Having too much fun in Tokyo Disney Land?

It was fear at the beginning, but once they realized that America wasn't going to finish them off and instead helped them rebuild their economy fear turned to respect. Japan was under the spell of the wicked witch of the East and once that spell was broken Japan became a democracy and its people set free. There was lots of darkness before and during WW2 and ET lifted the shades a bit and let some light into the world, they will continue to lift the blinders from the human race little by little, and as the blinders go so will the shackles of institutionalize ignorance. Profound change visits Earth every few decades and fifty years from now people will look back and wonder about these insane times we are going through now days, or not.

January 19, 2006

You say that ET has involvement in wars. Has ET communicated to you when the next war will be? Do you know if it is imminent and whether it will be nuclear?

There has never been a day without wars in some corner of the world. There are dozens of wars going on as we speak. The only wars that make headlines are the conflicts super powers get involved with, because those are the ones with worldwide consequences. There is no major conflict in the works outside of the war on terror. A worldwide nuclear holocaust is not going to happen.

You say that my only purpose in life is to get through the illusion of problems and remain happy. This seems to me to be a lame purpose in life; I always thought that we were made for a greater purpose. BTW It's great talking to you again!

If you manage to dodge all the bad things life will throw at you and maintain a healthy and positive perspective on life you have achieve more than 95% of what the rest of the world population has achieved, and that takes some doing. Effective people are those that don't lose their cool in the battle of life. Most people lose their focus at the first hint of trouble and never regain it and then end up living the rest of their lives as unproductive, cynical people. Consequently, they have wasted their lives and opportunities to help themselves and others, not a good thing in the big picture of life, or our true purpose of why we are here on this planet.

I wish it would speed up, so many of our brothers and sisters die or are deprived from the basics we all should be entitled to everyday because of our selfish & ignorant ways. I wish they could help us be compassionate beings rather than being caught up with economies and self worth. All in good time, I guess. Millions will die to realize million didn't have to.

Some people have to die before they learn how to live. Those that have died are more alive than those that are on this planet now, and think that they are alive. Life and death are both illusion and part of the process of existence. People on this planet are here because they are not perfect and need some work in that area. The trip to perfection is a long and treacherous journey and not achieve easily in one lifetime, most people require many lifetimes before they get their foot in the door.

I'm still a bit puzzled. Wouldn't an infinite loop of existence imply that the same "beings" that we see in the physical universe are reborn repeatedly. Keeping this in mind, wouldn't that mean that there are a finite number of beings that have ever existed in this physical realm? That means that my soul would have already experienced being me an infinite

number of times and will again an infinite number of times in the future? The same with every other being in the universe? I'll assume I misunderstood your answer, but how, in this situation, would we be able to never experience the same life more than once? I appreciate that you have not yet left a question unanswered!

The universe is trillions of times larger than what cosmologists speculate. It will not keep expanding and then like a slinky fall bank to square one and start all over again as the prevailing theory suggests. The Big Bang theory is incorrect and such a phenomena never gave birth to the cosmos. Because the universe is so large and the possibilities endless, it's not a far stretch to believe that you will only live your life once, but that's not to say you can't relive your life endless numbers of times. Go to any beach in the world and pick up a grain of sand. Throw the grain of sand back into the ocean and go to another beach. What are the chances that you will ever pick up that same grain of sand again?

The grain of sand analogy can be refuted that's why memory is wiped clean when entering into planets like Earth, so that you can concentrate on this life regardless if you lived it before, and it will be like your first time. Much of existence is that way, you don't know that it's forever and you can't know until you die or unless ET showed you while you were alive. Human based reasoning, mathematics and physics, do not apply on the other side. Here on

Earth the existence of a soul contradicts all scientific absolutes and theories, the soul simply does not compute.

Let me say I have been reading this thread for a while. I must say it is interesting to say the least. (Please excuse me if this question has already been asked). If I may ask, what is your outlook/plan on the rest of your life since you have this knowledge of beyond/what is to come? Will you return here again for a repeat? Or will you choose to move on to bigger and better things in the next realm/dimension? From what I've read, It is your choice. What will your chosen "specific" job be if you do decide to move on past this realm/dimension. I'm pretty sure you have clear idea here also.

I will not returned to this planet for a long time, unless I am sent back or certain other circumstances pull be back. I am planning a long vacation before deciding on my next assignment, if any.

From my assumptions you have filled your "loved ones" in on any short comings they may have in this life? After all, we are here to claim "perfection" to move on, correct?

My children are on the right track, but not for perfection. Reaching perfection on Earth is a rarity, but you can move on from here to other more challenging planets to try your hand at perfection.

For me I'd like to know I'll see my loved ones again after death. No matter where I go. You said we take that with us to. Only upon our return to Earth will we have our memory wiped. What about if we move on? Will it be wiped again?

When you die you will see friends and family on the other side that are in the in-between place, staging area, before you or they go elsewhere, and you will be fully aware of those you left behind, as much as you want to be until you enter a new life. If you return to Earth or another planet like Earth your memory will be wiped. The higher the level you achieve the more you retain of your memories regardless of where you go.

I can say I have seen a UFO close up. They are real. No E.T. encounters that I know of yet. My personal feelings are that of self awareness of this untaught unknown have been there from the beginning. Don't know how or why it just is. Greater purpose? Maybe. I'm optimistic. Great thread!

Chances are if you have seen a UFO up close, you have been inside it.

January 20, 2006

I've been thinking about what you've been saying about what happens when we die. Right now, I am aware of myself and I only have the knowledge that I have gathered in this lifetime. I eat, drink, talk, and sleep etc. This person is me! Now then, when I die do I instantly become me again in the 'staging area'? Will I have all the memories that I have attained through this life. Will I be able to say to myself that he was right?

You never stop being you when you die and you will be aware of more than what you are aware of now. All your memories will be intact and crystal clear unlike they are here on Earth. You will know I was right.

In the staging area, I have the choice of where my next destination will be or I can stay in the staging area if I choose. Is this staging area where poltergeists exist? You have said previously that poltergeists can be humans or Extraterrestrials, and that when we use the Ouija board this is who we communicate with. So logically speaking this must be the place you are referring to.

In the staging area you and others will decided what's best for you, to take it easy in the staging area, relax and enjoy the respite, or go visit other planets in physical or spirit form including this planet, or move on to other advanced planets. If you are really good you might even get to be a super star. Yes, you can be a poltergeist, come back here, and mess with those playing with Ouija boards.

Someone asked you about déjà vu in a previous page. I think you said that if you think that you have been somewhere before, then you most likely have. Are you talking about this lifetime or a previous one? If you are saying that people that have experienced déjà vu really have been there before in a previous lifetime, then that means that pretty much everyone has had a previous lifetime, because I don't know anyone that hasn't experienced déjà vu at least once in their (current) life.

There are more than six billion souls on Earth, do you know for sure that they all have experienced déjà vu? Nevertheless, some strange things happen inside an infinite never ending universe.

Can you explain away the radiation that scientists claim is from the big bang and the fact that its been documented that scientists have already observed the birth of the universe through state-of-the-art telescopes?(I can't remember when or through what telescope but I remember I read it on cnn.com) Are these stories just a cover up?

Cosmologists are paid to come up with such stories, what else they got to do or go on. There is no way for them to know what

242

that radiation is or where it originates. It could be radiation from massive stars and galaxies being recycled and giving off enormous amounts of radiation across the spectrum. This radiation originates from what scientists believe to be the edge of the universe because that is the furthest their instruments can pick up exotic particles, which is about thirteen billion light years away, they think. Now anything that has travelled thirteen billion light years to reach their instruments would require more energy than what is in this vast never-ending universe altogether. The whole idea is absurd, but it pays their bills.

So the quest for perfection is virtually unattainable in this life?

You tell me, how many perfect people have you run into or read about throughout history? I'm not talking about those who think they are perfect that would be at least half the population if not more.

Then why even try, some may be asking? If eternity greets us after what we perceive as death, big deal! Let's just party or play the chance game, after all there is no end.

There is no end to the universe, but not so, for souls. We may live forever, but how we live is what is at stake. Most souls are salvageable. BTW, there is nothing wrong with merriment as long as it's not infringing on others merriment.

The whole suicide thing - if you instantly come back, then suicide again some years later, or if you will 'perhaps' a suicide loop, you say you will be faced with harder challenges. Is it safe to say that this soul will never get better - essentially living a life of never-ending hardship? If they suicide in the first place, you can only assume they will do it again if the next life will be harder than the first.

Hardship is not the cause of suicide if it were there would be no people in Third World Countries, they would all kill themselves. BTW, suicide is low in those countries compared to the rest of the world where life is easier. People commit suicide to get back at a parent or lover, they do it out of anger and revenge, and it works, suicide is devastating for those left to pick up the pieces. Many people have thoughts of suicide, but the vast majority don't carry it out, and -there is no suicide loop, they will cut you off the vine. All suicides are not wrong, terminally ill, and other circumstances like honor, Samurai warriors and others defeated in battle. The reason behind suicide makes a difference and is taken into consideration.

On a final note, if all you are saying is true, and the human mind is barely conscious, why bother even informing us? Your answers point us in a direction that is pointless to even question.

The saying, "search and you will find" is a legitimate statement, but ambiguity can skewer the findings. Everyone is searching for answers and most will not find the ones they want. All will get a big surprise when they wake up from this life.

It's somewhat reassuring to a degree- just enjoy and make the most of this one folks, the best is yet to come.

Isn't that what life should be about? Not worrying about every little thing 24/7 as most people do.

January 21, 2006

What makes you the expert in this field exactly? Seems your preaching how things are in *your* universe - but what gives you the position of all knowing? Can you base one shred of this on any doctorate? (And do you have a tin foil hat?)

Are you making fun of my tin foil hat?

I've had a near death experience myself, but that's another story. I'd like to know how you come to your conclusions - with life, the universe - and just about everything.

Near death experiences, are great for getting basic insider information and confirmation that there is life after death, but they are very brief journeys into the next life, like entering a foyer of a house, but not seeing the actual rooms in the house. Most people that have near death experiences don't remember much about them, but do remember feeling unconditional love, which is real. There are those that have experience the other stuff too, like hate, hell and negative beings. ETs are emissaries from the other side, other planets in other star systems, and dimensions in this universe. I would say that they are of the spirit type of existence except that everything is a spirit existence of one form or other. Matter is only another level of that kind of energy.

Thanks for the answers. Now, if the "we are good we might be superstars" answer. Can you iterate for us here? Good how? I'm sure a few of us would love to be a superstar.

Most of us know what bad is, hate, envy, stealing, killing, lying, cheating, etc. Good is the opposite of those things, helping others just for the heck of it, being happy in our lives, encouraging others and yourself for the fun of it. Having fun and being happy when you would rather not be, and taking advantage of the gifts life gives us all, etc.

What do you mean take it easy in the staging area? Exploration will be on everyone's mind I'm sure. Will fear be a factor at all?

Taking it easy means exploring, spending time with loved ones on the other side, not working, you do work on the other side. Not everyone hates their work even here on Earth so work is not necessarily a four-letter word for all souls, especially those moving up. No fear in that zone of existence unless one is moving down and receives a preview.

Why would we ever want to leave? Especially since our loved ones are there for us already. They didn't move on when they could have? Our other living loved ones will be here soon to. You said it's our choice. Is there some sort of alarm that goes off saying your loved one is getting ready to kick the bucket get back to the staging area for a reunion?

No one wants to leave that place but some don't have a choice. Some leave for personal reasons for instance to be super stars on planets like Earth and for any number of challenges or experiences including fighting in a wars. Those in that plane of existence are aware of loved ones as much as they wish to be, no alarms will go off.

Also, you said you plan on a long vacation. Like you know exactly your plan. That you wouldn't be back unless you were called back? So it's not all our choice then?

Not everyone has a choice. We don't let our young children walk across the street by themselves, we also don't let them decided whether or not they will go to school, if we did most of them would chose not to.

Can you travel with loved ones or only alone? Can we travel back in time to see events we did before? Another question is will we be given any answers to all these questions we have been asking for years about all our on Earthly thought mysteries?

You can travel with anyone you wish if they are there in that zone. You can revisit any moment in any of your previous lives. Some things will be answered, other things you will need to find the answers yourself.

Do we eventually reach a plateau or an end of all knowledge? Or do our souls get reused over and over an infinite number of times. Repeating this infinite loop? Never to jump off track? Because we may be summoned back? That would be such a bummer.

The plateau is infinite and there is no end of knowledge. Souls are very durable and not easily extinguished, but they can be. Life on Earth and on other levels is difficult when there are unresolved issues in your soul. While in the in-between zone, you can see these issues more clearly.

You asked what I remember about my NDE. I'm not sure, but when I was going that way - up, down , sideways - i had no idea of direction I was going. I just felt very calm, but after the calmness I was a more lateral thinker (as if I had crossed a defined line, but became more aware of everything about me), but when I did go to the other side briefly I can only assume I was there. I felt incredibly tired - and it seemed I was ready to leave this plain. I can't really explain it any other way. Existence, as far as I'm concerned is an energy - everyone's an energy - a spark, but if I continue I'd only be babbling on about things I really do not understand.

Some non-soul type questions for you:

1) You have said that most ET encounters are very traumatic to humans. Can you explain why? Is it just because of human reactions or is it on account of what ET does and doesn't do? (Abductions do suck as opposed to asking nicely).

ET encounters are for a number of reasons, but many are used to, how should I put, take you behind the barn. They are intimidating for a reason; sometimes you are forced to confront situations you would never confront on your own.

ETs don't look like ETs on the other side because the mind sees them differently. During Earthly encounters humans see them with a human mind and the human mind does not comprehend the supernatural.

2) You have said that ETs also can disguise themselves as humans and interact in society. IF that were the case, then at least some of them know how to not be intimidating to humans (and pass for them in casual interaction) and understand enough about human psychology to make this possible.

ETs know how to interact with humans, intimidation, when it happens, it's intentional.

If both are true, then it seems that ETs don't have to necessarily make encounters traumatic and unpleasant if they

don't want to. But if they do as you say, I get the feeling that they're real jerks.

Many of us humans see authority figures as real jerks, police, school principals, parents, the boss, drill sergeants, prison guards, etc.

Parents sometimes do things that seem mean to children, but they also do things that even children realize is very nice. How do we end up with just the mean ones?

Some ETs are two-faced, they can be both good and bad, but they are always right and looking out for your best long-term interest.

Are there "unpopular" lives? I mean, who would enter the body of an aborted baby or a baby who dies at birth? I'm sure there are people who have short pointless lives of permanent suffering. Or who, if people are so loving and benevolent on "the other side", would enter the life of a serial killer/rapist/cannibal or what about Hitler?

For the most part the soul is not inserted until the baby is born, the body is only a machine, and we don't enter cars while they are on the assembly line do we?

It's not always the choice of the soul where they will be placed. Once souls are inserted, they have to deal with their situation no matter what it is. People such as Hitler are souls that have taken on horrific jobs, but there is more to it.

Do souls have any influence on the beings that host them? If not wouldn't that just make their lives like a long movie?

The human body has a soul and that is the being, the you.

I've always been fond of Einstein's saying: "God does not play dice". This implies that everything in the universe happens one way. If it happened another way, then it would be disobeying the laws of physics. I may be more open minded than the next guy but I would have to shake hands/tentacles/paws with the Extraterrestrials you talk about before I could begin to question this. Keeping this in mind, from what I know, a soul is a celestial/spiritual entity with no mass or attributes that apply in this physical realm, therefore, how can it have any influence on the brain, a purely physical entity? The brain operates through sending/receiving electrical impulses through the body. There's nothing "spiritual" about that.

The brain is a machine that controls the body, the brain is the command center, the cockpit, without a soul the brain is a machine without a pilot.

Electricity and matter are one and the same, a creation and a subservient feature of the spiritual soul. The only real thing in the body soul equation is the soul.

Who chooses where their soul is put? Is there a superior being that chooses? Surely, this would mean there is some form of religion or something of that nature.

There are higher powers many strata of them a chain of command of sorts. Those that are religious may see it as such when they first get to the other side. After they have acclimate they will see things differently than they do here on Earth. There is nothing wrong with religious beliefs, or most beliefs, such concepts were instituted by higher beings.

I was born and raised a Catholic. When I married, I changed my religion to one of the protestant ones, the one my wife and children belong to. I even taught my children to be good Christians, yet I do not adhere to any religion or secular beliefs.

So in short, the soul does have influence in the physical realm? Do I want what my soul wants? What would happen if someone didn't have a soul?

You are your soul; the thinking part of you is your soul, your soul with blinders on while you are on this planet. Going to church and following the commandments is a good thing because for many the other side will be like heaven. However, heaven is not exclusive, all are invited to the father's table, so to speak, even those that don't believe or lack a religious base. Bodies without a soul are a waste of space.

"ETs are two-faced; they can be both good and bad." How do you know? How would I know?

I know because I was told and shown certain aspects of how they operate, it's the good cop bad cop routine on an intergalactic scale. Knowledge is a two-edge sword, too much and it can disrupt things in our human lives.

So far, there is no evidence ETs are doing anything other than what they want.

It's their show.

Parents who spank their children when they're naughty also ask them what they want for dinner and what they want for Christmas.

ETs, for the most part, remain behind the scenes, that's why everyone has human parents/ guardians to take most of the credit.

When they take people and then zap their memory: what is the point of "intimidation" or "giving them a lesson" if the people don't remember it?

The conscious mind remembers little, the unconscious mind remembers everything and changes take place in a subtle way. What kind of changes you may ask? That's between you and ET.

You give a very multifaceted message. I just want to concentrate on one aspect: you constantly refer to a view that the world is made of layers upon layers of levels of consciousness. Your view includes the concept that higher levels may have different semantics than lower levels, so that dialogue becomes almost pointless.

Now: a human and an animal are separate entities. But the human can implant electrodes in the animal's brain to crudely control its movement: so the animal becomes in a sense an extension of the human. Or: the Extraterrestrial and the human are separate entities. But the Extraterrestrial can sometimes inject information in the human's life stream, that will modify the field of choices that the human has when responding to situations: the Extraterrestrial makes use of the human.

The motivations why they do such things could be the same: just as the psychologist is trying to increase his knowledge, the Extraterrestrial may have the same difficulty across conceptual levels. You say that the Extraterrestrial is all-

knowing, and the galaxy is a wonderland and everything, but the Extraterrestrial may be using us in scientific experiments to understand what he's made of, just the opposite situation from what you imply with your rosy picture. Have you considered the possibility that they have not told you the truth?

I have been aware of ET all of my life I even remember then dropping me off on this planet. Nevertheless, for the first four decades of my life, I didn't want to know about them and I did my best to block them out of my life, totally impossible. They have literally taken me kicking and screaming into a life I didn't want. In short they forced me to clean up my act, I wasn't always the nice guy I am today. Evil beings wouldn't have gone to all that trouble to make me respectable, would they? What these ETs have shown me leaves no doubt in my mind that they are on the same level as deities. They are not out there trying to figure things out, their cities are beyond fantastic and everything is magic or what we would consider to be magical. Love radiates from everything they are involved in including themselves, when they don't have their bad face on, which they only put on while on Earth dealing with the obstinate humans.

Here on Earth we all know the truth is difficult to come by, but most of us wouldn't know the truth if it fell on us like a brick wall, truth is a tough concept down here, but not on the other side.

I can agree with many of your observations, especially the one that "love radiates from everything including them". But my problem can best be expressed as (and this is not meant to be cynical or anything): A domesticated chicken says to a wild chicken: "look how good the Extraterrestrials treat me, they have only my best interests in mind, it's all for my own good". We all know the sad fate of domesticated chickens. How could they (the domesticated chickens) think otherwise?

To me, the presence of love is not by itself reassuring, because love is the blood of deities. It is just the light they shine upon us to better observe our souls. Think of a human scientist shining light on a cold-blooded creature, how the light feels good for the creature.

The chicken domesticated or not is at the mercy of man, man and woman can keep the chicken and make it a pet or they can fatten and eat it. Using the chicken as a metaphor for humans and man for ET, the chicken is SOL and lives at the whim of man, there is nothing the chicken or for that matter, man, can do about it. I happen to know ET is not cannibalistic, but altruistic. Should ET be as you say, then there is nothing humans can do about it, being that they are omnipotent, as humans are when it comes to chickens.

January 22, 2006

I just saw a thread on cow, human and even dolphin mutilations. In their autopsies, apparently they had cuts that were so fine that they could only been performed with cutting tools on the atomic level. Although these sights don't really bother me the pictures are quite gruesome and gory (There are shots of a person whose face seems to be completely ripped off). Could this be the "evil" Extraterrestrial's work (surely it could be done by "good" ET as I doubt it's in no ones best interest to be brutally murdered)? Is it the government? Or have you not heard much on this subject (it is a somewhat obscure area of Ufology)? Do you think it is related to the chupacabra myth?

Secret governments do abduct people and animals for various reasons, but they don't have to leave evidence, neither does ET. They can't allow full disclosure, but UFO sightings, mutilations, and Extraterrestrial crashes, are part of the mind games played on humans by both ET and covert organization. There is more about this but not for now.

January 23, 2006

I find it a bit difficult to digest that the pinnacle I can achieve in this lifetime is to be a "superstar". I would hardly consider the movie and music stars here to be the best we can possibly achieve. Many of these said stars end up committing suicide anyway, so they can't think they are that great either!

You don't achieve stardom because you reached a higher level of nirvana, you can be a star in the same way you chose to be the hero in a video game, for fun and games. Once you are on the other side you have certain options and life choices you can choose from for your next life. Perhaps you might want to be a leader of a country, a general in some army, a schoolteacher, or a janitor. Depending on what level of consciousness you are at determines how many things you can pick from, and the quality of those things. You can also be someone who is selfless, like a mother Theresa or Gandhi, or return to Earth to help a family member or friend. After you make your choice, you will be placed into circumstances that lead you to those positions in life.

What you choose is not a guarantee of success or happiness. You will have to make those things happen for yourself. Once you are in the shoes of a world leader or super stars like John Belushi, Jimi Hendrix, and Janis Joplin you will learn that those lofty positions are not necessarily easy street, as you pointed out.

February 1, 2006

I'm not sure what to say. Some of what you describe is very familiar. I only remember some things. I think I've suppressed a lot. I don't know why anyone would lie about this stuff. It's scary as hell just typing this much. I remember a ride with my grandparents but it's not them. They are explaining things to me and I'm asking a lot of questions. I'm not bothered that it really isn't my grandparents. I remember talking about how gravity is like sound, a wave that can be generated or altered. I've played music since I was little. I remember remembering missing time and wanting to forget again. I know this sounds strange. It's come up again recently but years have gone by since I thought about it last. Some of the drawings I made as a child were difficult for my parents to understand. I would draw machines, places I visited, flying people, and anatomy. As an adult, I've studied the psychology of children's art - universal images that all children draw before they are taught. There was no basis in experience for some of the things I drew. I could draw anything very well from a very early age. My mom encouraged me to be an artist. I was tested with an IQ of 155 in 5th grade. I was placed in a special program for 2 years with a few other students until the state money ran out.

I remember sensing daylight at night and the feeling of someone entering the room but not being able to turn around.

If I'm in bed, I can't open my eyes. It's just very bright pink. This has happened a number of times but I'm more aware of it happening when I was very young. I've read about REM sleep and how this might be a split moment in time as your brain is waking up. I don't know what to think. It seems very real and it used to happen a lot when I was younger. I remember opening my eyes in the middle of the night and looking directly in the face of someone who is not human. I don't look away. I don't hear voices. I'm scared but curious. There might be someone else with us. I'm not sure.

I was hit by a car while holding my father's hand when I was about 8. Witnesses said I was thrown 10 feet in the air and landed in a thud on my neck and back. Without thinking, my dad rushed me to the hospital. I had a couple of bruises. I seem to remember watching it like a movie. I didn't feel alone. I remember other conversations with people I cared about (never quite looking in their faces for very long) and asking why and how, what might seem like spiritual questions now. I can't remember any answers but one and it's going to seem a little odd. I'll try to explain. The central point of my understanding is this. We are containers, collecting experiences and growing our soul in preparation for something more. What we see and touch is like a dream made real only because we seem to want to believe it. I'm sure I'll either mess this up or offend someone so please be patient with me. I believe god/the divine is flowing in, around and through everything. In a very real sense, there is no separation. When we choose to take part in this, we are realizing something greater than ourselves. My experiences seem to climax with those thoughts. Afterward, I wanted the strange things to stop. As far as I'm aware, they have. To be honest, I do still have dreams, occasional odd sores that heal very quickly and a feeling of being connected to something larger. I'm a night owl, getting a lot of work done then. Sometimes I'll leave the studio and feel like someone is watching. It scares me but meanwhile, the work is getting better. There are no accidents. It has all the manifestations of a religious conversion and spiritual awakening. Perhaps that's because it is.

Much of what I think I realized happened within a year of getting married and trying to have a baby. I was scared of bringing someone else into my experiences. I wanted to forget. I now have 2 children and am very happy. Both are very intelligent and talented in music and art. To set an example, I made a leap of faith years ago, leaving my established professional career for an opportunity to pursue my creative work. I surprise myself sometimes at having been so successful at it.

I can only hope that your experiences are genuine. I don't have any questions.

I haven't talked to anyone else about these things in nearly 12 years. My wife is VERY patient but we don't discuss it much anymore. I think she accepts it as being real. We've both seen too many things happen in 13 years of marriage together to dismiss as coincidence. What we both visualize together often comes around. Call it creative visualization if you like but it works...important to stay positive. I've often wondered about the psychological effects of this whole thing. Did my young desire to understand the relationship between things, recognizing patterns, manifest in a science fiction fantasy? I don't know. I'm willing to consider that may be the case. Did the nature of my curiosity guide my interaction with something I still don't understand or want to admit to? Again, it doesn't really matter. I have to believe that whatever brings us closer to making peace with our place and purpose in this world can only be a good thing. I hope this helps someone. Not that I'm contributing anything particularly original to the discussion. I feel a little better just saying it.

Do all life forms have souls? Do dogs have souls (somehow, I doubt this)? What determines what kind of life form is "sophisticated" enough to host a sole?

They have consciousness but to what level depends on who or what is inside of them. Machines that accompany ETs have the same kind of awareness that some animals display yet they are nothing but smart equipment that perform services. In many ways similar to what pets provide, companionship, protection, entertainment, or beasts of burden as in Seeing Eye dogs, horses, mules, camels, etc.

All life forms are sophisticated machinery without souls, however a soul is a soul and a soul can enter into any machine including pets and insects. This is done for a verity of reasons and purposes including entertainment or punishment. The machine one enters into determines what that soul can or can't do.

Most machines are autonomous robots and function without anyone at the controls. The human machine is the exception; it is designed specifically to be inhabited by a soul.

Are you implying that not all physical bodies host souls? For example, are there some dogs that have souls and some that don't? Wouldn't this mean that soulless beings would exhibit a "soulless" behavior as opposed to their soul-hosting counterparts?

Most non human physical bodies are soulless they operate on a high level of intelligence, what we call artificial intelligence or instinct, one and the same btw, yet souls can enter them for short durations. There is no such thing as soulless behavior you are either a soul or a toaster, insects and animals are complex forms of ecological hardware, toasters.

February 7, 2006

There is a chance that this is all a lie, but I highly doubt that. The ideas or "theories" that he has posted are very advanced and don't sound like anything that is made up or fiction. For a while, I have wondered a lot about the universe and about our lives. I didn't really have to many people who can answer my questions without believing I was insane. Most people don't want to think outside of the life they live because they're afraid of the truth. But you've helped me understand some of my questions and provided much help. Good job! I have a few more questions. First, what does gender represent? Is it just something that exists in this life? And if we are all the same gender before and after this life then why do most men like women and most women like men in this life?

Humans are wired to reproduce and have fun. Sex breaks the monotony of this life and also keeps the population going. Gender exists on other levels but in different capacities than it does here. We can be both genders or stick with one throughout our existence. It really is a complex issue.

Second, are souls constantly being created and if so then where are they coming from? Who's creating them?

Stars and planets are being created by the billions as we speak, a process that has no beginning or ending. New stars and planets replace dying ones. Unlike stars and planets, most souls live forever, some souls die for a number of reasons including extinguishing themselves. Freewill having got the best of them and they refuse to go on.

Who creates souls? A god? A committee of super beings? A soul machine? A mad scientist? Souls are created in a similar way as we procreate here on Earth, but through immense love. On Earth, it takes the love of two people to produce a soulless human body (a soul is inserted later by higher beings).

A number of souls that have reached a high level of unconditional love create souls, and such souls become integral parts of that family of beings for eternity.

Last, are there people brought into this world who already know about what exists and what the real truth is? And if not can they discover everything in a single lifetime on Earth? How can they discover this without the ET's help? Do they have to reach a higher consciousness and 'Pry open their third eye'?

There are many. No one can discover everything in a single lifetime. Do first graders figure it all out their first year in school? And even after college or high school learning is a constant requirement to move forward in this life and all the rest of existence. Without ET's help nothing happens, ETs are the extended families. It's a big universe and a very big consciousness, the higher we go the more we can grasp.

February 9, 2006

Sorry if this question has already been answered. I didn't exactly read all 30 something pages. How do you explain the mutilations that are supposedly happening to both cattle and humans?

Animal mutilations are common very few are cattle and none are humans with souls still in them. Mutilations are done mostly by human covert operations to extract certain enzymes from animal tissue, stuff they need in the field, the animals provide fresh material, wild and domestic animals are everywhere and are an easy source for biological elements as well as for food.

How do you explain crop circles?

Two old men with a plank and rope go out every night after being kicked out of their local pub and vandalize innocent wheat fields, that's what many in the media are buying and peddling to the world. Crop circles are often made by ETs and some are made by humans in ships and equipment provided by ET. Crop Circles are coded messages like billboards for other ETs and humans who work for ETs, some are nothing more than graffiti made by bored humans playing with cool Extraterrestrial stuff, and a few are made by humans for advertisements or bragging rights.

Concerning humans using ET equipment who are allowed (or at least can get away with) to mess around with this technology? I'm a tad jealous. What do you have to do to be trusted with this much power?

Such jobs are not available through your local employment agency, ETs chooses those who work for them, no standard negotiations, job interviews, or contracts, most don't know that they work for ETs.

What sort of messages would Extraterrestrials leave for each other in these crop circles? Surely, even for Extraterrestrials, this is a bit of an extravagant way of communicating (and I suppose rather primitive)?

Not so primitive that no human outside the program has been able to decipher.

Don't they know of a "kinder" way of communicating without destroying people's livelihood? What kind of "benevolent" being would do this?

Not a single grain is damaged when ET makes Crop circles.

One last thing that bugs me whenever I look at this thread. If existence has existed for eternity, hasn't everything already happened? This question is so mind boggling for me that I'm not even sure what kind of answer I'm looking for. I've always

believed that nothing has a probability of 0. So if that's true then wouldn't that mean at one point of time (actually an infinite number of points in this infinite timeline) the entire universe was ruled by a race of evil oven gloves? (Yes, I know it's a rather odd question but I just tried to think of the most absurd random thing that came to mind for the sake of argument)

The nearest star to Earth is only four light years away and no human will ever visit that star while alive or in a human body because it is excessively far. Can you grasp the size of the universe? The best human minds can't. The universe is thousands of times larger and more complex than any human mind can imagine, or has imagined. The possibilities are endless. The ability to comprehend such possibilities while residing in a human brain is limited.

The whole idea of randomness is nothing but a human toy, something to play with while in this playpen called Earth. The only reason I can give this information is because most people will not believe it and most people shouldn't believe it, distracts them from the life they need to focus on here on Earth.

But in advanced technology can we make our own machines that are so realistic that instead of "your soul entering a baby" your soul can enter a complex realistic machine? So instead of

giving birth to a baby then a soul enters, we make a machine and program it then a soul enters.

Humans could make such a machine through cloning but they do not have the ability to transfer the soul from one body to the next without the intermediary ET. Should ETs allow humans to successfully clone a human, a soul of ET's choosing will be placed into the body and not the choosing of any human. ETs have always used clones for themselves and for humans that work for them to enter into. Will humans ever create a mechanical replacement for themselves for the purpose of extending their lives? No, it's not allowed.

Humans are placed into baby bodies so that they have a new slate to work from without the distractions of other past lives and experiences. Once you leave this life, you don't need a mechanical or physical contraption to exist. We already exist forever.

If everything is possible then a human WILL reach that star, the next closest galaxy, and eventually every star in the universe!

Everything is possible, but not while in human skin.

Even if that's not true, I find it hard to believe that we won't ever reach the next closest star while living here on Earth.

You're saying that humans will NEVER become as advanced to reach our neighboring stars?

The soul is advance beyond what we are allowed to do here on Earth. The soul has been to neighboring stars and other galaxies. Humans on this planet will "not" travel outside this solar system while they are alive or in human bodies. Earth is not Hollywood, and Star Trek type of travel is not in the cards for Earth, but it is for other planets higher up the scale.

We have machines that jumpstart your heart to keep you alive. And we also have some medical advancements that can put your heart on machines to keep you alive LONGER. How is this not a "mechanical replacement" with the "purpose of extending their lives"? I'm not trying to prove you wrong I'm just saying if we are way so far behind in technology compared to others and already have things to keep us alive longer, then out of this whole infinite universe some other planet must have already reached even further improvements of this. Perhaps even keeping them alive for ever (unless the machine no longer works)

You asked if humans will build machines that they can transfer their souls into, that's way different from a heart pump. Billions of planets have technology far more advanced than what's here on Earth. Life goes on without machines or human type bodies. For most, life is forever and although you may not travel between the stars while on Earth and in human form you will travel to other stars during other lives. Most likely you have unless you are fairly new to the universe.

Your view is of those who are borne with loving parents. But what of those who are borne and do not know their parents? What of those who are born from single parents?

Lust is a form of love and it takes two people to create a baby even if it's by accident or in Vitro fertilization. Nevertheless, human don't created souls with their lust, love or in Vitro. Creating a baby is a no-brainer; some don't even know how it happens. Not important, the body knows how to procreate a biological machine (human baby), without much mental input, our hormones do most of the work.

We can create something that carries a soul, which is known as a human being. These human beings are made by having sex. I guess my question is will humans ever create something else that a soul is put into. I'm not saying that the humans transfer the soul out of the human and into a machine, but whatever it is that puts our souls into a human body, can it put it into a machine that a human has made. For example, Sperm and Egg combine making a baby, soul then enters baby. Is there another way? For example, Human makes machine, soul

enters machine instead of a baby. I guess I'm asking can a soul ever enter something other than a natural born baby?

Humans did not create the human body, the human body is self-perpetuating, and sex is the mechanism. ETs can insert a soul into anything even into a piece of wood. Humans on the other hand, we all know how clumsy we are. Would you want to be put into something a human made? Even by so-called advanced humans? Our technology changes and our knowledge increases but we remain human, with all the human flaws intact.

Also, I was wondering what did you believe in as a child and as you got older how did this change? Did you believe in what your family believed in because you were scared they might be right? (For example, did you question your religion in your head, but were too scared to ever say anything aloud because you were scared of going to a hell or something like that?) And if you eventually changed your ideas from theirs or told them what they believed what'd they think?

I don't want to get personal so if you feel offended in any way ignore those questions.

My mother was very much a Catholic in her beliefs and I did believe in Christianity while growing up, but I never was good at it. I went to church as a child and stopped going when I became a teenager, I started back up when I had children of my own to give them something to chew on. I was never afraid of going to hell; it never made sense to me that a loving god would send his children to eternal damnation for any reason, let alone, for lacking in belief. I never talked religion with my parents.

If we are the same souls just like ETs have and ET's have the upper hand cause they've been put into a body that is on a much more advanced planet then why can't we figure things out like they can. What is keeping this planet behind?

This planet is not behind it is exactly where it should be. All the problems in this world are here to be resolved but most of us will do good to resolve our own problems. Problems were created for the purpose of challenging us.

Why do we forget everything during our lifetimes spent on different planets? How are we supposed to reach anything if every time we enter a planet we forget everything and are just given a new obstacle (our lives) with the same question (what are we here for?) from a different point of view? I know that you said we will remember everything after each lifetime, but if we can't remember it during our current lifetimes then we can't really accomplish anything until after we die.

Perhaps the only thing you need to do while on this planet is finish school, find something you are interested in and make the best of it, get married and have a family and enjoy this life as much as you can, stop worrying about all the little details.

How can you trust everything the Extraterrestrials have taught you? What if your completely wrong and when we die that's it everything is over?

When we die, it's not over, it's never over unless somewhere down the line you decided to pull the plug on your life and give up.

As much as I want to believe you my mind always continuously questions everything. I would like for everything you said to be right and that when I die I'll go to another lifetime when I'm ready. I really don't want it to just end. But as usual I'll come up with another question which will doubt everything until it's answered. Why can other people become so easily convinced in a religion without ever having to question anything? At first, I thought maybe it was a good thing that I'm not so easily convinced on one main idea. But now it's just interrupting this life that I'm going to have to put up with for awhile.

Everyone is full of questions about life even the clergy, even if they don't show it. Relax and enjoy the ride. You're not going to know everything so take what you can use and move on with your life. Life really is not that big of a deal. People that succeed usually have failed often but they get back on the horse and keep trying that's what it is all about, never giving up

February 10, 2006

The state of existence and of this universe that you describe seems to have the characteristics of one created by a being. There seem to be a lot of "rules" and these sort of rules don't occur naturally. If you can, explain.

I presume you mean one god, but even in the Old Testament god used the word "we", insinuating more than one being or creator, and he was not speaking of the Trinity. There are rules for everything as you pointed out, otherwise there would be anarchy/chaos and we would cease to exist. In essence, souls belong to a family with good apples and bad apples and the family works to help the bad apples or weed them out.

And when will you tell us why you are telling all this? You admitted yourself that your story is too unbelievable for us to believe at face value.

I'm telling it because I was told to tell it. Regardless of whether people believe or not, information is being put out there. People talked about human flight way before it became a reality.

Is anyone aware of how myths are created? Common myths, including religious ones, have some common truth. I understand that people want proof for things but it's a mistake to dismiss all of a story because some of it is false (or merely

incredible). There's an old saying for this: "Don't throw the baby out with the bathwater." Read enough history, religion and mythology and there are common lessons for everyone to benefit from. So why do we argue about relatively unimportant details. Why are we obsessed with technology?

I've taught drawing classes. Everyone sits in a circle and draws the same teapot. Everyone's perspective is different. Everyone's teapot is different based on each person's ability to represent it with the technology they have at their disposal, charcoal and paper. All of the drawings are true. Perhaps we should be asking different questions. I'd prefer to think about what's in the teapot. Is it warm? Is it delicious? I think so. That's a start.

Suppose none of what this person has posted is factual. I won't argue to support any of his claims. I will argue that the source of the information isn't as important as we've come to believe. Wisdom and knowledge can both come from children. What possible basis in experience can explain this? Likewise, I think it's possible that we sometimes receive small bits of truth from the most unlikely sources. It's easy enough to dismiss any or all of this story if you like. Simply walk away and start your own thread. I somehow don't think that will happen. How can we stop being who we are? Anyone reading and posting repeatedly, is finding something compelling here.

February 11, 2006

Care to touch base on the 4th dimension?

The fourth dimension is the mind's ability to conceptualize endless possibilities within the three dimensional realm of existence. It's a dimension where our soul/mind can access the subconscious mind and not be able to make heads or tails of what's in there.

Furthermore, you talk about ET's in all your posts as hearing all, seeing all etc.. In your own post, you stated there are hundreds of galaxies with hundred of Earths etc... How is there only ONE race of ET's? There must be MANY races of ET's. SO which one is "feeding" us information?

There are many planets with intelligent life, but not all of them have the freedom to leave their solar system. Those that can leave are able to visit other planets like Earth on tourist visas but they can't interact with humans. Then there are renegades that get through the cracks, that seem to escape or fly under the radar of the authorities and visit this plane of existence. The ones that feed us information don't come with name tags, they operate behind the smokescreen of all those other Extraterrestrials reported by abductees.

Your posts are very entertaining, however very flawed and to someone that might have access to classified information you might seem delusional and a great author?

Are you such a person with "classified information? The readers of this thread would love to know.

Please elaborate on which species of ET is helping us and creating us, as you put it and why the other 52 known species of EBE's are not creating us, "feeding us information" etc.

There are billions of species and thousands that visit Earth every day, most come here for the heck of it, others to visit the place they once lived on in previous lives. There are many ETS that seed/feed information to this planet, I don't know them personally.

One other thing, please give me your take on the AIDS/HIV virus and what your take is on that. Thank You for your time.

AIDS/HIV is like everything else that plagues humans and was created by ETs as part of the immunological tweaking.

So what you are saying is that Roswell never happened or dead ET's are left on board with the junk pile.

Roswell happened and the ETs recovered were biological machines with no souls. Most of what abductees come in contact with are these types of Extraterrestrial equipment.

I just made a space craft out of the "pixie dust" I got from ET for Christmas. I want to visit Zeta Reticulli to see what it's like there but you said I can't leave the solar system, but I'm a risk taker so I'll do it anyway. What do you think will happen to me as I whizz past Pluto?

If you reach Pluto, you will have accomplished more than most humans ever will. I would tell you to come back and enjoy the tickertape parade they will throw in your honor. But if you decide to keep going farewell my friend see you on the other side of life. However, your body and your ship, even if it's up to ET specifications, will drift in the darkness of space for thousands of years, assuming it breaks out of the solar system, and it will eventually get sucked into one of the many Black Holes, the universe's recycling bins.

So what is the need for biological machines?

Biological machines do the grunt work, the tedious jobs like the robots that build cars along side of humans on the assembly line. Humans use robots all over the place and are getting close to making artificial intelligence so that robots can think on their own like most of the robots ETs use.

What really happened at Roswell in 1947? I would like specific info and not that a crash occurred. One crash? Two crashes? How many BMs as I will call them. Where? When? How? Why?

The more info here would be greatly appreciated. Please do not hold back on the info. More is better.

There were two ships and six biological machines. The crash was staged for the purpose that it achieved. It made every newspaper in the world, a disclosure of sorts. But too much knowledge is not a good thing and the cover up was implemented by ET not the army air force. The concept of life from other planets was firmly planted in the human psyche. Meanwhile, a large amount of new technology was handed over to America using the crashed ships.

So you're saying I could leave the solar system but I would get lost? Well what if ET was sitting next to me telling me which way to go?

ET could take you but he would have to place your soul into a special container, the human body is not designed for that kind of travel.

How come the human race is doomed to be confined to their own solar system while other species are not? Do all civilizations have a limit to how advanced they can become?

Many solar systems are isolated for many reasons, which would fill hundreds of libraries if written down. The human race is not doomed it is made of hundreds of generations and each generation gets to experience certain things. Your children will venture further into space than your generation and their children even further. Your generation will be part of building the first structures on the moon and perhaps on Mars, but the vast majority of your generation will not venture into space at all. If you wish to increase your odds of getting into space in any meaningful way, you should concentrate on fields of study that will place you in those coveted positions. Humans will not travel further than Mars until the next century, unless they are taken by ETs. Most solar systems have limits on their travel, but millions don't have any limits.

How was this incident covered up by "ET". I would finally agree that the incident was too much for our government to cover up by our own means. On the fence here.

ETs talk to certain leaders every single day, they make suggestions and those request are carried out without hesitation or resistance, sounds creepy but that is the way it has always been done.

What technology have we been given by ET? Sounds like the book I read by Phil Corso. So is his book legit?

All of our technology came from ET. Corso told the truth, as he knew it; however, he was given little information about ETs and only disclosed some of that.

February 12, 2006

I can believe your story of being abducted and I can even believe the fact you went on a "joy ride". BUT my biggest concern here is as you put it "ETs let you see and let you know only what they want you to know", a simple man with a family living the American dream has the answers to life's questions because EBE's let you know?

That is correct and if you don't believe me then the world as we know it will come to an end (sarcasm).

When EBE's come here they do so for information.

ETs don't need anything we have and do you really think beings with the ability to travel hundreds of light years came here to get ideas from us?

They DO help us with technology and such BUT they are not our creators, we evolved as cells through hundreds of millions of years and are still evolving now.

We did not evolve from slime over millions of years, Darwin laughs every time someone says that.

To touch base on my comment about EBE's coming to Earth for information; they do not come here with the intentions of leaving with new technology or a cure for EBE's ailments, they

come here as we would to gather information, something we do to whales, monkeys, and such.

They know everything we know and more, because they are the architects of us, the whales, monkeys and everything on this planet. We humans on the other hand are curious because we don't know much about anything.

We will not obtain any Earth shattering information from them but we study them to better understand what they are, why they are here, and all other questions that may arise.

Humans studying ETs is equivalent to ants studying humans, ants would never get it, neither would humans.

When humans make the jump into space and we discover a race or species more primitive than us, we wouldn't be able to gain anything from them, but we would help them, just as EBE's do now for us humans.

Humans will never be allowed out of the playpen known as our solar system, the only primitive life forms we will encounter are on this planet, all we need do is look in the mirror to find them.

You also stated that ET's manufacture out bodies, why do we have many traits our parents did? our grandparents did? Do

they do this with DNA? And then implant them into our mother's womb?

Everyone shares the DNA of their parents. ETs created human bodies a long time ago, our bodies are self-perpetuating—with the use of sex as the carrot to keep the humans containers from depleting.

February 13, 2006

Well what an active and enjoyable weekend some of us have had eh? I come back Monday morning and find that there are five pages of posts on my favorite thread. "What joy," I thought, thinking that it would be five pages of intelligent discussion. Instead, to my horror I find five pages of utter crap. You people should be ashamed of yourselves that you cannot behave like intelligent adults. It was like reading a conversation from children in a playground.

Abusive content is not included in this book, for those wishing to read all the content this discussion generated go to the internet site mentioned at the beginning of the book.

ETs with souls are like us on the other side but while they are on this plane, they use physical bodies that are much different from ours. They can go from what we call a physical state to an ethereal state, which they do while in flight or passing through walls. The natural state for all souls is an orb of energy. From this orb of energy state we can take any shape and travel anywhere we choose in the galaxy.

What makes us different from ETs then? I thought you said in my next life I could choose to go to another planet like this one. Surely that makes me an ET as well?

More or less but not in this lifetime, if you were abducted and were allowed to remember some of those you encountered during the abduction you might recognize your abductors as old friends or family from another life.

I've taken my meds so I'll ask a question. In regards to seeing loved ones on the other side, let's say 'I' was in a dysfunctional long term relationship here on Earth, and my partner & I split up because she was unfaithful. Now I will not want to see her ever again, but on the other side she wants to see me - what happens in that scenario? Will I be forced to see someone against my will? Excuse the simplicity of the question, but the paradox baffles me.

On the other side all your fears and anger are gone with the wind. While you are there in that in between zone, you will be the best of friends. However, many centuries in the physical realm may pass before you cross paths again giving you plenty of time to get over whatever bothers you about her. Everyone you come in contact with on Earth has a connection to you from the other side. You can't control what type of person she is nor how she feels about you, but you can control how you feel about her. You don't have to be with her but you should forgive any transgressions or ill feelings you have about her, even when it's her fault, otherwise you may have to deal with that issue again in another physical life. Every issue we have must be resolved in order for us to move up; especially anger between two people.

I saw this thread a little late. I don't have time to go through each page and see what you have said to each person's questions, so if I ask you a question that someone already asked, I would appreciate your answer. 1. You said that Extraterrestrials created us. Why?

Human bodies are what they strap the soul into like a seatbelt on a car, so that we can experience life on Earth, the challenges and everything that goes with individuals lives.

2. You said we would never be able to leave our galaxy, or solar system (I forgot which one you said). Is it because we will never be able to get that technologically advanced or because the Extraterrestrials just won't allow us? If because the Extraterrestrials won't allow us, Why?

Humans will not leave the solar system. We need ET technology to get out and they are not giving it. Nevertheless, it will take the next thousand years to explore this solar system and the next few thousands of years to build cities on many of the moons in this solar system.

Why do we have large cities and small towns? Why not build up all the small towns and make them large cities? Because some people like small towns and some like large cities.

3. Is there an afterlife for us (and if so, explain a little). Thanks for your time.

Life never ends unless you opt out or are thrown out; most souls remain in the universe for a long time, even forever.

I have watch your thread a long time now and you have great information, yes everything you have said at least it's 70% actual true. I too have seen this, I am from Mexico and yes have seen UFO's and ET's up close. The Greys has mostly known them and like you said are mostly robots, automated. They don't have any soul at all, that's why everyone who encounters them feels like they are not alive (myself too I have seen them and felt the same). The only thing you have not address is about this robots, they don't have a soul and they want to have soul...you know this and I know it, that's why the experiments because if they can have soul they can live forever. The Greys don't have one and if they die, they die period, no eternal life for them, that's why some of them are seeking to have a soul and they are doing the bizarre abduction types.

February 14, 2006

You say that those facts come from the New Testament not history books, but Josephus mentions the Christians in the Jewish Wars.

More than half of religious scholars believe that the Jesus of Christianity was inserted after Josephus died and not by Josephus himself. Josephus was a Jewish general and one of the major fighters against the Romans, but as the Jewish Zealots got out of control and became the biggest threat to Judaism, his loyalties changed and he became a Roman. He was a Roman historian and therefore his fellow Jews believed him a traitor. Josephus did write favorably about the Romans and their conquests against the Jews, otherwise he wouldn't have survived for long. Had he wrote about Christianity that too would have offended the Romans. Had Josephus believed in the Jesus story, that Jesus was god and came to rescue the Jews from the Romans he wouldn't have been so loyal to the Romans.

Unlike many deities of that time and to the present Jesus represents all that is good in mankind and beyond. Jesus also represents the fact that there is life after this one vie the resurrection account, he died and lived again and returned to heaven. The story of Jesus was designed to give hope to a desperate people during very desperate times and it still serves that purpose today.

However, alongside good ideas and concepts travels the bad, the Crusades, deception, false beliefs and gods. The Holy Roman Empire replaced one tyranny with another, but that's what life on this planet is all about, conquering. We are here on Earth to learn and to prove to ourselves what we are made of and you can't do that in a perfect utopian world.

On the subject of ETs I have had an experience with my mother coming home from Football practice when I was in middle school. We saw a diagonal line of three cigar shaped craft hovering over clumps of forest in between cornfields in Indiana. We pulled the car over and watched them for a few minutes before they (very rapidly) ascended out of sight. Since then, I've had several "Sleep Paralysis" episodes where I'd awaken unable to move with the feeling that something was trying to enter my body and a feeling of total terror but never saw anything and would eventually "awaken."

Sleep Paralysis is what the doctors call it because they can't afford to admit it's ET without losing their license to practice, or they simply don't know about ET contact, or believe in such things.

My question is, do you think that particular locations are more susceptible than others are to this type of activity. In just

about all of my sleep paralysis episodes I'd dream\be (even if I wasn't there) at my family's lake cottage. My father told us stories about things that used to happen to him when he'd stay the summer there as a boy - bed shaking violently while he was in it, orbs coming out of a mirror in his bedroom and floating off across the lake. I have also been witness to some strange events there as well. My grandmother was extremely into the spiritualism aspect of "religion", she preached heavily about reincarnation and that our current lives are means to solving personal problems much as you have discussed. She also mentioned that each of us have guides that we neither see nor "hear" but were always with us and would help us with things if we asked them. She had said that they had told her their names(me and my 2 brother each had one) and we just had to ask them for help if we needed help finding something we had misplaced or needed guidance or whatever.

Some locations are more convenient that others especially if they are going to have extended encounters with you. When they want you in a certain place or location they make things happen that will get you there, new job, vacation or whatever it takes. Many ETs are family members or friends from the past and they can be helpful, but asking for help and then receiving help may not seem like they are being helpful. For instance, if you suffer from stage fright and ask for them to help you with it they may put you in more uncomfortable situations where you have to stand up and talk to people, that's how they help.

Did ET's help us with EVERY advancement? Even the things we use that have no purpose of moving us forward?

Everything is under ET control because ET is part of us, our extended family. Everything is created by the life force that is made up of ETs, humans, and all other intelligent beings in the universe.

I've found your thread to be very fascinating. I have a quick question. Is a light to mass converter possible?

Yes, it's called a leaf, high tech stuff those leaves are.

When will ET step in, in regards to wars and global conflict? And will we know they intervened? Thanks for all your hard work in keeping up with and responding to this thread.

They step in all the time, and we never know it, or in most cases, appreciate it. With all the ongoing wars, there is always room for a lot more.

February 15, 2006

How can we be sure that anything is true? How do you know that you'll wake up from this dream and find out you are something completely else? You say that it's true cause the ET's told you but, well ok, but maybe they are part of your dream too.

There are places, planets, existences, where people similar to humans know without doubt that the things you ask are true. Some of those people, entities, are on this planet and they are talking. Humans have the capacity to know inside their soul what is true and what is not, the first step to unlocking that information is believing it's possible.

The big danger of knowing is that if you become too enlightened while on Earth, you can become on outcast because you still have to live around people that are not and people are uncomfortable around people that are different from them.

I'm just not getting how anyone can be 100% positive that their theory is true and that they won't wake up from a dream and return to their real life. But then again that kind of IS your story. That we will all die and wake up in the "in-between" world, which is where our true life exists.

While here, your true life is here. What you do on this plane of existence is part of what you are, knowing the real truth is not essential for moving forward.

Is there a common vision for the future of mankind that is shared by us collectively?

Peace and survival, which neither can be achieved at this level of the physical realm.

Are we actively changing this future now?

People are becoming more comfortable with the idea of space exploration. Some are frustrated because it's taking so long and alternatively many see man in space as a waste of time and money. There is no consensus or unified push in any particular direction as a race.

Are we collectively progressing up a kind of spiritual ladder?

Humans were more spiritual a thousand years ago than they are now; many are more aware, most are more confused.

Are we destined to be become spiritually self aware in our physical life?

Some want to believe that but how many of us see that happening in the people and the world around us?

How do ETs explain multiple dimensions?

Human brains see multiple dimensions, ethereal beings don't.

How is the soul multidimensional? Does it exist independently of time and space?

Time and space as humans understand it doesn't exist. ETs exist in multiple dimensions in a similar way that we humans exist in three dimensions. They can easily enter ours but we can't enter theirs.

Long story condensed. My wife and I had detailed dreams the last two nights. Hers was apocalyptic. UFO's took over everything, running for survival, abandoned house, abandoned children.

Sounds like she saw War of the Worlds, Hollywood's version of ETs, not going to happen.

My dream the following night: a black calf/sheep threatened, guide it through a difficult mountain pass, nearly die, somehow, a class is watching, lose my balance, a hand reaches out and saves me.

I'm not a dream interpreter, but in dreams we confront many things in our present life and bits and pieces of former lives. Loved ones that have passed can also meet with us in our dreams.

Which religion would the ETs most closely advocate? What do they think/how do they view the Muslim religion, especially the extremist end of it?

They originated all of them, the good the bad and the ugly ones. We have minimum-security prisons and maximum-security prisons, similarly some humans on Earth need minimal control some need more control over their lives.

What 'belief' do the ETs have in regards to spirituality? Do they know "everything".

Those that are running the show pretty much know everything or at least they think they do. They are incredibly humble for know-it-alls.

Or are they still striving to understand and truly interact with the very essence of the origins all of creation, of "GOD"?

The only ones striving to understand are on planets like Earth, and at the levels of humans, or fallen souls.

Have the ETs fought wars on our behalf in regards to the protection of our planet from "ROGUE ETs"? Have they diverted asteroids and shielded us from destruction in a way.

Yes to both. Any asteroids hitting this planet in a major way would not be by accident.

Last night I dreamt I was in a classroom and in that classroom were other humans, and I befriended one of them, a girl, and she showed me her true self and she was an ET. She looked like a human, with a larger head, indentions in the temples on the sides of her head, was flesh colored, and had an illuminated brilliance about her, almost like that of an angel. Her eyes were slightly larger and looked similar to our own the nose was also flatter. She smiled at me and sent me 'vibes' that felt very comforting. Thanks again for all your hard work.

Did you get her phone number?

"The governments are not calling the shot, never have never will." "If the Extraterrestrials wanted to make contact with the general population there is nothing stopping them, they don't want to."

Have long believed that. What guesstimate might you make as to when--given current trends and geopolitical moves toward the tyrannical global government--when would you

guesstimate that more overt disclosure would be made--by whom?

ETs do personal disclosures all the time and they have no reason to do an overt disclosure to the general population anytime soon, if ever. Once humans are in space in significant numbers they will know a little more about the big picture. Presently, ETs are enticing humans to go into space by showing themselves more often to the astronauts and the space agencies.

After thousands of humans are in space the existence of ETs will be unquestionable, but ETs will continue to remain out of reach, the carrot is very important in enticing the donkey to move and keep him moving without it ever reaching the carrot.

Seems like we are moving into another era then. Is the recently discovered 10th planet ancient NIBIRU?

No.

Have you read any of Sitchin's books? Sitchin knows what he is talking about right?

I haven't read any of Sitchin's books.

February 15, 2006

I don't want to bother you, but, it seems like most of these ET's are kind of wimpy guys with fancy space ships, controlled by superior beings still on a planet and not subject to the horrors of space travel.

It's a job and somebody has to do it. They don't travel in physical bodies so space travel is not horrible for them.

Is it possible to communicate with people on the planets directly?

Not possible for humans, but ETs can communicate with anyone anywhere.

Here on Earth you can take a knife and hurt someone very badly with it, maybe even killing them. Do ET's feel the same pain...physical pain? Or are they a different life form and aren't affected in the way we look at physical pain?

Some ETs can be killed and damaged but not by humans, their physiology is not like ours, they don't feel pain.

If one of us were put up against an ET would we have the upper hand in strength or would they? Or is strength a thing of the past for them?

Like a lion tamer in a cage with lions, the lions could tear him apart but the tamer has the mental advantage. ETs have that advantage over humans. Has anyone ever beat the crap out of an ET and showed it to anyone? Of the thousands of abductions, it has never happened, not once. Except for in the movies and in books.

February 16, 2006

WOW! I can't believe this has lasted 46 pages. I enjoyed the read for the first 15 pages, but being at work, I couldn't really continue. I actually believe Lou, as crazy as it sounds it just makes sense. You have to think, in 1900, there was NO technology what so ever, but in 2000, only 100 years later we are where we are at today. No one questions that? From 1900, back to the beginning of time there was absolutely no technology, but all of a sudden within 100 years, we became what we are now. And everyone must know, that if Extraterrestrials came face to face with mankind one day, the world would destroy itself, what would be the cause? Religion and Fear of the unknown.

February 17, 2006

Well that was some ride! Again, with no real truth behind it, or real facts. You have somehow managed, with the use of various words, to get my attention. Sometimes the power of clever words can capture everyone's imaginations. Do I believe him? Answer, he said much of what I already thought. Reading this was like reading the inside of my mind. All of this I have had in my head for many years. IT'S CRAZY. I KNOW others feel the same.

I have a question for you, psychic ability the ability of some (so they believe) to talk to the dead. Is there a connection between ETs and psychic ability? For some weird reason, I think there is. Again, I can't believe how much of this all makes sense to me.

In reality, the dead are more aware than we are so in essence, we are dead and they are alive. The so-called dead can hear and see us. Whenever you think of someone that you knew that passed over, died, they can hear you if they are in the in-between zone, some souls remain there for a long time. They can't interfere with our lives too much, but depending on how determined you are for some help or answers they can enter your dreams and in some situations be the instigators of your abduction, it's the only way to physically touch someone on the other side. If someone from the other side meets with you on a ship and tries to slap some sense into you, your conscious mind will be terrified, but your unconscious mind will get the message, sometimes.

Would there be a connection between Extraterrestrials and psychic people?

Like everything, there are real psychics and not so real psychics. Real ones have the ability to communicate with ETs and other spirits, some good some not. The problem with some psychics is that they don't know who it is they are talking with on the other side, and ETs reside on the other side, but can peek their noses into this side.

I don't consider myself a psychic, I don't meditate or go into a trance or use chicken bones, nor do I read the star charts to predict the future. Nevertheless, some need those things to pick up signals from their spirit guides, other entities, or to entertain themselves and others. Anyone can talk to beings on the other side the difficult part is on the receiving end down here.

If you see them again, or if they just happen to communicate with you in the future, tell them to swing by and pick me up! I need a vacation. To a different planet would be nice.

Do you have frequent flyer miles with them? You know, been abducted a few times? That really helps.

February 22, 2006

I just finished reading this thread from start to finish your account is fascinating! I have so many questions; I don't know where to start. I'll try to formulate something worthy of discussion and post later. One thing that strikes me straight away about this thread is how jerky some members can become. This is the man with the information that we all want to hear, yet, if I don't skip ahead to what he actually says, I've wasted my precious time reading all the crap and whining from detractors, and it is more than distracting - it's maddening. While reading this I thought to myself a thousand times "shut up you idiots and let this man say his piece, I want to hear him - NOT YOUR IDIOT MOUTHS RUNNING"! Just wanted to get that out. I feel better. I look forward to hearing more from you and hope you haven't lost patience with this thread!

I couldn't agree more! This thread is so thought provoking. I've really enjoyed reading it, and can't wait to hear more from you. Keep this thread alive!

Has anyone in your family ever seen this unquestionable evidence that you claim to have? Thanks.

They have, but they are not aware of it now. ET stuff has peculiar properties that leave no mental finger prints or physical litter. Once the items leave the ship they have short life spans, some last a few hours some a few days before they deteriorate and vanish into the air like a gas. The material most of these alien things are made of is high in energy and extremely unstable in Earth's environment by design. However, some items can be stabilized and last much longer when ET chooses to give them added properties. You can't keep ET stuff hidden in a drawer, basement, or garage unless it's a duplicate made of materials that can be found on this planet, but these duplicates have few or none of the properties of the original. So where do I keep my stuff? If you don't want the food to spoil you keep it in the refrigerator, if you have ET stuff you keep it inside their ships.

February 23, 2006

I know you like dropping little hints, but oh my, is that a BIG ONE? Are you saying you keep your ET stuff in an ET spaceship? Any chance of getting a photo of it?

There is a reason no one has photos of the inside of ET ships, the energy levels are too high and bizarre, the image doesn't stick to any known material, digital cameras are no exception. The most advanced photographic equipment on Earth is the human mind and you see how difficult it is for those who have been abducted to remember their experiences while on ET ships. Some do better than others do because there are exceptions to every rule and ETs make the rules.

Many people are expecting disclosure in a large way, but the vast majority of people on this planet are not, nor are they truly aware of the possibility of extraterrestrials residing on Earth in sizeable numbers. A large armada of ETs making themselves known would scare the crap out of a lot of people. The numbers of humans ready for wholesale disclosure are not there and will not be for some time, if ever. In the mean time, personal disclosure goes on every day. However, many of those people have a difficult time with it, including those that believed they were ready for anything; have discovered that they can't handled it.

My little stories and those of others are thrown into the mixture of the Extraterrestrial scenarios, which is mostly slanted towards the frightful Extraterrestrials from science fiction books and movies. Most people are comfortable with the Hollywood types of Extraterrestrials because they can be defeated by humans, unlike the real ones.

Do you think that all ETs are friendly? What about the awful experiences you read from people that have been abducted by ETs? Their stories are deplorable, and surely not the appropriate behavior for friendly, superiorly-intellectual beings?

As I pointed out in my last post many people have found being face to face with an ET the most terrifying experience in their life short of a nightmare. No one knows what is going on between an ET and the person they are in contact with, it's between the two of them and no one else. Teachers can be intimidating and in some countries, they are tyrannical. I went to a Catholic school when I was young and an encounter with a nun was to be avoided at all cost. Nuns could do with a simple twelve-inch ruler what no one else on this planet could do, put the fear of god in you. Heck, the most powerful military in the world, the US military, is terrified of all ETs and they have regular contact with many of them.

First of all, thanks for sharing your experiences with all of us! I have seen several UFOs during my lifetime. I'm 51, by the way, which is young in today's terms. Most importantly, I feel young and much wiser than ever. Enough about me. I am wondering what ET thinks about our music. Are they impressed or satisfied with our abilities? Which of our art forms do they like the best?

There is plenty of variety in music on this planet and a number of ETs from across the galaxy. Here, however, we are in a primitive state of being and their tastes are much different from ours. I don't recall hearing elevator music while going up into their ships.

Do they understand our sense of humor? Do they understand irony? What do they think is funny?

They understand humor and irony and to them everything is funny. Nevertheless, their innocent laughter can cause fear in us. Have you ever laughed at an animal, animals don't get it and become afraid of us crazy humans.

What do they think of our emotionality? Do they share our emotional pain in any way? Do they admire and/or applaud any of our emotions like love, anger, jealousy?

They are helping us with are erratic emotional problems, they empathize with us, they admire the act of love, despise anger and loathe jealousy and hate.

Are humans in a reincarnation type situation where we keep working at each life until we get it right and then move on to the next level?

That is the purpose of this life.

Does ET harvest human hormones like adrenaline?

ET drones and sometimes humans working for ETs harvest biological material from humans.

Why do they abduct and scare the hell out of humans if they don't have to? Why not just keep the abductee unconscious, they would certainly be much easier to deal with in that state.

They do in many circumstances, but sometimes they need them to be conscious for psychological acrobatics that they will be put through, and a way for them to leak out that they are here.

They are monitoring something about us with the abductions - what is it?

It varies with each individual; it could be a health issue, a learning experience, a kick in the butt, a reunion of some kind or simply a pleasure ride, a treat. They are not monitoring mankind as we would monitor a new species.

Getting the attention of the abductees is one thing, but what about really messing them up with all the probes and raping them and awful stuff like that. That's going a little beyond attention grabbing isn't it?

You are receiving only one side of the story when some abductees tell it, have you met any humans that don't exaggerate a little or a lot? No one is raped in the literal meaning of the word. Sex happens during some encounters for the purpose of hybrids or other population enhancing programs. The individual may or may not agree to what is happening but it's not rape in the sense that they are being violated and abused. Things are done for a reason and they have been doing them that way forever.

Tell us more about what they are like. You say they think everything is funny. Fox example, what did you see them laugh at? Do they laugh with or at each other in front of you? Do they laugh at you?

They have no reason to be gloom, they know who they are and their lives are near perfect if not perfect. To them everything is amusing. Kind of like drill sergeants they put on a mean face for the recruits but back at the office they joke with each other…about the recruits.

Are ETs all "sweetness and light" or do they exhibit a bad side?

They can be sweet and cuddly, but also your worst nightmare.

How could they allow innocent victims to suffer? For example, the torture and murder of a young child should be pretty hard to sit through - how could they allow that to happen?

They see the big picture and know that all pain and suffering is temporary. Do we go off the deep end every time a child falls and scrapes his/her knee? Some children act as if it's the end of the world especially if there is blood.

If *they want to help us all out, why not brain-scan everybody and cull the psychopaths for us?*

This is not that kind of planet, on this planet pain, fear, terror, and psychopaths are part of the program. It's an incentive to keep us moving forward and try to keep our nose clean. Everyone will die it's the only way to get to the next level, up or down. Besides, if they weeded out the psychopaths, there wouldn't me many people left down here.

My first post here at ATS, I arrive amazed and humbled by the many brilliant minds/intellects I've witnessed (figuratively speaking). You might say you've inspired my first post, this message board or any other. The Serpo fiasco brought me to

ATS, accidentally, don't remember what brought me to Serpo, but I'm sure happy to have found ATS.

Your story/experiences/beliefs/etc., and more importantly, you're telling of it/them, is masterful! They say brevity is the soul of wit, and you sure took that piece of philosophy to heart. For all I know it's a complete fantasy. However, if we all find that it is, it won't break my heart, don't think I'll even feel insulted. If it is, you're a "twisted" brilliant mind - nuff said on that.

To Wilbur (the only post name I specifically remember because I thought Mr. Ed would have had a little more class and tolerance responding to this thread) and the others that feverishly tried to debunk Lou with considerably less "proof" via credibility than Lou has. (An opinion I'm aware, albeit an educated one), allow me to offer this: it seems to me that ATS doesn't attract a majority of lost souls you so gallantly (though childishly) offer/claim to want to protect from Lou and those who post like him. Most of us here (I presume) are big boys and girls who neither want, need, nor desire your protection. Your tirades are (at least to me) an unwelcome and time consuming diversion from the brilliant/interesting and well thought out questions and responses on this thread (true/real/made-up/fantasy or not). Also your abnormal fear of reprisal for bad spelling/grammar was nearly equal to your fear of Lou!? Take a lesson then from Lou - confidence in your beliefs, manners, and tone carry a great deal of weight and appeal to intelligent others - making "you" decidedly worth listening to. Hooked on Phonics, dictionaries, and "Spelling For Dummies" might offer many a great deal more confidence prior to their next post. Lou, I'm all eyes, great stuff.

1. I've bought into nothing on this thread, I find the subject matter profoundly interesting and intelligently presented (both Lou and many of the questions asked of Lou).

2. Interesting and "telling" that you re-posted Lou's brief rant on you however, failed to re-post your paragraph+ rant on him that provoked his remarks. His credibility (at least with me), i.e., doesn't attack but will certainly defend when he's attacked, (and damn I sure like his wit when he's defending!), his offering of information, not forcing down anyone's throat, and he will certainly answer every pertinent question asked (that's rare), that's credibility.

3. Ten Years in the military, twenty years in law enforcement, I have firsthand knowledge of ET life, long before that and for as long as I can remember, I had a core belief, a sureness that all this space (the universe) isn't here for the inhabitants of this one, small, blue planet. I have no direct experience or confidence in organized religion. What's going on right now

with people killing each other over newspaper cartoons (among many other things) adds further to my doubts in such respects but then certainly adds to my confident belief that "man" went down the wrong road where God is concerned a long time ago.

February 24, 2006

Lou, my first question to you: paraphrased somewhat from your own words "you're better off not knowing this, it may interfere with your life here". Do you state this and then tell us/answer questions because you believe most here at ATS can "handle" the revelations you offer? If not I would believe your only other objective here is entertainment, selfish or for everyone.

As we all know, everyone capable of reading and presumably somewhat discerning is invited on the internet and on boards like this one. Whether or not everyone is capable of digesting, what they find on these types of sites is another matter. Certainly, there are dangers, physical and more so, physiological. Should we protect our children from threads like this one? Perhaps. Can young minds handle some of the stuff that is written and discussed here? There is only one answer, yes they can and in many cases more so than mature, set-in-their-ways adults.

I put my disclaimer, "you're better off not knowing" for those who need to keep their existing belief system intact in order to get through the day. All beliefs have value, and no matter how you view the world you will get through it one way or another regardless of the validity of those beliefs. Most people are looking for new ideas and realities, hence the popularity of Hollywood and writers willing to fill every need and desire we have. Nevertheless, I am not here to cater to the lost souls desperate to find the holy grail of their existence, I'm here to simply tell my story, my experiences with the supernatural. Not to entertain, not to enlighten, but because they are true and real and if by doing so entertains some, enlightens others, or pisses them off, so-be-it.

So Lou, did you ever get to talk to the ETs to see if they can hook me up with some ET healthcare? Thanks again for your contributions, please keep it up.

They got the message; your situation is not by chance or just plain bad luck, which btw there is no such thing as good or bad luck. In ET's world, which everyone is a part of—sickness and pain are tools they use. They know your predicament, and they know how to fix you and regardless of what you think that is what they are doing. Sometimes they incorporate the medical profession but not everyone in this world has access to that, again by design.

Lou, are you saying that hybrids are real? Do they look human? Do they know they are hybrids? Why are hybrids created? This thread gets ever more interesting.

Hybrids are real and some of them have human features. They are hybrids because they are a product of human and extraterrestrial material. Their souls are not hybrid they are souls occupying a different machine. They have a higher awareness than humans once they enter the hybrid machine. Certain souls are captured after they leave the human body, died, and are placed into the hybrid units and sent elsewhere.

Lou - thank you for the response. I have seen no attempt by you at self-promotion, on this thread or any other I've seen so far, in regard to books you've written or anything else. Also, with every word of yours I read, my mental "credibility checklist" with a plus/minus column is in full swing! Try as I might, I can't place many minuses in that column, and find that when I'm tempted, it's only because you've relayed a piece of information that "really" stretches my sense of credulity (then I think about it, can't disprove it, have to leave the minus out of the column), you are incredibly consistent.

MY interest in your books (that I assume/may have read somewhere on another thread) were about a different subject entirely), are related to what else that mind of yours has to offer. Again, not looking for 10-64 on this ET subject for you, just an avid reader and a vessel far from being full. Obviously, books are written for many reasons. Outside of entertainment and profit, and with a slant towards intellectual honesty (my father wrote 5 books, none published, his ego and pride got in the way when he refused to accept an offer to publish in paperback in the late fifties). To first share what's in your

head; then if it's good enough, you obtain that sense of accomplishment and profit to boot when people buy.

If I follow your logic correctly, ET helped you write those books, directly or indirectly, regardless of the subject, the wisdom in them must be great and meaningful to share. If everyone/anyone else is interested let them ask as I have and use your good judgment to determine their reasons/motive(s) for the request as I'm sure you'll do with mine. Many thanks.

Lou, my story is that I'm either a fool or a babe in the woods. I could write a book on the stupid things that I've done which show lack of humility and intelligence, conceit, false pride, insecurity, selfishness, and dumb-assery that was many times just plain dangerous to my health. How does ET view a fool?

They must love them because they are in charge of several billion of them here on Earth.

Do they enjoy watching me and my reaction to being embarrassed, humiliated, the last one to see the "shit" hitting the fan? I seem to find myself in those situations more often than not.

They don't enjoy seeing us wallowing in the mud but as soon as we tire of it they will hose us down.

Or, am I a stranger in a strange land? Am I actually an Extraterrestrial sent to this planet to interact with these crazy humans? Did they plant me here with my crazy family and expect me to do well? Are we humans the "protégés" of ET?

We all are strangers in this land called Earth, some have been here before others have been sent down here to repeat lives until they get it right. They do expect us to do right, and everyone, down deep inside knows what that means. We are protégés, students, family and some of us have gone astray but no matter which road you take they all eventually lead back home.

If we are protégés, then I send my apology to whichever ET is watching me! I know I'm a fool. What I need is more money to make this awful experience down here on Earth with these crazy bastards more bearable! I'm serious.

Have you met anyone who couldn't use more money? Money is a gift and a curse, but mostly a gift. Life really sucks without money and billions on this planet know the sting of poverty. Many that have money haven't searched for it, those that search for it hardly ever finds it.

February 25, 2006

What is the best way of getting the attention of the ETs and to really impress them (and God)?

We are not here to impress ET or God, or anyone else for that matter, but if you do manage to impress the gods, the drinks our on you.

How do you earn one of the 'treats' from the ETs in regards to interstellar vacations? Thanks again!

That's a tricky proposition. It helps to have someone on the other side, family or friends that have passed away and have achieved a level that allows them such privileges, if granted, it would be one of them that would be the tour guide. But that's a two-edged sword, they could use that time to chew you out, they call it tough love. You don't know why you are here in the first place, they do, and they more than anyone knows what we merit.

Lou, are we a "farm" of humans? Are we unknowingly involved in some sort of competitive activity on behalf of our owners (ET) - are we pawns?

We are not pawns; we are what they use to be.

What attributes does ET think are particularly attractive in human beings? What behavior do they applaud?

Integrity

Lou, are there evil souls? If the answer to this is no, then this whole story does not work.

Your dilemma is that for there to be good we need evil otherwise how do we distinguish between the two. Have you read the book of Job? In that story god uses evil, Satan, as a tool to test Job. In other words, god created evil so that man could choose between the two.

I find this idea of souls having an influence on the body/entity that they occupy hard to swallow. It doesn't make sense... unless there are evil souls as well.

What is a human body? Mostly water and a few minerals that's all. When the body dies it goes back to the Earth from which it came, the soul is all that remains. The soul can exist on its own or it can be caged into another body for more cultivating. Evil is a human concept and was created by ET as a tool, some humans use that tool very well, as do ETs.

What I mean is: If you claim that souls have an influence on the bodies they reside in and all of them are overflowing with love and compassion then why did Hitler exist?

Souls are not overflowing with love and compassion if they were they wouldn't be on Earth. We souls have some love and compassion in us, but nothing to brag about. How many people have you met that are overflowing with it? If so, for how long are they able to overflow with it?

Why does any tyrant like Hitler exist? There have been thousands throughout history and there are hundreds and thousands running around today. They are the face of evil; they are pawns of god/ET, for those that believe in god or ET, and even for those that don't.

Why didn't he end up being an author (of books unlike Mein Kampf) or... a butcher? Instead of a maniacal dictator hell-bent on ethnically cleansing huge populations? What about serial killers/ rapists?

Hitler was a soldier, a painter, a politician and an author, but he excelled at maniacal dictator. He orchestrated a cast of millions to do his bidding for him. When it was all said and done more than fifty million people lost their lives and countless others were left destitute and crippled. Hitler was the face of pure evil and millions chose between good and evil during his time on this planet. Many of those that chose evil never participated in that war or killed anyone, but neither did they stand up against him or what he stood for. Many of those who chose evil have since died and have been returned to this planet for their evil deeds. Some of the worst have been terminated; they literally have lost their rights to a soul. We all choose between good and evil. Many that choose evil will not lose their souls, but some will wish they did.

Serial killers and rapists are wolves amongst the sheep. Are they evil? Without a doubt, they are, but if they get a book deal or a movie made about them the books will be best sellers and the move a hit. We claim to deplore violence and at the same time lust over it. Such things are subtle speed traps that catch the most violators of freewill—with hands in the cookie jar. We don't need to do the crime but most certainly we will do the time if our hearts are as black as the rapists and serial killers.

I seriously doubt anyone on this thread is lighting incense, candles, chanting, praying to ET, or sculpting effigies in what they imagines is Lou's likeness.....get a grip man! For all I know this poster is conducting an experiment from the Ci office of the DIA to see how many people he can snooker! Who cares? He's dog-gone good at it and I want to learn what's next. If you've read the entire thread, there's at least a little philosophical and romantic truth here for anyone (made up or not) he's good, stop trying to protect us educated folk!

I contribute to this thread instead of all the self-aggrandizing spiritual mumbo-jumbo, i.e., ask a question - what plane of spiritual existence is Elvis on now? Will Monica Lewinsky have to return and corrupt another president? Of course, these are

just examples. Point is, if you want to trip Lou up, engage the intellectual exercise - blow his cover, prove him wrong, deny ignorance! Gentlemen!

Lou - have you ever relayed any of this information in any other forum anywhere else? And, are you aware of others that have shared your experience(s) but have chosen to stay mum?

Not to this extent as on this board. I'm not aware of others, but I remember playing and interacting with other children on alien ships as a child.

February 26, 2006

Hmm...Now that I am stuck in that track of thinking, I must know -- is Dennis Rodman really an Extraterrestrial?

As far as I know, Rodman is a US citizen and not an illegal alien.

More seriously, when's the last time you had contact with the ETs?

Had breakfast with them this morning.

And if that question has been answered before (I'm too lazy to read forty pages), then what is it that makes you believe what the ETs tell you?

How do you know that your mother, father, preacher, teacher, president, boss, closest friend is telling you the truth? Sometimes you don't, most of the time you don't, but family members are less likely to lie to you.

What do you do to ensure that your own personal beliefs don't alter what you hear/see?

I have a political slant, which I have shared on other threads, but will not on this one. ET is neither left nor right in the political spectrum, they are in fact apolitical, I am the opposite I am very political in my views.

If you're familiar with Near-Death Experiences, then you know that such events can depend immensely on the views of the person. (For example, in a group NDE, one person will see the Buddha, another Jesus.)

The souls on the other side are pure energy and some exhibit more light than others, some are radiant. When a Christian comes in contact with a radiant being they presume it to be Jesus, when a Buddhist sees a radiant being they see Buddha, a Muslim would see Allah, etc., even when it's the same ET being.

Now this isn't an NDE, obviously, but ET contact does seem to have some parallels, to an extent. (Both are...well...out of this world and beyond what a human is used to experiencing; perception can be altered.) So, what do you do?

I wear my tinfoil hat.

Ok, Lou - what/where is/was the genesis of all this? When did it all begin? Are you privy (from ET or otherwise) to this knowledge? Thanks.

There was no big bang, the universe is not expanding nor will it contract and fall into itself as many cosmologists believe. The universe will never end. This universe is so large that human instruments will not find the edge, ever. And because time and space are illusions so is Genesis. Energy did not come into being it has always existed and it will never cease existing. Everything is and will always be.

So if I am understanding this correctly, ultimately I am (or my soul is) here to fulfill some kind of "job/test" that leads to some form of reincarnation or transmigration of the soul. Now in this "staging area" I choose what kind of "job/test" I want to take in my next life. My soul is then placed in a body ("machine") created by "ET", that I can only assume would be capable of performing that "job/test".

Now let's say that this body develops cancer (rust?) with no obvious cause (lung cancer from smoking for example, just *poof* let's say prostate cancer) and "ET" takes me aboard the ship and fixes up the cancer, however I remember nothing of the experience, my cancer is just "magically" gone. So I never know why the cancer is gone. So what would be the purpose of this?

Each time you come back even with a purpose you still have that pesky freewill to deal with all over again. If you choose to smoke or jump in front of a moving car you might alter the original contract. Remembering has nothing to do with anything, other than it can give you an advantage, sometimes you get them mostly you don't.

I was suppose to learn some greater truth about who or what I am by the visit with the "ET" while I get cured? Nope, don't remember a thing and of course if I was suppose to "ET" would have made sure I remembered that part because "ET" doesn't make mistakes.

ETs never make mistakes, humans make careers out of making mistakes. Most of us know, it's called gut feeling, instinct or intuition, all of those are gifts that clue us into many things without giving us all the details of the big picture, known as life, which may or may not be revealed during encounters.

I was never supposed to get cancer as part of my "job/test"? That's not possible because that would mean there is a flaw in this body ("machine") but this body ("machine") was chosen so I could fulfill my "job/test" and it was created by "ET", and "ET" doesn't make mistakes (flaws).

If you avoid cancer-causing things, you may not get cancer, but if you did everything right, and still got cancer, then it was part of the contract/deal. Death is an exit from this board game and we don't always get to finish the game especially if we have detracted from it to a point that going further is pointless.

I was suppose to get cancer and then have it "magically" disappear after wasting thousands of dollars, countless days/months/years, and causing, ultimately, unnecessary

stress on myself and those around me and left wondering why. I'm somehow special while hundreds of thousands of people in North America (and probably well over the 1 million mark worldwide) die from cancer each year?

Nothing is wasted; all that we have, money included, is given or taken from us according to our purpose in this life. And millions die from cancer and a host of other things and reasons every day. But no one dies one second sooner than they are suppose to, or lives one second longer than they are allotted.

Does that mean that religions such as Hinduism that teach Metempsychosis are wrong? How could they be wrong? They were created by "ET". Did "ET" just decide to make up some BS for millions of people to believe in and even die for?

We can call it BS, but ET prefers to call it illusions, everything in this game called life is an illusion. What we do in this illusion is real and we take that with us when we die and leave Earth.

Please explain the apparent contradiction from your last post - "There was no big bang, the universe is not expanding nor will it contract and fall into itself----it will never end. This universe is so large that the edge will not be found by human instruments". If the universe does not end then there should be no "edge" for human instruments to detect.

Human instruments can't detect the soul; they cannot detect the real existence which is full of boundaries, "edges", on the other side there are no detectable boundaries.

My original question is more along the lines of - from what pitcher did all this soul creation pour into this cup of humanity, within the awesome expanse of the universe?

There is no pitcher, we enter and leave this stage alone. There have been many civilizations on Earth, the early ones have been wiped clean from this planet millions of Earth years ago, like an old house that is hundreds of years old Earth has seen many remodels, upgrades, and inhabitants.

What is the reason for the repeated birth/existence/destruction of these civilizations on Earth? Does each civilization peak? Reach it's goal?

There are no goals to reach, after awhile it withers away like fruit fallen from the tree and the infrastructure dissolves back into the ground from where it sprouted, with some help from ET.

Then a new infant/soul civilization takes its' place?

Not an infant/soul civilization, but more a place where undesirables are sent initially, eventually they form the villages, cities and nations, the rest is history, and then human types.

Is Earth (like other worlds) a romper room proving ground? Thanks.

> Earth most certainly is such a place.

Here, in the temporary dormancy of this thread, my fellow ATS knowledge junkies, allow me this observation: Some (certain other posters) seem almost intimidated and threatened by the author and content of this thread. One even mentioned he was brought to tears by the revelations and questions/information exchange!!!??? Huh? (Maybe a Hurricane Katrina thread would be more comfortable for such members where you would be with like minds quoting Celine Deion, lamenting the evils of non-liberal government policies, and knowing collectively and agreeing with each other that multi-culturism, human diversity, and tolerance for those who earn/deserve no tolerance, is the real strength that binds us). Putooey! I submit that Knowledge doesn't corrupt or pervert, not even false knowledge. It's the intellect that can't discern the difference that is in danger. Maybe Lou has concocted this entire story because he woke up one day and all the alphabets in the cereal bowl spelled it out for him! Maybe, it's all true. Who knows?

Not once have I seen the author of this thread dictate to anyone that they agree with him and/or demand acceptance (can you say this about other authors of dubious, questionable, fantastic, or hard to believe topics?) and smooth digestion of the information presented; hasn't forced me to swallow any ipecac yet either!

Lou (in the spirit of ATS or any other forum for knowledge exchange) has, in the least, entertained, informed, inspired, provoked thought, and done it all with some incredibly unique ideas expressed with a refreshing and ongoing invitation for rebuttal.

I think if anyone here is intimidated by Lou, it's not the information, it's that they can't measure up or match the level of intellectual prowess (again, story raving madness or not) that Lou so effortlessly displays here. Let's not forget the wit too! That almost always - provoked wit - when he's attacked for doing what we all come here to do. Now, we are all here on ATS so we all walk that fine line now and then. Let's keep going and see what side we end up on.

February 27, 2006

I am curious about this. Would this be an occasional thing they would do? Like sit down (intrude) at your table in a restaurant, appearing completely human, yet saying things that are somewhat otherworldly, maybe even being so blunt as to say they are not from here. Would they just have normal chit-chat, or say things that drop hints?

They wouldn't drop hints, that's against protocol, if they met with you in that manner it would be to give you some advice or direction. It may sound like chitchat but they transmit information directly into your subconscious mind subliminally.

Or could an ET take on a more permanent position in someone's life, appearing human, eating, sleeping, having a normal job, and even marry and have children with that person / human ? And you would never even know it. Or would you?

Yes, and you would never know it, suspect it perhaps.

Lou, This is a fascinating thread. I guess I could be described as a 'believer', though I also possess a healthy amount of skepticism - I think that you have to nowadays, faced as you are with the deluge of hoaxes, rumors and conspiracy theories that have spread with ferocious speed since the emergence of

the Internet. I have many thoughts and views on the subject of life on this planet, but it would take me a lifetime to explain and share them all. Suffice to say, I have never wholeheartedly accepted what religion has endeavored to force us to believe - that the Earth and stars were created in a single moment by a single being of unimaginable power. Indeed, by its very nature, Religion is self-contradictory. It teaches us that 'God' has no measure of time or space - everything is and always has been for him. If that was the case, why do we live finite lives? Why are we isolated by distance? If our only way of overcoming our isolation is through the appliance of science to create new technologies (think FTL travel) or medicine, then surely Science is proving more useful to us than Religion ever did.

As you say, we are a complex species living in a complex world. Man has traditionally been egotistical, convinced that we live in the center of the Universe and that God is almost obsessed with the short lives of every one of us billion humans, and every small act we do. I have always found this hard to believe, but have instinctively felt that we are a small part of a much bigger picture - a picture we can't always see, hear or feel. There have been huge leaps and transitions in society over the years which have never been fully explained, sudden advances, fires which seemed to ignite without a spark. In a way, everything you say explains it all.

Is it true? I don't know. What I do know is that even if you have made it up, it has certainly opened some of our minds to the possibility of thinking a little outside the box - and that's always a good thing.

Hi Lou, Are you saying that ET would have the same physiology as a human?

For them it's like going from one vehicle to the another one. Sometimes I drive my wife's car because she has me blocked in, if you get my drift. ET bodies are not like human bodies but they can enter into human cloned bodies like we change shirts.

If so, wouldn't the practicalities of everyday life get him exposed eventually? Wouldn't he have to take a physical to get a job, etc.?

They are in total control of any situation they are in without those around them knowing it.

Hi all! Brand new to ATS; just discovered this thread this past weekend. Sorry this is so long, but I have so much to get off my chest, and so many questions for you, Lou, and anyone else with insight: First question: You said several times in these 50 pages that souls don't enter babies until they are born. Years before my children were born, I had a vision of two children,

an older boy and a younger girl, who were waiting for me to find the right guy to be their father. I finally did. Within one week of conception, before I'd even tested positive (though I knew I was pregnant), my son came to me in a dream and showed me a scene from one of his lifetimes. It appeared to be many centuries ago in the area of the Great Wall of China. So the question is, was my son's soul in his body when I had that dream, or was he out floating around with the intention of entering the body later?

They enter at the very last minute; sometimes they watch the birth of their body and don't enter for a few hours after or as in some cases a few days after. Sometimes they are allowed to "float around" and watch before making an entrance.

Interestingly, when my daughter was 3 (son was 5), daughter saw an aerial photo of the Great Wall with someone walking on it. She said it was her brother. We haven't yet been to China in this lifetime. Then she saw another photo of the Great Wall from an entirely different perspective, and said that's where her brother used to live. I asked her who else lived there. She said she and I did.

Many of the people you meet in this life you shared lives with on other planets and other times on this planet, you might have been her daughter in China.

Second question(s): Have I been abducted? Have my children been abducted?

Yes, you and the children and probably your husband as well. However, I would not tell him that if I were you, nor would I tell the children, let them ask you.

She described the beings as vampires because they suck your energy.

They are not vampires but most people that are abducted don't remember what really happened, and many of the things that go on while in the ship are extremely strange to the human mind and sometimes we have difficulty describing what we perceive.

Since then, daughter has been sleeping with me. Many nights when we go to bed, I feel the bed vibrating slightly for a few minutes. What's that about?

No one can hide from them, if they wanted to do you or her harm there would be nothing to stop them, but they don't, they are in fact looking out after you and her. Don't know about the vibrating, unless she is frightened and she is shaking, nothing really to be afraid of.

In the last few years, I've had numerous dreams of angelic young men (they look young but feel very wise) for and from whom I feel great love (not sexual). They don't ever smile in

those dreams, and it never seems to be the same person, but I feel as if I know them from somewhere. Who/what are they and why am I having these dreams?

That is something only you can figure out, but most of us never do concerning the meaning behind the dreams.

Last question: What are orbs? I was up on a mountain with some friends who were trying to take orb photos. I had a sudden feeling of thousands of beings coming in from behind me. My friend turned to take a photo with her digital camera, and there were thousands of orbs in the photo, almost obscuring the people in the photo. My feeling was that they were ancient beings from this Earth. What do you think/know?

Orbs are souls, when we leave our bodies we are spheres of exotic energy.

Is there any way for me to make my daughter's and my encounters with ET any less frightening?

Yes, when you know they are not going to hurt you why fear them? The ride is much more enjoyable when you are not afraid, nevertheless, ETs are so strange to us humans and keeping our wits about us in their presence takes some doing. Abductions are numbered, you only get so many and then they stop.

Large cities don't seem natural at all. I think villages i.e. Indians are more of a natural setting. AM I wrong?

With large populations, large cities are the only way to go, sanitation, clean water, resources, parks, diverse activities, etc. Earth will have a population of over twelve billion by the end of this century; cities will be much larger, more efficient and safer.

So when the ET uses a human body as a "vehicle", to be among us incognito. Do they just make a human form and go into it, or "take" one from an unsuspecting person to use?

They create a human body from DNA that they acquired from an abductee, its new and never used or reused.

And I ask this to touch base on a poster who just asked about telling one's family and you said not to, best to let them ask you.

My advice was to never tell family members things they aren't ready to hear because people get divorced for things of this nature and much less.

What is one to make of it when they (family members) do approach you about this, but not to ask, but to actually tell you "you were abducted" and you are selected as part of the Extraterrestrial plan. Even though you never, ever discussed this with them. It is out of the blue. And they are giving you

things to stir your thoughts, things like Extraterrestrial related books and photos, and telling you things about the Universe. Then denying it after.

Someone is messing with you and I doubt it's ET, could be of the homegrown variety masking as family from beyond.

And if it is not imagination, and not a mind game, what if it was real, how is one to cope with having been threatened ? And how then can it be acceptable to believe Extraterrestrials are "nice"? Are there good Extraterrestrials and bad ones?

ETs use the good cop bad cop routine but they mostly do it on their ships and then they wipe your memory of most of it, only your unconscious mind knows the pertinent information that was imparted to you. ETs work in mysterious ways, but rarely in the way you have described. ETs don't kill for no reason, and even with a reason rarely do. But there are exceptions to every rule and there are other elements in the soup that I will talk about on a later date.

By the way, thanks, this thread has helped me get over some of my fear. The ETs are just so...unknown. Sometimes that's really hard to face. Any tips?

Because they have your best interest as their job there is no need to fear them. Children fear going to the doctor because it's a strange place with strange people and sharp needles, yet the doctors are not there to hurt them, well, hopefully not intestinally.

How can someone best come to understand the ETs?

No human way possible. Do we truly understand other humans and what makes us tick? How then can we hope to understand a far superior life form as ETs?

How does the soul relate to a premature birth?

Like any other birth, when the body is ready the soul is inserted.

You said long ago that all Presidents and world leaders have met ETs. Did the leaders "know" that they were ETs? Or did they think they were meeting humans?

Some knew/know, others met with the human costumed ETs.

Lou, you are the "Man" (Juvenile, but I don't want to date myself) Oops. - Just when I think you've tapped out, exhausted the interest, the wonderful minds and questions (as well as the answers) come roaring back; you even appear to have escaped the some of the Trolls for now (I think in consideration for their own pride and sense of self worth, they're off seeking easier, less challenging prey). I too apologize (as I saw another

poster do) If I ramble too long incident to a question, just so much here that's compelling to comment on; the environ of believability is a fickle domain on such a subject, you fare well; my compliments and sincere thanks.

My question, and I hesitate to ask (reminiscent of fingers lingering on a chess piece), not because I'm worried about what you "will" say, more that I'll be disappointed in what you "don't" say (yea, yea, I know, I deployed his safety chute for him, so shoot me!). How do the ET's regard "love"?

They love it, had to say it. Anyway, there is nothing higher than love it encompasses everything. ETs have a much higher appreciation and understanding for love than we do.

What a "skull" session! Revealing answer aint it folks? Anyone have "hoax" alarms wailing? Me neither and I'm no cheering section. (The member worried about her children - less worried now? I should hope so? Truth or fiction? If all fiction, since when does [relative] spontaneity of answers on such a subject breed empathy, concern, thoughtfulness, and "there is nothing higher", "it encompasses everything"..... This thread is whacked! (Intellectuality purposely diminished, selfishly, heck I'm no super brain), It's a square peg in a round hole, I'm flabbergasted fascinated and I love it! (Ok, I'm sitting down again, sorry).

Compared to the usual, the expected from other's ET lore - "Love doesn't apply to ET that's a human emotion" (waiting for a response I was rolling the bones and kind of expected that one), or something more complicated, or ambiguous or cosmically creative, or... - help me out here, jump in anytime - its' all very refreshing.

My prior posts still stand, you know where I protect my pride and ward off any concern for being duped? And, I'm going to do it again.....here: If this is a feeler for a new sci-fi novel, well....then....ok; I'm mature enough to accept that (be kind of neat if we were all the confirming inspiration for a successful sci-fi yarn, huh?!). However, if Lou has spun all this because his wife (more successfully) continues to block his car in the drive, and he's bored! If that's the case, then I picture the celestial ladder of good and bad stretching far into the heavens (top rungs = good, bottom = bad) and Lou desperately trying to cling to the lower rungs cuz we're all kicking him as we climb. Barring that scenario I'm more mesmerized than ever, Keep it coming Lou.

February 28, 2006

I cannot believe one mentality can so explicitly explain complexity, and remain unknown. Only the prurience of a subverted intellect could affect this. God help us all, Tiny Tim, if the collective intellect turns out to be subverted!

Lou, do you happen to know what this means...Jesus said, "This heaven will pass away, and the one above it will pass away..."

It's a parable that concerns the divisions of mankind, the Gentiles and the Jews. Which later divides again, the Israelites were one people coming out of Egypt eventually the twelve tribes organized into two factions Judah and Israel (two heavens). The people of Israel faltered and their nation was destroyed by the Gentiles, the nation of Judah survived and those where the people that existed in the land of Palestine when Jesus came into the picture. There would be another division, a priestly division of the Jewish people the Sadducees and Pharisees. Jesus spoke mostly against those two groups, blaming them for leading the Jewish nation astray.

The Sadducees believed that God would establish heaven on Earth and place them in charge of the Gentiles. The Pharisees leaned a little more on the spiritual side of the god question, but also believed that heaven was only for the Jews.

Both orders were mistaken, but it would be the Pharisees, which the majority of the Jews belonged to, that would provoke the wrath of Gentile Rome, which nearly extinguished the Jewish people completely. Therefore, the *physical heaven on Earth concept and the spiritual-exclusive-heaven passed away.*

1) Do you now believe there is such a thing as 'fate' (i.e. we make it ourselves), or is everything basically controlled and pre-ordained by these ETs? Given that you said, there are many, many different types of ETs, who controls them?

Life is a combination of fate and freewill and there is no contradiction. We are pretty much all the same but at different levels of awareness. Most that are free to travel the galaxy (ETs) don't need to be controlled they know what is right and wrong. Nothing gets under the radar for humans or ET, from the collective conscious.

2) It is obvious they don't monitor time in the same way that we do; however, time must pass for them in one way or another or they wouldn't exist in the same dimension that we do. Do they have the ability to travel back and forth in time, at least in the sense that we understand it?

As the case with Santa Clause, time travels with ETs, a concept without explanation.

3) How much of the known Universe have they explored?

There is no unexplored part of the universe, the universe is 100 % explored.

4) Is there anything the ETs fear?

The IRS, but nothing else.

5) If they are here to slowly assist in our development, why have they allowed many of our scientists to go down the route of the big bang theory (wasting years of work) when it's plainly wrong? I can see no benefit to this.

Earth is a playpen. Try telling a child that the toy he is playing with is a useless waste of his or her time. All the toys we get to play with do help us grow, more or less; therefore, not a waste of time.

February 28, 2006

Last night while reading one of your posts, the TV in the other room went on. Why do I tell you this because you're the only one that would believe me, because it really happened. Since living alone makes it hard for someone else to have done it and having the cabinet doors closed makes for the remote not easy to have turned it on. But odd things have happened to me too in my so called life here on Earth. With that said my question is---The 12 Zodiac signs have been long ago signaling who we are and the makeup of ourselves according to the planets and stars. Do you know if the ET's take that into consideration of who they choose to align with and are more likely to have contact with... I'm a true Cancer.

The Zodiac is fun and sometimes ETs or other errant spirits will communicate with people and give them advice. However, since you don't know where that advice is coming from it would be risky to bet the farm with it. ETs do not choose people according to their date of birth. Nevertheless, many people display traits in line with their signs. Coincidence? There are no coincidences.

Thank you for the answer Lou. Still having a bit of trouble tying it in. Here's the full quote. Could you please help explain how your answer fits in with the rest of the quote?

"The dead are not alive,"

The non-Jews (Gentiles) those that don't believe in the God of Israel are considered dead and not alive/worthy.

"And the living will not die."

Jews and those that believe in the God of Israel and in Jesus, will not die but live forever in God's kingdom.

"During the days when you ate what is dead, you made it come alive."

Refers to the OT when the Israelites entered the Promised Land and killed or converted the non-Jews in the land of Canaan. The Israelites disobeyed God and did not kill every woman, child, man and beast as they were instructed to do by God, instead they attempted to convert some and enslave those they did not kill. In essence, those that they spared, "they ate", an allegory. What belonged to the Jews became sanctioned and therefore were alive like the Jews, and their offspring would torment the Jews for several generation.

"When you are in the light"

The light is the grace of God shining on the chosen, the Jews. For the Christian they are in the light when they accept Jesus as their savior.

"What will you do? On the day when you were one, you became two. But when you become two, what will you do?"

Talking about the nation of Israel, Israel became two nations, Israel and Judah, and they fought each other and became weak. Israel corrupted itself with the paganism of those they had failed to destroy. The Jews became easy pickings for the non-Jewish nations of Assyria and Babylonia.

As did their brethren, the Israelites, the Jews of Jesus' day, became divided and were basically in two camps, the Pharisees/Sadducees (priestly clans) and the (Zealots) orthodox combatants/militants from the priestly clans, their division cause them to parish, divided they fell.

Lou, this thread is interesting in many ways. In particular, I find it very interesting that many of the members contributing to this thread have joined in the month of February 2006. I suspect they were prompted to join ATS expressly to communicate with you. What a compliment to you and the insight you bring to the subject of ET.

Again, I speed-read through the detractors and debunkers' diatribes preferring, as do most, to read an intelligent exchange of information and ideas whereupon each of us will make our own decision whether to believe or not believe. I have more questions for you later and sure don't want to

overload you. I enjoy reading what other members ask as well.

Thanks for the feedback!

I just don't get it. I'm too human. I'm part of that species that has no control over anything, has never accomplished anything of note, and must rely on 'ET' to validate my lack of self-esteem.

Did you believe you had control before you got snared by this thread? Most people don't like the idea that Earth is a playpen, they prefer to think of it as a hell-hole, it's actually both, but no one has to believe what I write. If you are waiting for me to come clean, OK, here it is, I tell my experiences, what I have seen, what I learned and what ET tells me. That's my story and I'm sticking with. My story is never going to change so if it's too crazy or ridiculous to believe—then don't.

Now unless I misunderstood this. I have a hard time believing that they take DNA, grow a fetus, then grow a full-grown human, and keep it in stockpiles, should they need to use an impersonator. I mean to appear "real" what do they do? Feed it, teach it to walk, talk, send it to tanning booths to give it tan-lines and wrinkles, build muscles (which would atrophy btw if they are not used) and put a few zits and whiskers on their

faces, do their hair, etc. Do they upload a lifetime of memories for them to have real reactions, feelings etc?

They are in tubes of liquid in a sort of cryogenic state, zits and all.

Now do you not think it would be much simpler to seize control of a person's mind, and say what they want to say, do what they want to do, and then exit the body they used, and the person is none the wiser? After all, you say Extraterrestrials can wipe out your memory. So it is established they have shortcuts via the brain that this is how they operate.

They can and do, but that's not the way they normally operate.

I would believe my own hijacking of the brain theory. The way a hijacker takes control of a plane and flies wherever he wants. He doesn't go to all the trouble to build a plane.

It's no trouble for them.

If they are making Clones, then this is making an identical body of another body. So what is the motive of a clone? This would mean they need to send in an identical person to replace the person they stole the DNA from.

They have thousands of clones. Interspersed in a population of 6 and a half billion people they've had no problem remaining incognito.

If they are not using the clone for this purpose of impersonation, then they really don't need to clone. It then makes the entire abduction process of stealing DNA needless. Why ? Because again, why go to all this trouble of flying ships to peoples' bedrooms at night, then taking them hostage & extracting DNA. If I want money, and I want lots of it. Why would I go rob people's wallets as they sleep? It would be a lot easier to do it all in one swoop, rob a bank. There are sperm banks, egg banks, and you only need one cell anyways.

They have been doing it for millions of years on many planets, they must have figured out how to do it right by now, besides there is more to it than DNA.

You said, "The Extraterrestrials are garrisoned on this planet and on the moon. They have bases in several countries in cooperation with those governments. They let us play with their toys, take them for a spin, learn a few things along the way on how to improve our technology." "Humans are on the verge of stepping into space, there is a lot of stuff to know about that next big leap."

Lou!! Much KUDOS to you. I have not read this entire thread, but up to this point, you DO KNOW. Allow the bashers to keep on; as if they were close to the wisdom, they would 'feel it'! Why did I just find this thread?

Glad you are here!

I am actually quite open to believing there are people among us who are not real human beings. I am just curious how it is accomplished. If "They are in tubes of liquid in a sort of cryogenic state", ok fine. But this does not explain how they can be removed from the liquid and begin to use this physical human body. If they were in a "dormant" state, how can they use their muscles? The muscles would atrophy, and shrink and be useless. They could not exit the liquid and walk, much less talk. Have you not seen a paralyzed person? The part of the body that is not "in use" shrinks, because they are no longer using their muscles. Even when we put a mouse in a cage, we give it a wheel to run around on.

You are projecting human level technology on ETs. ETs are gods, wizards that can transform our physical reality with a blink of an eye.

You can't just say "they can and they do"! And expect everyone will nod their head in agreement. It just doesn't validate the claims. Or it is best to answer "I don't know".

I can say that because that is the way it is. I don't expect anyone to believe me without proof and proof is not forthcoming for the vast majority.

I am only confused because you said, "Their bodies are not like human bodies but they can enter into a human clone like we change shirts."

We and they are spirits, their spirit can move from one body to another as simply as we change shirts.

Then you said, "They create a human body from DNA they acquired from an abductee, its new and never reused."

I could have said they created it from pixie dust, but then everyone would laugh at me, and no one laughs at Lou. LOL

And now you say, "They are in tubes of liquid in a sort of cryogenic state". I'm counting 3 different answers here.

All three apply to the questions you asked.

If they are using cloned bodies, and clones are exact replicas, then they are not an ET , but simply a human copy. Where then, is the part in their body that is ET? The brain? Or the term "clone" is not applicable. Are they in fact a Hybrid? Humanoid? Do they scoop out all the insides of a human body

and put their tiny little bodies inside it? The changing of the shirts answer?

The human body and the bodies ET often use are simply machines. When they enter a clone or another human or whatever costume they choose, what enters is their spirit, which resides in the machine, they don't become the machine as we humans tend to do. In other words, if you drive a Ford car you are not a Ford car you are a person driving a Ford car. If you prefer something other than a Ford for the analogy, say a Chevy, that's ok too. They discard such bodies, vehicles, like we spit out chewing gum when we are through chewing.

If ETs knew that when they die they return to the "other side" wouldn't they be completely fearless of death?

ETs don't fear death, it's not in them to fear anything.

If ETs can move from body to body why doesn't it just abandon the body altogether and just be a floating blob of exotic energy?

They do it to have physical contact with humans, they need to be quasi physical themselves and they do spend most of their time as balls of energy, it's the only way they can unwind after an encounter with humans.

If I were to somehow destroy an ET's body while it was "vacant" or soulless (perhaps it was busy talking to people in bars while in a human body) what would happen to ET?

ET would get another clean shirt to put on, they have a closet full.

Why are there so many reports of "Grey" Extraterrestrials if the majority of ETs, apparently, don't appear to resemble them?

ETs are masters of disguises and so are their droids.

Was there a particular species that you had contact with most or that you found the most advanced/interesting? Out of curiosity, what did they look like? I need something "tangible" just describe the features without dodging the question.

The one that I see most often looks a little like Jimmy Durante, or maybe that's what I want him to look like, they can shape shift. I don't dodge questions, you dodge my answers.

I'm not sure I believe, but I've been having strange dreams lately and somehow found this site/thread.

Lou, several years ago I witnessed a giant rectangle-shaped ufo floating just above the tree line as I drove down a crowded

interstate at 5pm. Incredible! It was about the size of a tennis court and had at least three levels of encased panels or floors. It was made of reflective material that seemed to mirror the surrounding green trees and landscape - so it was dark green/gray. I saw it for about 20 seconds as it floated along the tree line and disappeared over hills. There were large power-lines close by. Who would populate a large craft like that? Have you ever seen this type of ufo? Do you know them?

Not sure what you saw, but ET ships come in every size and shape and some are ships filled with tourist from other star systems and in this solar system, some are filled with human/ET hybrids shipped out to other places.

What would they be doing flying around in broad daylight?

ET ships fly around the clock, they have the ability to hide behind clouds or go invisible, cloak.

Could I have been the only person that saw it? I don't think they abducted me because I had to be at class in 10 minutes and I was on time for it - so why did they let me see them?

They let you see them to let you know that there is more to life than what is on this planet, not all human brains are capable of understanding that phenomenon, hence the tantrums on this thread.

In addition, each time I have seen ufo's, I felt absolutely no fear whatsoever. In normal situations, I'm the first one to sense danger. Each time I've seen a ufo, I was completely calm - very calm. I think maybe I have more to fear from mankind than from ET. What do you think? Thanks for your help.

You know what humans are capable of , hate and envy being the big ones. ET neither hates or envies and most of the fear people report is unwarranted and in some cases exaggerated.

Jews and those that believe in the God of Israel...Who is the "God of Israel"?

According to the OT and the NT he is the god of creation, the god of scripture. Initially he was exclusively the god of the Jews. Then came the Christians and they now claim him as Jesus. Then came Mohammed and Moslems, who claim him as Allah. The Jews believe that they are god's favorite people, the Christians believe that they are god's favorite people, the Moslems believe that they are god's (Allah) favorite people. They may all be right, but none of them are each others' favorite people. If God is the god of love then it seems he wasted his time down here.

Ok. I just finished reading this thread in two nights. I wanted to get it all in before I posted anything. First off, everyone here needs to calm down. Lou, ignore anyone that is just plain giving you a hard time and not asking you legit questions

about your story. After reading this thread things started to get a little shaky since like page 38. And it hasn't stopped since! It's kind of disappointing when you are trying to read things and form your own conclusion with this child-like bickering in the background. Honestly for one, I want to hear what Lou has to say. (I know I'm not alone) Whether he is right or wrong, some of the things he said were still inspirational and some really good food for thought.

Now, IMO Lou, I found many personal truths in your story, and even picked up on your metaphors since day one that some others passed by. There really are many fascinating theories in here.

You rock the boat a little and some people get seasick.

March 2, 2006

Just thought I'd say I've found a summary of a book on the internet by a gentlemen that went through what you have. His mother also was visited by Extraterrestrials when she was pregnant, this being told to him by a high-ranking officer. Also came across a website that had a 1995 report about a reporter that was given info by a man by the name of Riconosciuto. He was back then a high-ranking person of interest in high intelligent and secret, dirty affairs. The list he gave the reporter had many interesting things in it, but when I read the sentence, I know the identities of the "sleepers" here and overseas. I almost fell over; I knew you were real from the first post. Seeing it repeated from those higher ups didn't make it believable just heightened it. Please we need you more with every post and every dumb question. I've thought a lot about you in the last 3 days I've found this site. Just taking in so much can be more then overwhelming. So to the unbelievers here stop sitting at your computers with your eyes wide shut and look things up.

Thanks for your comments!

Lou, please tell me that ET appreciates something about our music. It's the only thing I'm proud of. Thanks for sharing

your story with us. Personally, I feel better after having read your account.

Will I get in trouble if I say ETs inspire our music? Not that they are musical, but neither are they scientists and physicists, they are far about those things, but they have their fingers in everything we do and accomplish. If I have no other purpose than to let people know that the Extraterrestrials are not here to eat us or enslave the human race that would be enough. Hollywood and others need to keep the masses in fear of the unknown, paranormal and extraterrestrial because people are much easier to control when they are afraid. Is ET behind some of the fear mongering? Yes, they are, some people need to be controlled, in fact, many people insist on it, politically speaking.

What if I don't want to be afraid? What if I just want to understand, at least to the best of my abilities?

The ball is in your court when it comes to being afraid, it's kind of like dealing with a bully, you need to muster the courage for the confrontation. ETs are not bullies, not all of them, but they are intimidating. Not a real danger to you personally. A lot of information from them is given on a need to know basis and only they know what each of us need to know.

Hi Lou, you said, "The great thing about dying is that it only last a few seconds and then you are alive again somewhere

else." "The place you wake up in will be a temporary place a fantastic city that you will never want to leave."

I've just started reading your posts in the past several days. When I read what you said in the above posts I was totally shocked! My daughter died in 1989. I had a dream of her after she died. I asked her what it was like where she is now. These are the exact words that she said to me in a calm voice "It's just another "place" Momma". I just had to tell you this and I have much more that I will post later. Thank you for telling about your experiences.

I think you know that your daughter is in a much happier place; otherwise, she couldn't have given you the message that she did. The best part of life is that it ends and then we are with the ones we love, no fear no hate, it's a comfort no one here on Earth can experience. And the departed don't feel the separation, they are aware of us and can spend time with us. However, we certainly do feel the separation, even when we know they are in a good place.

Unbelievable. Just absolutely unbelievable. First, to the member who posted he/she thought about this thread for several days, amen, ditto, me too brother. The Porsche member......is the 911 really that corvette yellow? I'm glossy green with envy (trade for my BMW K bike? Just for a day or two?).

More importantly, that there are/were several points Lou made (didn't make a big deal about them either - rare), atavistic, deeply philosophical without being cliché, was a great observation to bring back into this thread, thanks. H E double - tooth - picks, maybe he's Falcon. Onto other things...

Anybody care if I remind everyone here that this is an "ANONYMOUS" discussion board; please think about that very hard. I "know" that Lou understands this, good god he made a very clear statement at the beginning of the thread that should have prevented all this nonsense. There simply are a few that must believe that making a fool of themselves is a worthwhile aspiration.

Lou, from your perspective, any thoughts on the large and fairly consistent "near-death experience" phenomena?

Near death is just that it's not death so the information imparted is limited. But many that have experienced it know without a doubt that there is life after death that life continues. However, they don't know where their next assignment is going to be or how long they can or will remain in that in-between place, until they die. Most NDE are similar to abductions, they are not accidents, and people are pulled into that zone for a short review, warning, or to be congratulated on living a worthwhile life. Unlike abductions NDEs tend to be pleasant, neutral, or horrible with more of the memory intact.

Lou, I am wondering why you seem to approve of the religions of Abraham (or seem to imply that ET used these religions in some way), when the Abrahamic religions are totally opposed to the idea of rebirth? If ET knows rebirth is real, why would they have backed the Abrahamic religions to which rebirth is an abhorrent notion?

It's part of the grand illusion. Was Abraham a real person? To answer that I will offend many people. So I will just say that it's my opinion that he was only a metaphor. Was Sodom and Gomorra a real place and occurrence? No it wasn't, it too is a metaphor for something larger. Why did ET let people believe the sun moved around the Earth? Because they didn't need to know more than that. There are people starving in India, but they refuse to eat cows. Cows were made by ET as an easy and convenient food source, but ET is also behind their beliefs, contradiction, certainly, illusion definitely, purpose, human diversity and more.

Lou, when was the last time you visited or talked with the Entities?

We are in regular contact.

They obviously know that you have already written this post. Have they said anything to you about it?

They are the source of it.

Is there some way you can communicate with them about this thread and have them comment on it? I mean, what's more convincing than an extraterrestrial commenting. Surely because of their intelligence above ours they could come up with probably a single sentence that would just shut us all up and prove everything.

Does everyone really want to know all the answers with one sentence? We have to finish our lives on this planet, if we know all the answers that would spoil the ending of the play for each of us, not happening.

Lou your making me nervous. I have relatives that I don't like seeing in this life, let alone in some afterlife or different state of being. Do I have to see these people again after I die?

Depends on how many negative points you have racked up for yourself while here on Earth. That's the incentive to fly right and not burn bridges.

I do have some thoughts about this thread. From what I have read so far, Lou seems to be describing many of my beliefs and they correlate to experiences that I have had in my life. I spoke of a dream that I had of my daughter before. Well, here is another dream that I had of her, many times.

For exactly one year to the day after she died I had many dreams of talking to someone, a male, on the telephone. In each dream I would ask if I could speak to my daughter. Each time I asked he would tell me that "it wasn't time yet". One time in particular, he said "she is working with children". I never saw this man's face so I don't know who he was. My daughter died suddenly and left behind 3 children. When the year was up, I started having vivid dreams of her. I could ask her anything I wanted and she would always answer back. I have always wondered who this person was that would talk to me on the phone in my dreams. Lou, could that have been an ET?

A personal guide.

I heard ET's could morph into a human image, is this correct? Or do they look like the commonly depicted large eyes and head etc?

Many of the entities that are reported by abductees are simply machines. ETs might be present but they usually stay in the background out of sight and communicate telepathically with the person. ETs often inhabit human type bodies and they can take on any appearance they choose, even canine, but not the talking kind like in the movie MIB.

If "they control and know everything", then they are fully capable of providing you with something to post that will prove your story. Anything will do, as long as there is no other logical explanation that could make it unbelievable.

They are big boys if they want to show themselves to the general public and remove all doubt they certainly don't need me for that.

How about a prediction?

I don't read palms, chicken bones, tell fortunes or do predictions, but there is no shortage of people that claim they can and some even make a good living at it.

OR, Arrange a flyover of a UFO. Give location and time, and someone who is not believing you of course, can look out for it and report back that it happened. The ET's who know all, can tell you where the disbelievers of your story lives.

I'm not here to prove anything, I tell my experiences and answer questions ET allows me to answer, nothing more. The only people that happen on to this site by accident are the non-believers and I have no answers for them, none that they are ready to hear.

Lou, what does ET do for enjoyment, pleasure, fun? Are they artistic? Are they athletic? Do they have houses? Do they have pets?

Those that live on this planet as humans do everything that humans do. They could be your neighbors and they would be the ones you least suspect. They have the human thing down very well and they do it better than humans do. ETs enjoy everything they do.

I have always been a believer and they did show themselves to me when I was a small child and I remember this as if it happened yesterday. I have come to the conclusion that they only show themselves to the believers because it would be a waste of their time to try and convince someone of their existence. The ones that believe they exist have already proved to them that they know they are for real and that they can trust us with their vast knowledge. Lou, you have been chosen to give us messages from them and that is good enough for me.

I don't know about chosen, but I do work cheap.

I have not seen undeniable proof so far in your story. It is just text across my screen. And I think this is most likely the case with others who you think are not believing your story.

I give answers to some questions but proof comes from ETs. If they chose to give you proof then they will abduct you, for lack of a better word, and show you the planets in the solar system. You may not remember the tour but those that got one know down deep inside that we are not alone and they search for confirmation, some end up on this thread.

Anyone can come in here and say all this, so you must expect some of us need more than that. Not everyone is naive you know?

On the contrary, this world is chock full of naïve people. Wars happen because of naïve people, religious institutions flourish because of naïve people, our learning institutions teach naïve people that they have originated from slime, a freak accident of mother nature and that we are decedents of apes, now it don't get any more naïve than that!

If these ET's that are posing as humans exist, are they normal inside ? I mean can they go to a doctor like anyone else and get checkups, eye exams, surgery etc and the doc doesn't notice? Or must they avoid this? Would they suffer physical injury just as a human would? Like break a bone, cut themselves?

Those that are full blown ET don't need to see a doctor but if they feel they need to for show, the doctors would be under ET's control. ETs that are half-breed don't normally need much care but if they do ET will fix them. Nevertheless, their physiology is nearly exact to the average human and most human doctors would never pick up on the difference.

Do they eat too?

When in human body suits yes they do eat.

Is there a telltale sign that some people may pick up on, that makes you suspect they are this way? Like someone who is more sensitive to things being amiss (you think they are not human), as others may not notice a thing. Is there something that is just not 100% human? No matter how good the "act" is. Like maybe they react very strongly and adversely to some things, or comments? Or maybe they go off places and no one knows where they go?

If the average person suspects someone is an Extraterrestrial, then they are most likely not, they tend to cover their tracks well.

Do they report back to the ship, planet? Or are here on a full life mission? And go back when it is done.

There are several places in the solar system and on Earth they can go to if they wish, even those on full-blown missions.

Are they aware they are an imposter?

Some are not aware.

Show us the Solar system? Mercury, molten. Venus, too hot to inhabit. Mars, barren. Jupiter, a planetary mess. Saturn, ditto.

Uranus, well, there might be Klingons there. Neptune, the wild card. Pluto, a rock. We already know about this stuff. If they have intergalactic and travel why would they only favor us with inter-planetary.

Seeing the solar system up close is more than most people can handle. Going beyond the solar system is not going to happen.

Yes, the world is full of naive people; do you think you'll find them here? Not likely.

Many people believe that we are alone in the universe, other than perhaps some microbes and therefore, yes the vast majority are naïve. Naturally, I'm not talking about anyone on ATS. LOL.

Solar system up close? I don't think that would phase anyone, we already know what's there.

Are you serious? Viewing Saturn from one of its moons, or Jupiter, most people would have a heart attack from the awe of it, some would faint, others would get on their knees and worship it. You have to see it to believe it.

Why aren't we going beyond the Solar system?

Because the human body can't handle the trip. The soul or essence would have to be taken out of the human body and placed into a container. In some cases, the soul is only taken out of the body and it floats around the ship or off ship as a spirit. Nevertheless, most humans are not leaving the solar system until they die and perhaps not even then, depends on where they are destined to go.

So you're saying that these ET's have limited physical procedures that they couldn't protect "us" against the travails of intergalactic travel? Man that sounds merely mortal.

Human bodies are not designed for intergalactic travel, Hollywood movies are not real.

Moderator loses debate and threatens to shut down this tread. LOL

Thought today about the patience of the moderator(s) here at ATS, and was impressed until now. I'm not just being critical, there's a point to be made here, and a very important one I think. Allow me first to say, that I'm brand spanking new to on-line forums, and in light of that, if there's something I'm missing, feel free to let me know.

A thread starts, (title may even be a metaphor) author states he is willing to share his experiences - about what nearly everyone agrees is a fascinating topic - offers to answer questions, CLEARLY STATES HE DOESN'T CARE IF ANYONE

BELIEVES HIM. On at least one other post by the author, he also states he doesn't expect anyone will believe him.

Mean time, other threads, "George Bush is a reptile", "Orange tinted skin under fingernails, have I been abducted by the grays"? "I'm channeling Don Knott's (recently deceased, may his soul be doing whatever it wants) and he says Lady Fish knows where Bin Laden is!" ...ok, so I made that last one up. But, these threads (and many other threads equally fantastic, incredulous and downright loony - opinion) are proceeding quietly, smoothly, with lots of ooo's, aahhhs, and agreement; some, if not many, "arguably" - the virtual epitome of foolishness, sad ignorance, downright stupidity, and madness. These threads for the most part are unmolested by moderators, soothsayers, "trolls" (perfect word to describe the practice) and wannabe skeptics (there are two kinds of skeptics and I'm prepared to differentiate between the two). Bills have to be paid though, ATS salaries, don't they?

Back to this thread. Questions and answers fly back and forth; the information offered is as incredulous, fantastic, and wild as anything you'll find on ATS. Sober, serious, obviously adult ATS members are flummoxed that the author can't be brought down, he can't be "proven" a nut, speculation abounds; I think it's safe to assume that just about everyone was thinking: This guy has to be a nut/hoaxer, but d*mn he's good! Equally mesmerizing is the Author's style, intelligence, knowledge of history, and I think for some, his thoughtful consideration of other members, and their questions, who needed that thoughtful consideration. Yes, some intense reciprocal sarcasm from the author, however, from what I saw, only when provoked. There are undeniable pearls of wisdom here as well adding further mystery to all of this.

At the very least, and I may mentioned before, we were all hearing one incredible story.

Before long, soothsayers, kooks, and skeptic-wannabes berate author on every page. Despite the aforementioned, you could almost hear the foot stomping, screaming tizzies of the morons who obviously couldn't by-god- stand to have a thread author get this much attention and them not be part of it. "GIVE US PROOF", "GIVE US PROOF", "I'll HOLD MY BREATH AND TURN BLUE", "GIVE US PROOF" wwaaahhhh! All on an "Anonymous" discussion board where thread author advised in beginning, that he didn't care if anyone believed him.

I tossed into the fray as well, I regret that now, and sincerely apologize to the other ATS members, there were many appropriate posts to end the silliness and get back to it; those of you who did that, were absolutely right. I apologize to the morons as well.

Now, "Mr. Moderator" (Intrepid) Official Representative of ATS - that jumped testosterone laden, gauntlet smashing down, "I've had enough", into this thread - the main reason I'm taking up all this space - what were you thinking? And, who are the "guys" you are referring to in the above quote?

Additionally, what does (as you surreptitiously advised the thread author)

"Read your U2U's", and then stated "I gave you a way out" mean? Do I really need to explain the implications of your actions? You represent ATS, its' ideals, policies, and certainly its' ability to attract members and earn a profit (at least I would hope; or is this all pro bono, advertisers included? Did you not create a tremendous and potentially damaging conflict of interest?

You throw in with the knuckleheads? The morons whose pap and want for recognition for their "Googling" expertise, thoroughly annoyed the living crap out of everyone else, failed to "out" the author, and most of all, most importantly, miserably failed to use their skepticism as a tool for what it should be used for - understanding! The knuckleheads bashed the author in the head with a rock, you looked around for more to hand them.

Please tell me (in regard to the kooks, skeptic wannabes, etc) where this analogy is wrong: Barbara Streisand (BS) comes on my TV espousing her considerable knowledge of politics and the art form that is "Yentil". Now I can't stand BS, but, instead of changing the channel or turning the TV off (I really should read a book, take a college course, hint hint knuckleheads) Nope! Instead, I chamber around into my Remington 12ga. and blow the holy crap out of my TV! I've killed the message and the messenger/medium that brought it to me, haven't I? From my doorstep, I trumpet my accomplishment, bask in the glow of my bug-lite and run around to my neighbor's houses to see what's on their TV's. If it's BS, then by golly, I'll save them too.

If the "Three Amigos" agree with your actions, I'm nobody special, but I don't belong here.

Most Sincerely and Respectfully

Bravo! Not just for this thread, but for all threads. When mods can't handle their jobs and throw bigger tantrums than those they mod over, one has to wonder about their motives.

March 4, 2006

Can I speak with the real Lou? Not the one spitting Extraterrestrial mumbo jumbo, but the human that was born on planet Earth. Can that Lou come out and tell us that he believes all this when the burden of evidence is that the ETs are not here to help us?

ETs have souls and the orbs are souls, if you wish to call them astral bodies that works too. ETs created the history you have become so attached to, that is why full disclosure is impossible. This thread has shown how unprepared many people are for the "real" truth, and not the made in Hollywood truth. So far I have only used simple words and those words have created havoc and confusion in the lives of people like you. Try and imagine what actual proof might do to billions of people like yourself.

If you are here as a messenger, than do you not think you could reach more listeners by having a # 1 bestseller ? ! Bet Larry King would have you on his show! Is it because you fear your story will be investigated by aggressive journalists? Exposure verse disclosure?

I'm not concerned about aggressive journalists they have yet to discover if Roswell is true and they have been at it for 59 years. And they had many live witnesses to that phenomena to kick around. In my case they only have me, are they going to cut me open to see what I'm made of? Or badger me for proof like on this thread? There was a heck of a lot of proof for Roswell, and yet what good has it done?

Lou - Insomnia wanes, but have a question: You can Google it till doomsday now but I've never heard anything more than a dodge from preacher/minister/etc. (makes them nervous though) since I was kid - Genesis 6:1. What's your take and do you know how/if it translates from the Torah?

Genesis is one of the five books of the Torah. The daughters of men imply false gods, the Babylonians, Syrians, and Egyptians had thousands of them and they were the people that had the most influence on the nomadic Hebrew tribes that inhabited the land of Canaan, from the word/name Cain of Cain and Able fame.

Lou, could you say how ET views abortion? If an unborn baby has no soul yet, does it matter?

Abortion is wrong for the simple fact that it is use as a contraceptive too often. On the other hand, all that is being eliminated is a little machine/container for a human soul. The power of life and death does not reside in human hands not even when we murder someone. We only kill a body not the soul, but it doesn't make it right and there are consequences for murder and in some cases, abortions too.

If your baby dies before birth, will you ever know that child after you die? Thanks for your thoughts.

When the baby dies from abortion or is stillborn a soul never enters the baby. Some people will get to know who they missed out of having in their lives, most will not.

Lou, I have read the 1st 25 pages of this thread, I have found your story very interesting and compelling. Have the Extraterrestrials been in contact with you since you started this thread?

Yes they have.

As I posted previously, my son came to me in a dream one week after conception. Could it be that those who are going to be born and not aborted or miscarried have souls that have attached to them in some way, put dibs on the body if you will, and those souls then only enter their bodies around the time of birth?

We don't scramble for available bodies to inhabit, each body is customized, made specifically for the new occupant, soul.

Do miscarried or aborted fetuses also have souls that will now have to find another vehicle? Or was their purpose to experience the abortion/miscarriage?

Miscarried or aborted fetuses have no souls assigned to them. Souls do not experience abortions or miscarriages, the fetuses are like clay pots that have not been fired in a kiln.

We are not here to change the world, we are here so that the world can change us, hopefully, for the better.

Printed in Great Britain
by Amazon